Praise for

THE UNMAPPED CHRONICLES BOOK ONE:
CASPER TOCK AND THE EVERDARK WINGS

"This whimsical, humorous, richly built world sets the stage for more courageous adventures. A delightful series opener." —*Kirkus Reviews*

"Perfect for fans of Narnia in search of more portals into new worlds." —*Booklist*

"Extremely satisfying." —*SLJ*

"A humorous adventure that resonates on multiple levels." —*Publishers Weekly*

"There is a rich tale to discover here. . . . This complex tale is anchored by familiar emotions while undertaking a thematic exploration of friendship and family ties." —*School Library Connection*

Also by
Abi Elphinstone

The Unmapped Chronicles Book One:
Casper Tock and the Everdark Wings

The Unmapped Chronicles Book Three:
Zeb Bolt and the Ember Scroll

Sky Song

THE UNMAPPED CHRONICLES

- BOOK TWO -

The Bickery Twins and the Phoenix Tear

ABI ELPHINSTONE

Aladdin

New York London Toronto Sydney New Delhi

ALADDIN
An imprint of Simon & Schuster Children's Publishing Division
1230 Avenue of the Americas, New York, New York 10020
First Aladdin paperback edition July 2021

Originally published in Great Britain in 2020 by Simon & Schuster UK as *Jungledrop*

Also available in an Aladdin hardcover edition.

Cover designed by Heather Palisi
Interior designed by Mike Rosamilia
The text of this book was set in Truesdell.
Manufactured in the United States of America 0323 OFF
2 4 6 8 10 9 7 5 3
The Library of Congress has cataloged the hardcover edition as follows:
Names: Elphinstone, Abi, author. | Title: The bickery twins and the phoenix tear / by Abi Elphinstone. |
Description: New York : Aladdin, 2020. | Series: The Unmapped chronicles ; [2] | Audience: Grades 4-6. |
Summary: "Twins Fox and Fibber find themselves in one of the Unmapped Kingdoms and set off on a quest to find the Forever Fern hidden deep in the glow-in-the-dark rainforests of Jungledrop"— Provided by publisher.
Identifiers: LCCN 2020002262 (print) | LCCN 2020002263 (ebook) |
ISBN 9781534443105 (hardcover) | ISBN 9781534443129 (ebook)
Subjects: CYAC: Fantasy. | Magic—Fiction. | Quests (Expeditions)—Fiction. | Twins—Fiction. |
Brothers and sisters—Fiction. | Adventure and adventurers—Fiction.
Classification: LCC PZ7.1.E465 Bic 2020 (print) | LCC PZ7.1.E465 (ebook) | DDC [Fic]—dc23
LC record available at https://lccn.loc.gov/2020002262
LC ebook record available at https://lccn.loc.gov/2020002263
ISBN 9781534443112 (pbk)

For Freddie, my godson

* * *

Here's to all the adventures we'll

go on together up north. . . .

Welcome to the Unmapped Kingdoms . . .

When you become a grown-up, several rather troubling things happen at once: your knees stop working as well as they used to; you spend large chunks of the day harping on about homework, vegetables, and bedtimes; and you fall asleep the moment you sit down in a comfortable armchair. But with all the dodgy knees, nagging, and nodding off comes wisdom. Or does it? Because if grown-ups were truly wise, then they would know about the Unmapped Kingdoms. But they do not. They are far too busy to believe in magic. And yet, if they did, they would realize that the world is very much not as they know it. . . .

You see, at the beginning there were no big bangs or black holes. There was just an egg. A rather large one. And out of this egg a phoenix was born. It wept seven tears when it found itself alone, and as these tears fell, they became our continents and formed the earth as you and I know it, although to the phoenix all this was simply known as the Faraway. But these lands were dark and empty, so, many years later, the phoenix scattered four of its golden feathers, and out of these grew secret—unmapped—kingdoms, invisible to the people who would go on to live in the Faraway, but holding the magic needed to conjure sunlight, rain, and snow, and every untold wonder behind the weather, from the music of a sunrise to the stories of a snowstorm.

Now, had a hippogriff or a unicorn been in charge, things might have got out of hand (for though these beasts like to boss others around, they are rarely on time for anything and are far too vain to govern fairly). But a phoenix is the wisest of all magical creatures, and the very first phoenix knew that magic grows strange and dark if used selfishly, but if it is used for the greater good, it can nourish an entire world and keep it turning. So the phoenix decreed that those who lived in the Unmapped Kingdoms could enjoy all the wonders that its magic brought, but only if they, in turn, worked to send some of this magic out into the Faraway so that the continents there might be filled with light and life. If the Unmappers ever stopped sharing their magic, the phoenix warned, both the Faraway and the Unmapped Kingdoms would crumble to nothing.

The phoenix thought long and hard about which magical creatures to appoint as rulers of each Unmapped Kingdom. The cloud giants were tall and strong, but they tended to fall asleep when anything important needed to be done. The snow trolls were kind and clever, but rather too keen on firing crossbows. And so the phoenix settled on the Lofty Husks—wizards born under the same eclipse and marked out from the other Unmappers on account of their wisdom, unusually long life expectancy, and terrible jokes. And although the Lofty Husks in each kingdom took a different form, they ruled fairly, ensuring that every day the magic of the phoenix was passed on to the Faraway.

The four kingdoms all played different roles. Unmappers in Rumblestar collected marvels—droplets of sunlight, rain, and snow in their purest form—which dragons transported to the other kingdoms so the inhabitants there could mix them with magical ink to create weather scrolls for the Faraway: sun symphonies in Crackledawn, rain paintings in Jungledrop, and snow stories in Silvercrag. Little by little, the Faraway lands came alive: plants, flowers, and trees sprang up, and so strong was the magic that eventually animals appeared and, finally, people.

Years passed and the phoenix looked on from Everdark, a place so far away and out of reach that not even the Unmappers knew where it lay. But while a phoenix may be wise, it cannot live forever. And so, after five hundred years, the first phoenix died and, as is the way with such birds, a new phoenix rose from its ashes to renew the magic in the Unmapped Kingdoms and ensure it was shared with those in the Faraway.

A period of peace and prosperity followed, and every five hundred years the Unmappers learned to watch for a new phoenix rising up into the sky to restore the Unmapped magic and herald the arrival of another era. Everyone believed things would continue this way forever. . . .

When you're dealing with magic, though, *forever* is rarely straightforward. There is always someone, somewhere, who becomes greedy. And when a heart is set on stealing magic for personal gain, suddenly ancient decrees and warnings slip quite out of mind. Such was the case with a harpy called Morg who grew jealous of the phoenix and its power.

Four thousand years ago, Morg breathed a curse over the nest of the last phoenix on the very night of the renewal of magic. The old phoenix burst into flames, like the rest of its kind had done before it, but this time the flames burned black and no new phoenix appeared from the ashes. And so Morg seized the nest as her own and set about seeking to claim all the magic of the Unmapped Kingdoms for herself.

But when things go wrong and magic goes awry, it makes room for stories with unexpected heroes and unlikely heroines. I could tell you about a girl from Crackledawn who stole Morg's wings, the very things that held the harpy's power, or about a boy named Casper from the Faraway, who once journeyed to Rumblestar to destroy those same wings so that the Unmapped Kingdoms and the Faraway might be saved from ruin. I could also tell you about the dragons that roam the kingdoms now and scatter moondust from their wings to keep what is left of the Unmapped magic turning until Morg dies and a new phoenix rises.

Those are stories for another time and place—and perhaps some of you have discovered them already. Now, though, a new story is brewing. . . . Because Morg is stirring in Everdark once more, with new wings built from the deepest curses, and her sights are set on the kingdom of Jungledrop, where grows—she has learned—a mythical fern that grants immortality. A plant that Morg believes will be most useful in her plans for the Unmapped Kingdoms. . . .

And as much as I wish I could introduce you to a boy and a girl brimming with charm for this story, I'm afraid I cannot. The Petty-Squabble twins have as much charm as a politician's underpants. But just because someone has a sharp tongue and a thorny heart at eleven years old, doesn't mean that they will stay that way forever. Quite the contrary. Children are remarkably bendy creatures, especially when they are thrust headfirst into an adventure. Just when you think you've got the measure of them, they twist and turn and end up surprising you altogether.

Even the ones who seem truly dreadful like Fox and Fibber Petty-Squabble. In fact, sometimes it is children like that who make the most interesting heroes of all. . . .

Chapter 1

Fox Petty-Squabble flopped onto the sofa in the penthouse suite of the Neverwrinkle Hotel. It was the summer holidays—or at least it was supposed to be—but rather than heading to the seaside, or relaxing with a barbecue in their garden, the Petty-Squabble family had descended upon the sleepy village of Mizzlegurg in the Bavarian countryside for a business trip.

Although originally from England, Gertrude and Bernard Petty-Squabble had moved their family to Germany shortly after Fox and her twin brother, Fibber, had been born. Bernard had a very wealthy German ancestor, a duke called Great-Uncle Rudolph, and when he passed away, the Petty-Squabbles found themselves inheriting his enormous mansion in Munich because they were his only living relatives. Bickery Towers was one of the biggest and grandest houses in all of Europe, which was just as well because being bigger and grander than everyone else mattered enormously to Mr. and Mrs. Petty-Squabble. So much so that they filled every summer holiday (and indeed every Christmas and Easter holiday too) with business meetings, because making heaps of cash was, to them, the only way to ensure they remained more important than everybody else.

And so, as today marked the start of the twins' summer holiday, the Petty-Squabbles had all set off from Bickery Towers that morning, complete with matching luggage, matching business suits, and matching scowls, before bullying their way through the day—as was their custom. The family motto, etched in gold across the trunk of their car, was:

DO NOT BE AFRAID

Then, in smaller letters below this:

TO STAMP ALL OVER OTHER PEOPLE'S FEELINGS.

Gertrude Petty and Bernard Squabble had been living by this code for as long as they could remember, and it had made them very rich indeed. Even before the move to Bickery Towers eleven years ago, Gertrude was running one of the world's leading antiaging skincare lines, Petty Pampering, and Bernard was the founder of Squabble Sauces, a global corporation that claimed to make cooking sauces that did all sorts of improbable things like reduce tiredness and increase intelligence. In reality, neither the skincare products nor the sauces actually fulfilled any of their bold promises. The Petty-Squabble empire was built on lies. But bullies and liars often go from strength to strength until someone is brave enough to take them down.

Needless to say, no one was brave enough to take the Petty-Squabbles down the day they left for Mizzlegurg, for they were very much in a stamping sort of mood. The family's long-suffering driver, Hans Underboot, took the brunt of it first. Mrs. Petty took it upon herself to dock his pay every time he obeyed the speed limit or got stuck in traffic, because she had an appointment at the Neverwrinkle Hotel that she really didn't want to miss. Then, upon arrival at the hotel, Mr. Squabble clouted the porter round the head when he asked if the family had had an enjoyable journey because that was *clearly* none of his business. And Fox sneered at every single person who crossed her path—the receptionist who smiled too much, the waiter who asked too many questions at lunch, and the pool attendant whose mustache was "stupid"—purely because that was how she had been raised to behave. To be kind was to be weak and to be weak was to be stamped on by everyone, which, admittedly, did not sound ideal to Fox.

Only Fibber had held back on the stamping. In fact, Fox had noticed that her brother had been unusually quiet since the end of term a few weeks ago. Suspiciously quiet, she thought.

Fox and Fibber were twins, not that you would have known it to look at them. Fibber was tall with sleek dark hair, like their mother, while Fox was short with a tumble of red hair, which had come from their father. But, though they might not have looked alike, they had one thing in common: a sharp tongue. And the only thing the twins liked more than insulting strangers was being horrid to one another, especially if it meant that they could show their sibling up in front of their mother and father.

This interfamily competitiveness had been handed down to the twins from their parents. For, while Gertrude and Bernard ultimately wanted to amass one giant Petty-Squabble fortune, they valued rivalry over romance. Working *against* family members, rather than *with* them, added a competitive edge to moneymaking schemes and got you richer quicker, as far as Gerturde and Bernard were concerned. And so they were constantly seeking sly ways to get one up on each other, and this rivalry overshadowed every aspect of Fox and Fibber's relationship too.

Moments after the twins' birth, Fox had given Fibber a black eye for being born three minutes sooner than her, and that was to set the tone for the rivalry to come. When they were barely a year old, Fibber knocked over Fox's crib back in Bickery Towers when his parents weren't looking. Fox then retaliated by biting the head off Fibber's favorite teddy, and Fibber had fought back by flicking the brake off Fox's baby carriage the next day, which very nearly sent his sister hurtling under a truck racing down their street.

The Petty-Squabble parents delighted in these feuds and even named their children in such a way as to heighten the sense of conflict: Fibber because they hoped he'd turn out to be a brilliant liar (which he did), and Fox because they hoped she'd turn out to be as sly as the animal itself (which she didn't, because being impulsive makes it near impossible to be sly). Even outside their home—in the local neighborhood and at school—Fox and Fibber's arguments had earned them the title "the Bickery Twins." So this sibling rivalry, fueled by their parents and widely accepted by everyone else, went on—through early childhood, preschool, and school—reaching a peak a few months ago when Fibber tricked Fox into flushing her homework down the toilet, causing Fox to dangle her brother by his ankles from a fifth-floor window in Bickery Towers (to the cheers of their parents down below).

But Fox was uneasy. Since the dangling incident, Fibber hadn't tricked or cheated or—his favorite—lied to his parents to get his sister into trouble. For months, she had waited for her brother to fight back, but instead Fibber had remained uncharacteristically quiet and thoughtful. So now, as they sat together in the hotel suite booked by their parents, Fox watched him with narrowed eyes. He was sitting in an armchair opposite her, his briefcase parked by his feet and a pad of paper open on his lap. Fox craned her neck to see what he was up to, but he inched his pad higher to shield the page from her.

Fox plucked at her braid. "What are you scribbling about?"

Fibber didn't look up. He didn't stop writing either. Fox was used to her brother's calm, collected manner when he was stamping all over other people's feelings, but she had always found it easy to bait Fibber into bickering with her when it was just the two of them alone together. These newfound silences were starting to unnerve her, because Petty-Squabbles who were silent were usually plotting something.

Like the aforementioned Great-Uncle Rudolph, who apparently hadn't said a word for forty-three years, then announced he was digging a tunnel from Munich to London so that he could kidnap the queen and hold her hostage for an unreasonable sum of money. Great-Uncle Rudolph had gotten as far as Poland before realizing he had been digging in the wrong direction; he was then silent for another forty-three years, for different reasons.

Fox tried to conjure up some mutinous moneymaking thoughts of her own, but she couldn't help feeling that kidnappings, robberies, and large-scale revolutions might be more effective when performed with other people. And Fox was very much a solo act, both at school (where avoiding being stamped on meant insulting classmates and teachers on a daily basis) and at home (where conversations were limited to business, smiling was frowned upon, and hugging was completely out of the question).

Fox pulled off her tie, wedged it down the side of the sofa, then looked across at her brother again. "You're working on the Petty Pampering business plan, aren't you?"

There was an edge to her voice now because she knew that if Fibber was putting in the hours attempting to rebrand the

Petty Pampering products, it meant she should be doing the same for Squabble Sauces. The twins knew that both companies were based on lies, but there was too much at stake to start messing around with the truth. Customers had slowly but surely been starting to realize they'd been duped, and now profits were falling and contracts were being dropped, which was why the twins spent every holiday traipsing round luxury hotels while their parents tried to persuade the spas and restaurants to stock their products.

But Fox and Fibber weren't brought along on these trips because Gertrude and Bernard couldn't bear to be parted from their children. Oh no. They were here to work. Their parents had cornered them at the end of first grade and informed the twins that only one of them would inherit the Petty-Squabble empire; if Fox came up with a way to save Squabble Sauces, it would be her, but if Fibber swept in and rescued Petty Pampering first, it would be him. So, just like that, the rivalry between the siblings deepened.

And Gertrude and Bernard didn't stop there. To spur Fox on to recover the family fortune as quickly as possible, her parents frequently told her that Fibber's cunning lies would, eventually, be the key to his success. While at the same time (unbeknownst to Fox) her parents goaded Fibber into believing that Fox really was sly enough to rebuild the Petty-Squabble empire without him even noticing and would push him out in the process. This meant that the twins were always jealous of each other and constantly convinced that their parents loved one more than the other. So they had grown up in the firm and somewhat terrifying knowledge that they were rivals, not siblings.

In truth, Gertrude and Bernard didn't care which child saved the family fortune. The only reason they had had children in the first place was in the hope that one of them might eventually make them lots of cash. Indeed, when Fox had asked her father what would happen to the child who didn't inherit the Petty-Squabble empire, his response—"They will be packaged up, mailed somewhere very far away, like Antarctica, and politely wished all the very best"—had not been altogether reassuring.

Fox reached inside her blazer pocket for her phone and began tapping away in the notes section.

"Just opening my list of secret, and utterly brilliant, ways to save Squabble Sauces," she muttered, loudly enough for her brother to hear.

Fibber looked up briefly, then carried on writing.

Fox tapped away with a smirk. "Just adding in a few more winning thoughts to clinch the deal."

Which was entirely untrue. There was no list of breathtaking ideas that would save the dwindling Petty-Squabble empire. Fox knew all the right words to bluff her way through the weekly family business meetings—"expenditure," "capital," "profit margin," "asset"—but she had no idea what any of these terms actually meant. And she was absolutely hopeless at strategic thinking.

For a moment, Fox felt the weight of something dark and unlovely shifting inside her. Fibber was a businessman-in-the-making. He was clever and smooth-talking—he could fool even the most intelligent grown-ups with his silky lies—and although at school he was far too arrogant to feel the need to make friends, he had, this term, endeared himself to a teacher, Mrs. Scribble, with whom he now took extra lessons during lunch break because she sensed in him some "*hidden potential.*"

The darkness inside Fox flinched. No one had ever thought that she was special. That she had "potential." What was she good at? Too much of a solo act to be picked for the sports teams, not bright enough to achieve top grades, and not nearly popular enough to be picked for Head of School in sixth grade next term. Everyone in her class seemed to be good at *something*, even the really quiet ones who (much to Fox's annoyance) looked perfectly ordinary, but ended up being fabulous at spelling, feverishly fast on ice skates, or shockingly good at the clarinet.

Fox had concluded some years ago that her obvious lack of talent was what made her unlovable to her parents. Stamping on other people's feelings every day was all very well—after all, Fox didn't fancy being kind, because being weak, as well as talentless, would only add to her misery—but the heart is a fragile thing, and sometimes people assume that the best way to keep theirs safe is to build a wall round it. And that was just what Fox had done. Hers was a very high wall that had grown up over the years without her truly realizing because it made dealing with being unlovable ever so slightly easier.

She stole a look at Fibber. Was he quieter than usual because he had, finally—and perhaps predictably—come up with a way to save the family fortune? Maybe he was just moments away from announcing his triumph. Fox contemplated her options. She could pin Fibber down, snatch his business plan, then—she thought fast—*eat it*? Or was it time to do a Great-Uncle Rudolph (without the tunnel drama): grab the plan and hold it hostage until Fibber agreed to say that he and Fox had come up with all the ideas together?

Before Fox could do either, the door to the penthouse suite opened. In stormed Gertrude Petty, wearing a white bathrobe, white slippers, and a white towel twisted up over her hair. She was wearing so much white she looked uncannily like a meringue, while behind her, red-haired and red-faced, was Bernard Petty resembling a volcano rammed into a business suit.

Bernard flung the door shut. Then he and his wife eyed their children with the kind of look that is usually only reserved for traffic wardens and large spiders. Fox gulped. She knew all too well that when her parents barged into a room like this, it was never good news. . . .

Chapter 2

"The facial was a disaster," Gertrude snapped.

She swept across the living room, plucked a grape from the fruit bowl on the table between the twins, threw it in her mouth, winced, and then spat it out onto the carpet.

"Just as the beautician was finishing up," she muttered, "I launched into my sales pitch for the new Petty Pampering line, whereupon I was told that the spa had decided to discontinue stocking my products, as of next month, because of complaints about the moisturizer."

Bernard rolled his eyes. "I *knew* that moisturizer would come back to haunt you. But did you listen to me?" He thumped his clipboard down on the table. "No. Too busy waiting for your son to sweep in and save the day."

Fibber shifted but didn't look up.

"Time is marching on," Bernard tutted to his wife, "and Petty Pampering profits are accelerating at the pace of an asthmatic ant."

"While Squabble Sauces," Gertrude shot back, "are run by a man with about as much skill as a newly born baboon." Before her husband could reply, Gertrude rounded on Fibber. "I thought you said we'd discontinued the moisturizer because it dyed customers' eyebrows green?"

Fox watched Fibber, every muscle inside her tight with dread. Was now to be the moment her brother stood up and revealed his groundbreaking plan to save the Petty-Squabble empire?

Fibber placed his pad of paper inside his briefcase and clicked it shut. Then, very calmly, he looked up. "I am pleased to say, Mother, that I am *very* close to presenting you with my incredibly detailed and unmistakably profit-soaring business plan that will ensure every spa in the world champions Petty Pampering products."

Gertrude smirked at her husband. "As we always thought, Bernard: Fibber will be the one to save this family."

Fox swallowed. She felt the need to say something brilliant so that her parents remembered that she, too, was in the room.

And so she coughed. "Father, my even more detailed and profity plan for Squabble Sauces is also almost ready. We're looking at some profit margin . . . capital . . . greatness ahead." She reached for her tie and put it back on. "*Asset.*"

"*Almost* ready isn't good enough," Bernard barked. "Not when the head chef of the Neverwrinkle Hotel is refusing to cook with Squabble Sauces ever again because of claims the slimming line we introduced last month gave half his guests food poisoning!"

"Are the guests okay?" Fox blurted.

Then she shrank into her blazer. *Why* had she asked about the well-being of other people? That was *not* the Petty-Squabble way. . . . Her parents had drummed the family motto into her so many times she genuinely believed that stamping all over other people's feelings was how you behaved if you wanted to get to the top. Only it seemed she was so dreadfully talentless that she even got stamping on other people wrong.

Gertrude looked on, appalled, and Bernard's reaction was no better: "Hard-headed businessmen and women do *not* waste time worrying about other people, Fox! Next you'll be telling us you're feeling sorry for all those affected by these silly water shortages."

Fox glanced at the newspaper on the table; the worldwide water crisis still dominated every headline. It hadn't rained *anywhere* on Earth for months. Rivers and reservoirs had dried up across Europe, crops were failing, and plants and animals were dying. Further afield, where droughts were commonplace even before this catastrophe, countries had now been without water for almost a year, so rainforests were withering, famine was commonplace, and communities were descending into violence. Meteorologists, scientists, and environmentalists had warned about the devastating effects of global warming, but no one had foreseen the speed of this disaster.

Gertrude followed her daughter's gaze. Then she picked up another grape, squashed it between her fingers, and flicked it onto the carpet for someone else to clean up. "So long as we have money—which we will have because things always work out for those who stamp all over other people in the end—we will always have access to water. Who cares about everybody else?"

Fox nodded. "I don't plan to lift a finger to help the environment *or* other people," she said firmly.

And she meant it. What she didn't know was that she was dangerously close to an adventure that would force her to do the exact opposite.

Bernard reached for his clipboard again. "I'm going back to the kitchen to throw my weight around some more." He looked at his wife. "And since Petty Pampering is on its knees, I suggest you do the same in the spa."

Gertrude raised a haughty eyebrow at her children. "As for you two . . . It's high time you started doing your share of the work rather than sponging off us. Petty-Squabble profits are at an all-time low, so when your father and I return, we want to hear your business proposals. No more dilly-dallying with half-baked snippets of information. We want hard, clear, profit-soaring facts."

"Disappoint us again," Bernard called as he and Gertrude marched toward the door, "and you're *both* off to Antarctica first thing tomorrow. So you will stay here until you have those business proposals ready for us!"

The door slammed shut and Fox swallowed.

But, without realizing it, Bernard Squabble had uttered two words that would prove to be his downfall. For telling a child to *stay here* is about as pointless as telling them to *keep quiet*. Commands like these are lethal for children because they have next to no control over their legs and mouths.

And though, at this precise moment, Fox was imagining

being stamped on by a colony of furious penguins, it wouldn't take long for the words "stay here" to echo through her body and stir her legs into disobedience.

She glanced at Fibber. Eating his business plan was no longer an option because he had stashed his papers safely inside his briefcase and only Fibber knew the code to open it. Stealing the briefcase and disposing of it altogether, however . . .

So, without more ado, Fox leapt up, grabbed the briefcase, and legged it out of the penthouse suite.

"FOX!!!!" Fibber roared. "Give me back my briefcase!"

Down the corridor Fox ran, desperately trying to cobble together a plan. Where did you dispose of items forever and ever and ever? Other than Antarctica . . .

She looked over her shoulder to see her brother hurtling down the corridor after her. There was panic in his eyes as well as fury. Fox ran faster, charging past the hotel rooms and slipping into the elevator just as it was closing. She heard Fibber bang a fist on the other side of the door, but he was too late. The elevator was already sinking down toward the ground floor.

Panting, Fox turned to the lady manning a cart of cleaning products in the elevator beside her. "How would you go about getting rid of something very quickly?"

The lady thought about it. "My husband once left a pair of dirty socks in a cupboard for twelve years before I found them. They smelled of dead badger." She paused. "So I burned them."

Fox gripped the handle of the briefcase. Was real leather even flammable? She looked up at the lady. "Got any matches on your cart?"

The lady laughed, then realized Fox was being serious and that there was a dangerous glint in her chestnut eyes. "What exactly is it you're trying to get rid of?"

Fox considered her answer, then held up the briefcase. "My dad has decided he doesn't want to let work stand in the way of a perfectly good holiday, so he asked me to dispose of *this*."

Fox's heart, despite the wall around it, ached suddenly. Not at the lie—she was used to twisting the truth, though she wasn't as good at it as her brother—but at the shape of her world, which was unnatural and unfair and unbelievably cruel. And, to her horror, she felt tears rising up inside her. She pursed her lips at the lady and thought of something foul to say.

"If you don't come up with a sensible plan for the disposal of this briefcase *immediately*, I am going to lodge a complaint to ensure the disposal of *you* from the Neverwrinkle Hotel by dinnertime."

The lady blinked and then sighed as if she was used to dealing with guests like this. "If the briefcase is worth something, and by the look of those buckles I'd say it might be, then I wouldn't get rid of it. I'd take it to the antiques shop in the village. They take all sorts of fancy objects to sell on to customers across the world and they'll give you a good price."

Although Fox had always been taught to think of ways to make money, she didn't imagine there'd be much need for lots of cash in Antarctica, but then a rather marvelous idea occurred to her. Perhaps she could use the money to bribe the postal service to send her somewhere else. Somewhere with fewer penguins and more people.

The elevator shuddered to a halt and the door opened.

"You turn right out of the hotel," the lady called after Fox, who was already sprinting away. "Then down the street, past the train station, and when the road bends left, take the first little side road. The shop is tucked in there."

Fox didn't turn to say thank you—partly because it didn't occur to her and partly because she could see Fibber leaping down the last of the fire-escape stairs and tearing across the foyer after her like some small, deranged business tycoon.

She flung herself into the cobbled street, squinting through the afternoon sun at the rows of higgledy-piggledy colored houses with peaked terracotta roofs climbing into the bright blue sky. Last summer, tourists had flocked to the village of Mizzlegurg, drifting around on bicycles and eating ice creams under the restaurant awnings, but since the water crisis, Mizzlegurg, along with so many holiday destinations across the globe, had become a quieter, less visited sort of place.

The signs of the water shortages were subtle, but there nonetheless: The flower boxes beneath windows were empty because there was a ban on watering plants purely for decorative purposes; numerous restaurants had closed because the increase in food prices due to failing crops meant fewer people could afford to eat out; the hotels were half-empty because they could only supply a limited amount of water to guests; and the reservoir just outside the village that generated water for the locals was running dangerously low, so each building had a water ration.

Fox ignored all of this and carried on running, knowing that Fibber was hot on her heels and that somehow she'd have to shake him off when the road split. The train station burst into view, just as the cleaning lady had said it would. Only it didn't have multiple platforms and trains all under the same roof, like others Fox had seen. In fact, Mizzlegurg Station had *no* roof at all. It was simply a train track flanked by two platforms and a little wooden hut, which might have been a ticket office—though it was as empty as the platforms. Behind the station, Fox could see mountains covered in trees that had once been tall and green and bursting with leaves, but which were now bent and brown and shriveled from lack of water.

She sprinted past the station, eyes peeled for the side street she hoped to vanish down without her brother seeing. And so intent was she on finding it that she didn't give Mizzlegurg Station another thought. But if Fox had been moving a little more slowly, and if she had been paying a little more attention, she might have felt the faint but unmistakable tingle of magic stirring.

Because, in precisely forty-seven minutes, an event was going to occur at Mizzlegurg Station that would change the lives of the Petty-Squabble twins forever.

Chapter 3

When the road bent left, Fox bolted down the side street, then practically threw herself into the antiques shop. It was quiet inside and specks of dust hung in the air, suspended in the sunlight above the clutter of antiques like thousands of indoor stars.

Fox glanced around. The shop was full to bursting. Where tables laden with old-fashioned weighing scales, copper jugs, and dusty cutlery ended, pianos, grandfather clocks, old trunks, and wardrobes began. There were spinning globes perched on threadbare armchairs, ship wheels wedged into corners, jewelry boxes stacked one on top of the other, and chandeliers hanging from the ceiling. Every nook and cranny was filled with *junk*. Fox blinked at it all in disgust.

Then she stiffened as she heard Fibber's footsteps thundering closer. Would her brother shoot on down the road into another shop or had he sensed, as twins often manage to do, that Fox had turned in here? She shoved his briefcase under a piano to buy herself a little more time, then seconds later Fibber crashed into the shop, sending a pile of antique books flying.

He turned on his sister. "*Where* is it?"

Fox could hear the panic in Fibber's voice, but she noticed he'd hung back on unleashing the usual insults: squid-face, moth-brain, scum-breath. Fox wasn't exactly a fan of these terms, but at least when Fibber used them, she knew precisely where she stood. She had no idea what game he was currently playing with his recent silences and his lack of stamping all over other people. She plucked a rusty telescope from a shelf and turned it over in her hands.

"I dumped your briefcase in a trash can on the main street." She paused. "So, if I were you, I'd go and find it before it's carted off forever."

Fibber snatched the telescope from Fox and hurled it over his shoulder. "I didn't see you hovering round any trash cans." He straightened his tie to show that he meant business. "What did you do with it?"

"If you keep pestering me," Fox muttered, "I'll dump *you* in a trash can."

There was a cough from the back of the shop, and the twins whirled round to see an old man emerging from behind a wardrobe. He had dark, wrinkled skin and a fuzz of gray hair, and in his hand he held a duster.

"I was once plunged headfirst into a trash can," he said, "by a boy called Leopold Splattercash." He shuddered. "Dreadful human being. Used to chew his own toenails." The man tucked the duster into his apron. "So, what can I do for you two, then? Bearing in mind that I don't, regrettably, stock any trash cans in this shop."

"You should," Fox mumbled. "You've got enough trash in here to fill hundreds."

The old man picked his way through the antiques toward the twins.

"Don't even *try* to sell us any of this junk," Fox said haughtily. Then she kicked the old-fashioned writing desk beside the old man, which sent the inkpot that had been resting on top clattering to the floor, and added: "Petty-Squabbles *never* buy secondhand; we don't need to when we can afford the best of the best."

She glanced at her brother, expecting him to say something equally rude, but he was too busy rooting through the antiques for his briefcase.

The old man picked up the inkpot, set it back on the writing desk, and blinked at the twins. He didn't often come across children. His customers tended to be adults, and he and his wife had never had a family. But he had remained optimistic about them nonetheless, because he knew, from personal experience, that when worlds and kingdoms needed saving, it was children who stepped in to sort things out. But the two in front of him now didn't seem the world-saving types. At all.

And so it was with a great deal of surprise that the old man noticed the blue glow coming from the half-open drawer of the writing desk the girl had just kicked. He bustled toward it and drew out a small velvet bag.

"Impossible," he murmured, tipping a marble into his palm.

The sun had dipped behind the street now, and in the gloom of the cluttered antiques shop the marble was sparkling with a fierce little light all of its own.

Fox plucked idly at her braid. "I suppose you're going to try and claim that this marble is one of a kind and worth stupid amounts of money."

Even Fibber, who was still worried about finding his briefcase, couldn't help but look up at the glowing marble. "What's it got inside it? Batteries? Miniature lights?"

"Magic," the old man whispered.

Fibber plucked the marble from his wrinkled hand, turned it over in his palm, then rolled his eyes. He was too old to believe in magic. But, just as Fibber was about to hand the marble back, the man reached out and grabbed Fibber's wrist.

"The world is not as you know it. But if I was to tell you the truth—that we only survive because of four unseen, unmapped, magical kingdoms that conjure weather for our world—you would laugh at me, just as I laughed years ago when I was told the same thing."

Fibber tugged his arm free, but the old man kept talking, his voice low and urgent as if, perhaps, he had been waiting for this conversation for a very long time.

"You'll have learned, of course, about the terrible hurricanes seventy years ago, which almost tore our world apart. Scientists have never understood why those hurricanes stopped as quickly as they started, but that's because it had nothing to do with science . . . It was because of magic."

Fibber shook his head. "This is madness."

Fox, for once, was in agreement with her brother. "I detest old people," she muttered. "The cardigans and the slippers and the nonstop knitting are bad enough, but the nonsense that comes out of their mouths is unbearable. If I were Prime Minister, I'd pass a law saying that anyone over the age of fifty should have their mouth duct-taped shut whenever they leave the house."

The old man ignored the twins' comments. "When I was a child," he said, "I stumbled across a magical phoenix tear. And that tear transported me to Rumblestar, one of the four Unmapped Kingdoms, where a harpy called Morg was wreaking havoc with the magical winds that grew there." He shuddered as he recalled it. "But, with the help of some friends, I, Casper Tock, banished Morg and her followers from Rumblestar, which, in turn, restored calm to our world's weather."

Fibber looked the antiques collector up and down. "You really think that *you* stopped the hurricanes because of something you did in a *magical* kingdom?"

Casper nodded. "Along with a girl called Utterly Thankless and a small dragon called Arlo, yes. Though I suppose we did have a bit of help from snow trolls and sun scamps, too. And Zip, a magical hot-air balloon." He looked from Fox to Fibber.

"I knew that one day Morg would hatch another plan to steal the Unmapped magic. She only needs to gain control of one of the four kingdoms for the rest to fall, so she won't stop trying."

Fox glanced round the shop. "I don't suppose there's any duct tape kicking around in here?"

The old man ignored her again. "My wife, Sophie, and I have spent our lives trawling antiques fairs across the world, looking for another phoenix tear. Then we came across this shop for sale and I felt the pull of something familiar." Casper's eyes shone. "It was the pull of magic. Tucked inside the drawer of this writing desk was that marble—a phoenix tear. I've been sure of it all along, because if you've encountered magic before, you know when it's sitting in front of you again."

The twins stared at the marble. The glow flickered mischievously in Fibber's palm, and for a second all thoughts about the briefcase, the Petty-Squabble fortune, and Antarctica were forgotten.

"Our planet is on its knees once again. If the rains don't come soon, who knows what will happen? All of us are to blame for global warming. We could have done more sooner and stopped ignoring the signs around us. But it's my bet there's dark magic afoot too." He paused. "It appears the phoenix tear's magic is stirring and, for reasons far beyond me, I believe it has chosen *you two* as the ones to save us."

For a moment, there was silence. Then Fibber snorted. "What a load of nonsense," he said.

"And as for us sweeping in to save the planet," Fox added, "you can forget it. It's not the Petty-Squabble way to start caring and helping and rescuing other people. What would be in it for us? No, it's stamp or be stamped on—and we very much like to do the stamping."

"Exactly." Fibber dropped the marble back into Casper's hand and glared at Fox. "So give me back my briefcase and maybe I won't stamp on *you*."

Casper tilted his head. "You mean the one under the piano?"

Fox stiffened as Fibber charged toward the piano and began rummaging beneath it. She looked from Casper to the marble, then back again at Casper. And in the old man's eyes she saw something burning as brightly as the marble he held: hope.

He dipped his head at Fox. "Take the marble. Then run, girl, run headlong into this adventure. The Unmapped Kingdoms have chosen *you*, and when magic sets its sights on someone, it's remarkably hard to wriggle free."

Fox blinked. The old man was off his rocker—he had to

be—but her plans lay in tatters, Fibber was on the brink of victory, and there was something about this marble burning in the gloom. Something wild and hopeful. She grabbed it from Casper's outstretched palm just as Fibber was raising his briefcase in triumph, then she turned and fled from the shop.

Fox tore back down the street. She couldn't go back to the hotel because her parents had been very clear: come up with a plan or be mailed to Antarctica. She had to get away from here. Immediately. And yet she had no idea where to go.

She hastened on down the street, then the train station came into view once again, and Fox felt the marble tingle in her hand. Without thinking, she turned into the station, rushed past the empty ticket office and onto the echoing platform, and there, like a gift—a glorious, hope-giving chance of a gift—was a train. And so strong was the pull of escape, of freedom, that Fox didn't stop to consider that this train was a very old-fashioned steam train and that the steam pumping out of its chimney was, in fact, bright green.

She gripped the marble tightly, hurried along the platform, and though she didn't know where the train was going to, leapt aboard. She turned to see Fibber dashing toward her. What was he *doing*? He had been desperate to find his briefcase and yet he wasn't, it appeared, desperate to hurry back to their parents to reveal the business plan inside it. Had he been lying about the contents? What if his briefcase didn't hold a genius business plan? Fox felt sure, though, that Fibber had *something* of value inside it, something he didn't want to lose.

The train started chugging forward slowly, and Fibber quickened his pace, throwing himself aboard just before the train gathered more speed. And Fox realized then that her world, which had seemed so ugly and unchanging before, now looked ever so slightly different. There were surprises and secrets bound up inside it: Why on earth, for instance, had her brother followed her onto this train?

But it was only when the train doors snapped shut and Fox glanced down the carriage that she realized her world was filled to the brim with magic, too.

Chapter 4

It was Fibber who spoke first, and his voice, usually snide and smooth, came out as a strangled squeak. "I'm dreaming. I must be dreaming." He whirled round to Fox. "Tell me I'm dreaming!"

Fox stared, open-mouthed, at the extraordinary plants sprouting through the gaps in the floorboards of the carriage: red-and-white spotted ones the size of tractor wheels; blue ones the shape of pineapples; tiny yellow ones that grew like clusters of fallen stars; tall purple ones that looked suspiciously like broomsticks. Indeed, there were so many plants, it was almost impossible to see the floorboards. There were vines twisting up round velvet-curtained windows and crisscrossing between the lanterns hanging from the roof, and scuttling up one of the vines was a creature the size of a squirrel with pointed ears and green skin. It took one appalled look at the children and disappeared from sight.

In among this jungly mess, as if they had every right to be there, were what appeared to be the contents of a sitting room: two large armchairs with a coffee table in between them, a velvet chaise longue, a bookcase full of leather-bound books, a chest (holding goodness knows what, but potentially more pointy-eared green creatures), and, at the far end of the carriage, a painting of a phoenix that was somehow moving about in its frame.

Fox gaped. "Is—is this what public transport looks like?"

Fibber clutched his briefcase to his chest. "I don't like it. Where are all the other passengers?"

Fox peered into the carriage behind them. More strange plants and furniture, but no people.

Fibber nudged his sister toward the carriage in front. "Go and look for"—he paused—"normal things. Like passengers. And dining cars. And ticket inspectors."

Fox studied her brother. His shoulders were bunched up round his neck and he was biting his lip. Fox realized it was the first time she had ever seen Fibber scared and ever so slightly out of control, and she wondered whether she knew him quite as well as she thought she did.

Fox narrowed her eyes at him. "Why did you jump on the train after me, Fibber? If you've got a fortune-saving business plan inside that briefcase, why didn't you take it back to the hotel to show Mum and Dad?"

Fibber flinched as a golden beetle landed on his shoulder, then sprouted wings and flew off. "I don't think now is the right time to be worrying about all that. We need to find out where this train is going and why on earth it's got a"—he squinted at the scene before them—"garden growing inside it."

Fox glanced out of the window. "Do you think we're meant to be going quite this fast?"

The train was moving at such a blistering speed that the countryside around them was merely a blur, and Fibber gripped his briefcase even tighter. "Go and find a ticket inspector or some sort of sensible grown-up."

"Fine," Fox muttered. "But while I'm gone, make yourself useful by searching this carriage for a timetable to work out where we're heading." She pointed to the chest. "Start with that."

Fibber turned to the chest, which was covered in purple moss, and recoiled.

"If I didn't know you better," Fox jeered, "I'd say you were scared of a load of plants. So I suppose *I'll* have to be the one to get us out of this mess." And with that, she stormed off toward the front of the train.

The bravery was just an act, though. Deep down, Fox was frightened. She passed through carriage after carriage. Each held plenty of plants and armchairs, but there wasn't a single person in sight. She thought of her parents suddenly. When would they notice that she and Fibber had gone? And would they even care enough to come after the twins? Perhaps they'd simply be relieved that they didn't have to worry anymore about children who never made them any money. Fox decided not to dwell on that thought because it was dredging up a familiar sadness in her. Instead, she pressed on through the carriages.

She realized that she had come to the end of the train when in front of her, rather than another carriage, there was a door with the following words carved into it:

TICKET INSPECTER

CURRENTLY NAPPING.

Fox wasn't sure whether this was a comforting thought or not. She also wasn't sure if "inspecter" was really spelled like that. But as she took a step closer and got ready to knock on the door, the carved letters jiggled, spread out a little, and another word materialized in the wood. Fox gasped.

TICKET INSPECTER

CURRENTLY NOT NAPPING.

The door opened the very slightest of fractions, and Fox found herself hoping hard that a sensible grown-up might appear. But that hope was dashed when she saw the being that slipped out. As it drew itself up in front of her, it seemed to be in the *shape* of a grown-up, but where flesh and bones should have been, things were decidedly wispy and white.

Fox screamed. The letters on the door had been right; this really was a ticket in*specter*! "You're a—a—ghost!" she blurted.

The ghost was tall and male and wearing nothing but a loincloth. "I'm a junglespook, actually," he said curtly. "My name is Tedious Niggle and, as the ghost of a nagging grown-up, I should just like to check that you brushed your teeth this morning, packed insect repellent for the trip, and have a sensible bedtime planned—despite the late running of this service."

Fox screamed again, then raced back through the carriages toward Fibber, who was swiping at a diamond-winged butterfly with his briefcase.

"It bit me on my finger when I flicked it off the chest!" he wailed.

Fox glanced at her brother's hands. All ten digits were

intact and there wasn't any blood. "You'll live," she panted. "My news is that the train is haunted."

"*WHAT?!*" Fibber's face paled and he shuffled nearer to his sister before realizing that this was the closest he had ever been to a family member. He took a few steps backward. "*This* is why Petty-Squabbles don't travel on public transport," he hissed. "What sort of ghost was it? One in a suit of armor? Was it wielding a sword?"

"No." Fox tried to breathe normally. "It was wearing a loincloth."

As if on cue, Tedious Niggle swanned into the carriage and made himself comfortable on the chaise longue. Fibber looked dangerously close to fainting.

"Welcome, both of you, aboard the Here and There Express." The junglespook crossed his legs (which he really shouldn't have done, given that he was wearing a loincloth), helped himself to a cup of tea from the teapot on the coffee table next to him (which was pointless because he was a ghost and the liquid simply slid right through him), and smiled. "This is a nonstop service for Jungledrop, the Unmapped Kingdom responsible for the distribution of rain to the Faraway."

Fox and Fibber exchanged panicked looks. The secret

lands that Casper Tock had talked about had been called the Unmapped Kingdoms. . . . Had the old man been telling the truth? But that would be impossible . . . wouldn't it?

"My profuse apologies for the fact that the dining car is out of order, the train sometimes splits without warning, and the driver has gone on strike." Tedious Niggle set his teacup down on a saucer. "Any questions before I deliver the rest of the onboard notices?"

Fibber was doing his best to come to terms with being talked to by a ghost, but the news that there was no driver was causing a great deal of sweating beneath his business suit. "Without a driver, when—when will the train stop?"

The junglespook took another pointless sip of tea. "Alas, the drivers on the Here and There Express are notoriously fond of striking. Come to think of it, I don't recall seeing a driver at all this decade. . . ."

He plucked a fruit that looked like a banana, but was blue, from a plant next to him, which had about as much impact on his digestive system as the tea.

"But the train is powered by junglespit—you might have seen the green smoke puffing out of the chimney back at the station? Junglespit enables the train to come and go as it pleases and even cross from Jungledrop to the Faraway from time to time. The Here and There Express always makes it to the right destination, though. In the end."

"But"—Fibber chewed his lip—"Jungledrop doesn't sound like the right sort of destination for us at all."

Tedious Niggle cocked his head at the children. "You certainly haven't dressed appropriately. I don't think I've seen anyone attempt a jungle quest in a business suit before. I'm not suggesting a loincloth for saving the world, although I can recommend them for comfort, but perhaps something a bit more flexible across the chest would have been wise. Not much use running away from Morg if you can't pump your arms. And maybe shoes with a bit more grip? After all, if you're searching for the Forever Fern to restore rain to the Faraway, you're going to want to scale gobblequick trees and the like quickly and efficiently."

Fox looked down at her leather-buckle shoes, then shook herself for even considering that Tedious Niggle might be speaking the truth. And yet his words were a worrying echo of Casper Tock's. . . . Going on an adventure to rid the Unmapped Kingdoms of this Morg creature and restore rain to the earth.

Tedious Niggle stood up. "So, a few more notices before

your arrival in Jungledrop." He cleared his throat. "Please do make yourself comfortable in the snugglers; they'll adapt to suit your personality soon enough. Keep your fingers and toes away from the trunklets; they're not normally too much bother, just the odd prank here and there, but they're almost always hungry, and their teeth are so sharp they can chew through stone."

Fox balked as the creature with pointed ears and green skin emerged from a vine and flashed her a toothy grin.

"And do apply sunscreen liberally when you arrive," the junglespook concluded. "It would be somewhat of a disgrace if, instead of saving the world, you got sunburned instead."

He laughed. The twins did not.

"The plants aboard the Here and There Express are used to Faraway folk such as yourselves; now and again, the train winds up in your world by mistake, you see, and although it usually vanishes before anyone can clamber on board, it does give the plants here a brief moment to familiarize themselves with the way you look and dress. The plants in Jungledrop, however . . . Just make sure you treat them with respect; that way you're far less likely to get eaten or trampled on."

Fibber let out a little whimper, then quickly covered it up

by growling, unconvincingly, at the ghost and the plants and his sister instead.

Fox's mind spun with visions of man-eating shrubs. "The plants are *alive*?"

"*Every* plant is alive," the junglespook replied, "but magical ones have more—how should I put it?—*personality*." He pointed to a cluster of tall flowers with yellow petals that looked a lot like sunflowers. "Take the timekeepers, for example. Silent types but ever so reliable."

The yellow petals jiggled in delight at the attention, and as Fox peered closer, she saw that in the center of the petals there were, in fact, clockfaces.

"Timekeepers only grow in Jungledrop. It's a stroke of luck, if you'll pardon the pun, that they sprouted up on the Here and There Express, too. But they have been telling the time for centuries. And considering one year in the Faraway is almost thirty years in the Unmapped Kingdoms, it helps to have a plant that can keep track of both magical and non-magical time."

Fox thought about her parents suddenly. If she and Fibber were stuck in the Unmapped Kingdoms for several days, weeks, or even months—Fox shivered at the thought—perhaps no one back home would even notice they'd gone because hardly any time would have passed there at all . . .

Fibber, who was evidently thinking the same thing, piped up: "I demand that you stop the train!"

Fox stamped her foot for good measure. "Immediately!"

Tedious Niggle raised a ghostly eyebrow. "This is, as I have expressly told you, a nonstop service, so I suggest you come to terms with that. You do, after all, have a great deal of work ahead of you." He straightened his loincloth. "Therefore, if I were you, I would conserve your energy; I cannot think of a single instance in history where stamping one's foot has made a difference to the outcome of a situation."

He drifted back out of the carriage. "Do not disturb me from my nap again, please," he called, "otherwise I shall come back, wielding all sorts of terrifying weapons: swords, axes, and maybe even a sledgehammer if I'm feeling particularly grumpy."

As soon as the junglespook was gone, Fibber whirled round to face Fox. "This is *all* your fault."

"*My* fault?" Fox cried. "I didn't ask you to follow me! I assumed you'd be running back to the hotel to announce you'd saved Petty Pampering! I have no idea what you're doing on this train with me!"

Fibber adjusted his tie, took a deep breath, then glanced at his briefcase. "I don't have a plan for Petty Pampering in here."

Fox started. Her suspicion earlier had been right. Her brother *had* been lying to their parents.

"But," Fibber continued, "it does contain a fortune-making scheme in regards to something else. All I needed was a little more time to complete it, and I *had* thought that a local train trip might just buy me those extra hours. But instead it seems I'm hurtling toward these Unmapped Kingdoms, whatever they might be!"

Fox scoured her brother's face for the trace of a lie. She'd missed it back in the penthouse suite, and now she was determined to look closely for Fibber's telltale sign: the way the corners of his mouth tightened when he was saying something untrue. But she saw nothing. Fox wondered jealously what ingenious idea Fibber had come up with that was *even* better than saving Petty Pampering.

"My plan will be the making of me," Fibber said casually. Then the corners of his mouth tightened, just a fraction.

Ha! Fox thought. So her brother had a plan, but he wasn't *totally* convinced it was going to work. She felt a shred of hope grow inside her.

Until Fibber added: "Even Mrs. Scribble said I was onto something."

If Fibber was telling the truth now, which he *seemed* to be, Mrs. Scribble hadn't been helping him with extra homework, but instead working with him to come up with a plan to secure his place in the Petty-Squabble family. That meant he was probably leagues ahead of Fox! Because who did she have on her side? Absolutely no one . . . Fox felt a familiar loneliness trickle through her.

She glowered at her brother's briefcase. For a moment, she had hoped she was back on an even playing field with him. But it seemed that, if Fibber did manage to get off this train, he could just go back to their parents, safe in the knowledge that one of the most respected teachers at their school would vouch for his idea to make millions and save the family fortune.

Fibber threw Fox a haughty look. "What was *your* plan? You said you had one almost ready."

Fox didn't fancy admitting that her plan had simply been to run away from the shame of being the Petty-Squabble twin without a scrap of talent. She flung herself into an armchair and refused to say anything at all.

When the armchair—or the snuggler or whatever Tedious Niggle had called it—started moving, though, Fox let out a yelp.

"What's it doing?!" she cried as the snuggler twisted and shuddered and transformed from a sagging armchair into a horribly uncomfortable steel throne with razor-sharp thorns down its back and spikes along the armrests. "I thought Tedious Niggle said these chairs would change to suit our personalities. This is like sitting on an iron!"

Fox was shocked into silence for a few seconds, but in that silence the snuggler began to change again. The thorns shrank, the spikes vanished, and suddenly the steel wriggled out of shape to become an enormous, fur-covered beanbag that purred gently.

Fibber, now slightly curious, edged closer to the other snuggler. He sat down with his briefcase on his lap. Immediately, the snuggler spun round and round before jiggling itself into the shape of an office chair.

Fox sighed. Of course Fibber's snuggler would turn into a hot seat for business while hers was nothing but a childish beanbag. Then she flinched. The beanbag appeared to be trying to cuddle her. At least she thought it was. She hadn't actually been cuddled before, but she'd seen it happen in films and with other families at end-of-school pickups, and it did seem that this beanbag was stretching furry arms round her waist. Fox felt a sudden and rather unexpected urge to cry, but thankfully, she was spared that ordeal because Fibber's chair was now spinning faster and faster and he had started screaming.

"Make it stop!" he cried. "Make it stop!"

When the snuggler did eventually stop, it was no longer an office chair but a beautifully carved park bench, made more comfortable with a row of brightly colored cushions. Fox thought all of this very strange. Tedious Niggle had said the snugglers would adapt to suit their personalities, but what did a cuddly beanbag say about her and a park bench reveal about Fibber? It made no sense. But, for now, there were more important things to discuss. Like understanding what on earth was going on.

The train was still moving irresponsibly fast, and through the window Fox could see that the light was fading. As if the carriage itself could sense dusk approaching, the lanterns burned brighter and some of the plants seemed to curl up as if going to sleep.

Fox turned to the bookcase and glanced over the book titles, hoping to find something that might shed a little light on their situation.

"*If*"—she paused to throw Fibber a death stare—"Casper Tock was telling the truth and this train is real and we are in fact heading for the Unmapped Kingdom of Jungledrop, I for one would feel just a little bit better knowing something about the destination ahead of us."

She lifted an enormous leather-bound book called *Navigating Jungledrop and All Its Quirks* by Mildred Amblefar into her lap. Fibber was making out that he wasn't interested, but given that the book started talking as soon as Fox turned to the contents page, it was impossible for him to ignore things completely.

"*For Lofty Husks, the ruling powers in every Unmapped Kingdom, turn to page three,*" a woman's voice—presumably Mildred Amblefar herself—said. "*For magical beasts (contains full-page illustrations of whitegrumps, swiftwings, and trunklets), turn to page ten. For rainforest plants (includes new discoveries about thunderberry bushes), turn to page twenty-three. For the Forever Fern, turn to page fifty-one.*"

Fox thought *Lofty Husks, the ruling powers* sounded like the most sensible place to start, but something about the Forever Fern seemed to beckon to her. After all, wasn't that what Tedious Niggle had said they needed to find?

She flicked to page fifty-one and the voice picked up the narration once again:

"*During my explorations through Jungledrop, I have discovered plants that grow pocket money and trees that sprout forgotten objects, but in all my travels I have never found the elusive Forever Fern. According to an ancient prophecy read in the wax of the candletrees, the fern can grant immortality. If the message from the candletrees is to be believed, an individual can take this fern and use it for their own gain or they can plant the rare pearl found inside it into an Unmapped Kingdom's soil to grant that kingdom safety and prosperity.*"

Fox closed the book for a moment. A fern that could grant immortality? That could be exactly what she needed! Squabble Sauces claimed, among other things, that their ingredients improved sleep and boosted intelligence, which was all nonsense. This, though—an ingredient that could offer customers immortality—now that would sell for millions. Billions even! And, although so much in the past few hours had seemed ridiculous and impossible and completely unlikely, Fox suddenly found herself believing in it all. Because if she could take something like this back to her parents, she would be loved and accepted and wanted by them, and that overrode all the impossibilities surrounding magic.

A very small part of her wondered whether the "safety and prosperity" of Jungledrop that the book had mentioned might be important, too. Then her parents' words back in the hotel sprang into her head. Worrying about other people was a waste of time. And what did their battle with this creature called Morg really have to do with her?

Fox glanced over at Fibber to see that he was staring intently at the book in her lap. Fox knew then that she had been right earlier: Her brother wasn't sure whether his plan was any good, whatever he had said about Mrs. Scribble. And now he was getting nervous because finding and selling immortality was a surefire winner, and if Fox found the fern before him, it would be a lifetime in Antarctica for Fibber. . . .

Without even speaking, the twins could tell that they both believed in the magic of Jungledrop now. Not because their world needed rain or the Unmapped Kingdoms needed saving—other people could sort all that out. No, they believed because their chance to impress their parents and avoid being ousted from the family depended on the Forever Fern.

Fox didn't know *how* she'd find it, but she wondered if the phoenix tear in her pocket might help. Perhaps the magic fizzing away inside it was the very thing that was needed to find the fern.

Fox gave her brother a steely look. "The Forever Fern is mine."

"Not if I get to it first, it's not." Fibber straightened up. "Finding a long-lost fern will require someone with a clear-thinking, strategic mind who can brainstorm confidently with the rulers of Jungledrop. Someone like me."

Fox scoffed at her brother, then she turned back to the book to read more about Jungledrop, but suddenly the carriage darkened and the train tracks began to rattle. The lanterns started to flicker on and off, until one by one they fizzled out completely and the train was plunged into darkness. The hairs on Fox's arms prickled with fear and she heard Fibber shift on his bench opposite her. She was surprised to find herself filled with a longing to hold her brother's hand, to cling to him and have someone reassure them both that everything was going to be okay. But pride stood in the way of her reaching out a hand, and years of jealousy and loathing were piled up on top of that, so Fox stayed where she was, alone and afraid and wishing for the light.

The Here and There Express rattled on, swallowed in darkness, and then, when Fox was beginning to worry that they might be trapped inside this tunnel forever, the train burst out into an explosion of color.

The trees that rose up around them were dark and mysterious, and what glimpses of the sky Fox could see through the tiny gaps in the canopy far above were velvet-black and pricked with stars, but the plants she saw shone with color: electric-blue ones with tentacles reaching upward and swaying slowly back and forth; purple ones in the shape of lanterns that hung from creepers and scattered golden dust; silver-spiked petals that clung to branches; green shrubs tipped with bulbs that blinked like eyes; and turquoise creepers that crisscrossed like a web of ice halfway up the giant trees.

Fox blinked in awe. This was a glow-in-the-dark rainforest.

The maze of roots and vines, bushes and plants was alive with detail and it was constantly moving. Not just the plants but the animals, too. A speckled squirrel nosed through the luminous undergrowth while butterflies with jeweled wings flitted above. A snake coiled round a tree flashed a golden tongue while a feather-tailed lizard scampered over the turquoise creepers. And high in the uppermost branches of the trees, silver monkeys played.

The train came to an abrupt halt that sent teacups, books, and trunklets flying, and the twins craned their necks to look out of the window.

Fox and Fibber had no idea what any of the plants and trees around them were, but when they saw Tedious Niggle glide out of the train and melt into his surroundings, they knew one thing for certain: They had arrived in Jungledrop.

Chapter 5

Fox jumped as the train doors burst open and a tapestry of noise hit her: the drone of insects; the metallic clank of tree frogs; the coos of hidden birds; and the barks and grunts of monkeys.

This was the voice of the jungle and it was, Fox concluded, offensively loud. "I wish it would all just shut up! It's impossible to think with that racket going on."

Fibber, still gripping his briefcase, peered out of the window again. "At least there's no roaring. I detest roaring."

Fox inched toward the doors, trying her best to remember what her geography teacher had said about jungles. Something about them being split into layers like a cake: the forest floor, where the insects, reptiles, and large animals lived; the understory, where most of the branches and vines were; and the canopy, closing everything in at the very top, where the monkeys and birds usually roamed.

"Tedious Niggle said we wouldn't get eaten or trampled on if we treated the jungle with respect," Fibber whispered from behind her.

"How do you respect something?" Fox hissed.

Fibber shrugged. "Insult it very quietly?"

Fox stepped off the train. For a second, the jungle fell quiet and still, as if it knew there were visitors in its midst, then the noise resumed as it stirred into life once again. The air was warm and heavy with moisture, and Fox blinked as she noticed freshly fallen raindrops glistening on the plants around her.

"*Rain*," she breathed. It had been so long since they'd had any back home that she'd almost forgotten what it looked like.

Fibber winced as his shoes touched down onto the carpet of leaves, sticks, and fallen branches. "There doesn't seem to be a shortage of rain here. So if Jungledop is meant to be in charge of sending it to us, why don't they just"—he paused—"bundle it all up and send it on like they're supposed to?"

"Maybe they're all incontinent," Fox replied.

"You mean *incompetent*," Fibber said with a smirk. "*Incontinent* means something else entirely."

Fox ignored him and tried to focus on the task in hand. *Find the Forever Fern before Fibber.* But as she looked round the jungle, she felt a stab of doubt. How, in this wild, chaotic mess, was she going to find it?

She peered at her surroundings more closely and it was then that she noticed just how different the animals were here. There was a dragonfly perched on a vine, holding a pair of miniature binoculars. There was a hummingbird playing a tiny piano, balanced on a branch. There was a sloth having a bubble bath inside a giant leaf. There was even a spider who looked very much as if he might be getting ready for a date: He was wearing a bow tie and doing all sorts of fancy things to his web involving flower petals and balls of fluff.

Fox watched, open-mouthed. Wherever she looked, there was something happening. The jungle, it seemed, never stayed still. Fibber was also looking on in wonder, and so intent were the twins on gazing at everything in front of them that they didn't notice what was happening behind them. Until Fox remembered Mildred Amblefar's book: She'd need it if she was serious about navigating her way through Jungledrop. She turned round to fetch it.

"The train!" she shrieked. "It's—it's gone!"

Fibber gasped. "This is what that naked ghost meant: The junglespit powering the train means it simply comes and goes as it pleases. . . ."

The twins took in the tunnel the train had come through. It was, in fact, a vast cave surrounded by undergrowth. Only the way that the roof of this cave jutted out into the jungle made the whole thing look uncannily like a mouth. There were even shards of rock hanging down from the roof in jagged spikes, like teeth, and had the twins explored the undergrowth a little further (which they wouldn't have because they weren't the exploring types), they would have seen two smaller caves nestled in the greenery above, which could, perhaps, have resembled eyes. But when you're not aware that some caves in Jungledrop take the form of dragon heads carved from stone, it is, admittedly, quite easy to pass them by.

"But—but how will we get home?" Fibber spluttered.

Fox felt her pulse quicken. "If the Here and There Express goes as it pleases, it'll probably come back as it pleases." She swallowed. "One day."

"Would've been helpful if it had left behind the whispering book," Fibber mumbled. He flicked several fireflies off his suit, then raised his chin toward his sister. "I suppose this is good-bye, then."

Fox ducked as a flying squirrel—wearing overalls—hurtled past her head. She looked at her brother and wondered whether an ally might be helpful on this kind of quest and if now might actually be a good time for her and her brother to work together. . . . And for the briefest of seconds, it seemed to Fox like Fibber was about to say something too, but then he stopped and chewed on his lip instead. The image of Antarctica spilled into Fox's mind again, and all thoughts of teaming up with her brother vanished.

"And good riddance," she said curtly.

Fox knew there wasn't an awful lot you could say to someone after that, so she turned sharply and marched off into the trees.

A squawky voice called down from the canopy. "The one with red hair is hoping the one with the black handbag will come after her. And the one with the black handbag is trying very hard not to burst into tears."

Fox froze in her tracks and looked up at the tree in front of her. Its branches were lined with yellow orchids and fire-red moss, but other than that they seemed empty.

Fox slid a glance behind her at Fibber who was squinting up at the same tree. And then the animal that had spoken gave itself away. High up on a branch above them was a yellow parrot. It had been completely camouflaged among the orchids until it ruffled its feathers, which, Fox saw, were purple underneath.

The parrot cleared its throat. "The one with the red hair is confused. The one with the black handbag—"

"—it's a briefcase!" Fibber cried.

"—is starting to panic and is realizing his choice of footwear is entirely inappropriate for the jungle."

Fox turned to see Fibber kicking a worm off the sole of his leather shoe. But just as she was about to question what on earth was going on, a young boy burst out of the canopy, riding a unicycle that balanced on top of the turquoise creepers as if they were tightropes.

He was smaller than the twins and wore shorts that appeared to be a patchwork of leaves while his waistcoat was made of feathers. What he lacked in height he made up for in hair, which was dark and messy and seemed large enough to house several bird's nests quite comfortably. His eyes burned with the wild kind of excitement and hope that comes with being eight years old.

"Heckle!" the boy cried. "I hope you haven't been rude to our guests."

The parrot cocked its head innocently.

"Sorry about Heckle," the boy said to the twins as he dismounted his unicycle and propped it up against the trunk of a tree.

He scampered down the branches as quickly and easily as if he had been scampering down a staircase until he landed with a thump in front of Fox. Close up, Fox noticed the boy had a blue raindrop tattooed onto each earlobe. But, other than that, he looked reassuringly like an ordinary boy.

He chattered on excitedly. "Heckle repeats what other people and animals *think* rather than what they say—which isn't usually a good thing. Last week she told a chimpanzee that his wife thought he was a—"

"—pig-headed know-it-all who never did his fair share of the washing-up," Heckle cut in matter-of-factly.

The little boy giggled. "And for that you very nearly got yourself eaten!"

Heckle pecked innocently at a leaf.

"I'm Iggy Blether," the boy said to the twins, "and I can't believe that *I'm* the one welcoming the Faraway heroes to Jungledrop!"

Fox couldn't recall anyone, ever, being excited to see her, let alone someone assuming she was a hero. It was quite a nice sensation and she very nearly smiled, until she remembered that smiling and being nice never got you anywhere, so she adopted her familiar scowl instead.

"They say you get the best view of the jungle from up on the Hustleway," Iggy continued. "But who knew I'd see the candletree's prophecy come true from up there too!"

Fox glanced up at the turquoise creepers and saw that there was, in fact, a strange sort of order to them. They zigzagged through the trees, connecting each one to the next to form a vast network, and in the far distance, silhouetted against the glow of the rainforest, Fox could make out dozens of unicycles nipping back and forth between the trees.

"There I was, out beyond the Boundary for Safe Keeping, way past curfew because Heckle had flown off—again—and I saw the dragon roar!" Iggy pointed to the cave the Here and There Express had come through and grinned. "I can't believe you're finally here to save us!"

Fibber took one look at the cave behind him and bolted through the undergrowth toward his sister. "Dragon?!"

Heckle coughed. "The one with the black handbag—"

"BRIEFCASE!" Fibber snarled before tripping over a log and falling flat on his face.

"—is worried he might throw up if the jungle starts roaring. The one with the red hair is secretly rather excited about the idea of being a hero, but is pretending not to show it."

Fox glared at Heckle, then turned back to Iggy. "What's this about a prophecy?"

The little boy's eyes glittered. "Eight years ago, a few weeks after I was born, the Lofty Husks read a prophecy in the wax of the candletrees and now *everyone* here knows it by heart because it's our last hope to be safe from Morg." Iggy took a deep breath.

"When trees fall dark and start to groan,
Morg has come to make her home.
Her power will grow until it seems
Hope is but a lost-long dream.
Then listen for the dragon's roar:
Help will come from far-off shores."

Iggy paused for effect, but the twins looked blankly back at him.

"The dark, groaning trees are the forest in the far north of Jungledrop, which we call the Bonelands," Iggy explained.

"This forest has been dying my whole life, and we Unmappers believe it's because Morg traveled from her old home in Everdark—a hidden land halfway between your world and mine—to Jungledrop and now she lives in the Bonelands."

Fox considered this. If the harpy was on the loose in this kingdom already, perhaps it was worth finding out a little more about her in case they came up against each other when they were looking for the Forever Fern. "So you've seen Morg in Jungledrop, then?" she asked.

Iggy shook his head. "No. But we've seen her spies. The Midnights, we call them. It's thought Morg is in the Bonelands because she hasn't got enough strength to get any farther. But her Midnights come snooping through Jungledrop most days after the sun has set."

Fibber stole a glance up at the night sky poking through the trees, then edged a fraction closer to the others. "So these . . . Midnights could be close now?"

"No one's sounded the alarm," Iggy replied, "so we should be all right, but it's not like in the olden times when apparently the Unmapped Kingdoms were safe places."

He took in Fox and Fibber's blank faces.

"I forgot that you wouldn't know anything about our

worlds!" he exclaimed. "You see, before Morg invaded the Unmapped Kingdoms, a phoenix ruled from a place called Everdark—so my parents tell me. They said the bird would watch over the four kingdoms, granting them their magic, then every five hundred years the reigning phoenix would die and a new bird would rise from its ashes to renew the Unmapped magic." Iggy sighed.

"But all that changed when the last phoenix died and Morg sprang up from its ashes instead. Now every Unmapper lives in fear. She tried to attack Rumblestar first, and now she's come here to Jungledrop. Her Midnights have been raiding the rainforest for as long as I can remember. . . ."

Fox looked around at the trees, plants, and shrubs. "What are they raiding? *Flowers?!*"

"For the first few years, it was our thunderberry bushes," Iggy replied. "The Lofty Husks said that leaving Everdark to come here would have taken nearly all of Morg's strength. So she used the last drops of her magic to conjure her Midnights, then she sent them out to steal our thunderberries to restore her power."

Fibber scoffed. "You're saying Morg got her strength back all because of a diet of berries?!"

From her perch on the branch above, Heckle cleared her

throat. "The boy with the briefcase, and indeed the girl with the red hair, are doing an awful lot of doubting when we really should be getting back to—"

"Shut it, parrot." Fox turned back to Iggy. "Finish telling us about these berries, then, in case it's stuff we need to know for our quest."

Fox wasn't sure how exactly heroes were meant to behave, but she assumed being bossy, rather than being pushed around by a loud-mouthed parrot, was probably a safe place to start. Stamp or be stamped on and all that.

Heckle ruffled her feathers, then muttered, "The girl with the red hair has some very strange ideas about being a hero."

Sensing that Heckle was veering into trouble again, Iggy carried on. "Thunderberries aren't like ordinary berries. They've always been sacred because thunderberry bushes are the most magical plant in all of Jungledrop."

He took a few steps into the undergrowth and pulled back the foliage to reveal a shriveled blue plant.

"We used to have thousands of them—blue bushes bursting with berries—before Morg sent her Midnights out across the kingdom to steal as many as they could so that she could take their magic. Thunderberries are so wild that our usual magic spells couldn't protect them, and now all the thunderberry bushes are"—Iggy swallowed—"dead."

"But what does it matter if a bunch of stupid berries get eaten?" Fibber snapped.

Fox was relieved to see that now Fibber was well and truly out of his comfort zone, his churlish nature was slipping back out again.

"Because these berries give us dye that we mix with rain marvels from Rumblestar to make ink," Iggy replied. "And that ink is used to paint rain scrolls—the very ones we send to *your* world to give *you* water—and we haven't had enough berries to make ink for *eight years*. I can't even remember seeing a thunderberry in real life!"

Fox thought back to the timekeeper plants on the train. If one year in her world was almost thirty years in the Unmapped Kingdoms, then eight years here would mean . . . She racked her brain, but she was hopeless at math.

Conveniently, though, Heckle had been reading her thoughts again. "The girl with the red hair is struggling with her arithmetic and would probably like to know that eight years in the Unmapped Kingdoms is just over three months in the Faraway."

Fox shifted. If the parrot was right, those timings tallied, exactly, with when the last of the rain fell in her world. . . .

Iggy sighed. "We thought the raids would stop after the thunderberries vanished. But then Morg turned her attention to our animals. Hundreds of them have gone missing over the last few years. It's as if the jungle is slowly being emptied of life! And we think somehow Morg has been using these animals to increase her power. Every day, a little more of Jungledrop is lost, because when the Midnights come for the animals, their dark magic causes a chunk of our rainforest to die. Omnifruit trees are now nearly extinct and many of our rivers have dried up—our main sources of food and water are vanishing before our eyes as the jungle shrinks around us! Beyond these parts, the rainforest is a wasteland and the Lofty Husks have said we've only got a few weeks left before the magic here fades away, too. Your world and ours are doomed if you don't find the Forever Fern fast because the Unmapped Kingdoms only stand if we pass on our magic to the Faraway!"

Fox felt a niggle twist inside her. This kingdom really did seem to be in charge of sending rain to her world, so if she found the Forever Fern, she could be the one to put an end to the water crisis back home. She'd be crowned a hero! She'd be valued and noticed at long last—possibly even loved! Her heart wobbled at the idea. And *yet* . . . she thought of Casper Tock. He had saved the world and what had become of him? Absolutely nothing. He'd ended up in a musty old antiques shop in the back end of nowhere. So if Fox gave up her plan and planted the pearl from the Forever Fern in Jungledrop, no one would know that their lives had been saved because of her. And what good was that?

Fibber, meanwhile, was eyeing Iggy distrustfully. "If you've had eight years of Morg causing chaos here, why hasn't anyone stepped up to sort things out?"

"We're doing all we can," Iggy replied. "The Lofty Husks are patrolling the kingdom for Morg's stronghold so that they can find a way to stop the Midnights. Everyone else is searching for another method of making ink for the rain scrolls. And the dragons are scattering moondust from their wings to keep what's left of the phoenix magic in each of the four kingdoms turning. But the candletree prophecy says only someone from the Faraway can find the Forever Fern and stop Morg."

Fibber smoothed his tie. "I'd like to speak with these Lofty Husks."

Fox elbowed Fibber out of the way. "Forget the Husks. And

all this talk about thunderberries and Midnights. I want to know more about this Forever Fern: How big is it supposed to be? What color do people reckon it is? Does it bite? There'll be no need to face Morg and her followers at all if this fern is found first."

Iggy reddened. "Sorry, I talk a lot when I'm nervous. Or excited. Or happy. Or sad. Or overwhelmed. Or underwhelmed. Or . . ." He blushed. "I talk a lot."

"We hadn't noticed," Fox muttered.

Iggy's face crumpled and for a second Fox felt a little bad for upsetting him. But her parents had gotten to the top by being horrid to other people and not caring about the consequences, and so Fox assumed, as a businesswoman-in-the-making, that she would have to do the same. She wondered briefly whether most businesswomen had training in being horrid to others to guarantee their success, because there were so many things to consider when stamping on people's feelings: tone of voice, the words themselves, and what on earth you were supposed to do with your hands. Fox settled for balling them up into fists and wedging them, aggressively, on her hips.

Heckle glided down from her branch and nuzzled into Iggy's shoulder.

"I should have known that heroes like to get cracking right away," Iggy mumbled. Then he drew himself up. "It's definitely best if you speak to the Lofty Husks first. They'll be able to arm you with whatever you need should things get out of control on your quest and—"

He stopped suddenly and his eyes grew large and afraid. Had Fox and Fibber known the rainforest better, they would have realized, along with Iggy, that the tree frogs were no longer croaking, the insects were no longer whirring, and the silvermonkeys had fallen silent.

An eerie hush had fallen over the jungle.

"Climb!" Iggy yelled. "Up the tree after me—now!"

The twins, used to being chauffeured out of situations when the going got tough, stared at Iggy as he pulled himself up through the branches.

"COME ON!" Iggy cried. "If the jungle goes quiet, it means danger's close!"

"What kind of danger?" Fox called up the tree. "Because I really need to get on with finding this Forever Fern and heading back home and—"

A thunder of hooves sounded. The kind of noise you feel in the ground as a tremble before it fills your ears and rocks through your bones. The stampeding grew louder and the leaves on the trees shook.

Both the twins flung themselves at the tree Iggy had gone up.

"Get out of my way!" Fox cried as she barged past Fibber and scrambled onto the first branch.

Her tie caught on the next branch and by the third she'd torn her blazer. She was doing better than Fibber, though, who was yelling about being terrified of heights and—in his attempt to climb a tree at speed while still holding a briefcase—had lost a shoe. But they hurried on up the tree anyway, as fast as their inexperienced legs could take them, because the jungle was on the move and it seemed to be coming for them from every direction.

Chapter 6

"Climb faster!" Iggy yelled. "There are spare unicycles parked up in the trees!"

"UNICYCLES?" Fibber cried. "I can't even ride a bike!"

But Iggy had already mounted his unicycle on a creeper and disappeared inside the foliage. Fox and Fibber froze on the tree they were climbing as the stampede of hooves grew louder, and left, right, and center, plants tucked themselves away and animals hid. Was this a herd of Midnights rampaging toward them? And had Iggy abandoned the twins to be eaten by these creatures?!

Seconds later, the little Unmapper zoomed back into view with Heckle on his shoulder. He was still riding his unicycle and behind him, following obediently, were two more unicycles.

"Hurry!" he called. "There's dark magic nearby, and though the Midnights have only stolen berries and animals before, the Lofty Husks warned that they may start snatching people away too. We're outside the Boundary for Safe Keeping, so the protection charms don't work here!"

The twins edged onto the bough where Iggy was waiting. "Just sit in the saddle and say 'Timbernook,' then the unicycle will take you to my village where it's safe."

Fibber gulped as he took in the drop below. "But what's to stop us falling off and . . . and dying?"

"Magic," Iggy replied firmly. "The unicycles are powered by junglespit, so you only need to say the name of the place you want to get to and they'll take you there by the fastest route! You don't even need to pedal!"

The stampeding hooves advanced and the leaves on the tree they had climbed trembled. Fibber, wild-eyed with terror, barged past Fox and Iggy. "Out of my way! Stampeding things always eat the stragglers first!"

Iggy shook his head. "Wait! You don't understand! The stampeding things are on—"

"—a mission to devour the whole jungle!" Fibber wedged his briefcase into the basket on the front of his unicycle, climbed on, then shrieked, "Timbernook!" and hurtled over the creepers into the understory.

Fox shoved Iggy aside, mounted the second unicycle, yelled her destination, then took off after her brother. Her unicycle darted along the turquoise creepers and zigzagged farther into the trees.

"The stampede has got nothing to do with the Midnights!" Iggy shouted at the twins. "What you can hear are the swift-wings! They're on our side and the whole herd is running because they're just as scared as we are by the jungle going quiet!"

"Impossible!" Fibber howled from the Hustleway ahead. "No one could be as scared as me!"

Fox glanced down to see a herd of extraordinary creatures bounding through the rainforest: They looked like stallions, except *these* stallions had wings tucked on either side of their bodies and eagle heads.

"Once we're back inside the Boundary for Safe Keeping, the canopy opens a little and the swiftwings will have room to fly off up to the clouds where they sleep!" Iggy cried. "See—look ahead! There goes Sprinter, followed by Lightning, and I think that's Flash with the silver wings."

The unicycles hurried along the creepers beneath the moonlight where the canopy opened, and Fox gasped, in fear and awe, as the swiftwings rose up all around them—a rush of swishing tails, gleaming bodies, feathered wings, and sharp, proud beaks. Then the trees folded over the sky again as the unicycles hurried on.

"The protection charms will keep us safe now," Iggy panted. "Morg knows there are several phoenix tears in the Faraway. She must have Midnights on the lookout to drag any newcomers in Jungledrop to the Bonelands, and that's why the jungle fell quiet earlier." His voice brightened the further into the trees they went. "Dark magic can't cross over into the heart of the kingdom where we live because these parts are still steeped in the oldest kind of magic." Iggy's eyes glittered. "Phoenix magic."

Fibber twisted round in his seat as far as he dared and looked at his sister. "Have you still got that phoenix tear?"

Fox thought fast. She wasn't about to lose her only advantage in this quest. "I"—she paused—"left it on the train."

"Typical," Fibber muttered.

The unicycles kept moving, wiggling their way over the creepers, as the rest of the swiftwings soared up through the canopy behind them.

"You might have told us at the start that the stampede wasn't anything to worry about," Fox called over her shoulder to Iggy.

"I did try," Iggy replied. "But it was quite hard to be heard over all the yelling and pushing."

Heckle, on Iggy's shoulder, ruffled her feathers. "Iggy is wondering whether all heroes have bad tempers at the start of their quests or if it's just the ones who arrive in business suits."

Iggy rapped the parrot on the beak, then sensibly moved the conversation on. "It's a shame the swiftwings couldn't tell you themselves that they're on our side, but none of the magical creatures or the animals in this kingdom can speak. Except, I suppose, the Lofty Husks. The swiftwings are incredibly fast at running and flying, though, so we Unmappers named them to suit their personalities."

Fox chanced a look behind her. There was just one swiftwing left on the jungle floor, and after a few false starts and a considerable amount of puffing and panting, it launched itself into the air. It wasn't graceful as the others had been—more winged donkey than flying stallion—but it wobbled this way and that until eventually it disappeared through the canopy.

"We call that one Total Shambles," Iggy explained.

Back within the boundary, there were dozens of unicycles flooding in across the Hustleway. Adult Unmappers, dressed in similar clothes to Iggy, hastened in from all directions. They were heading toward the same cluster of trees that the children's unicycles seemed to be aiming for. These trees weren't as tall as the ones Fox had seen beyond the boundary, but they were wider. Much wider. They had to be to make room for their beautifully carved doors, shuttered windows, winding staircases, and jutting verandas. For these fifty hollow trees were home to the two hundred Unmappers who lived in Jungledrop.

"Welcome to Timbernook," Iggy said. "I—"

He was interrupted by a growl so loud and close that both Fox and Fibber tumbled backward off their unicycles and plunged toward the forest floor. They fell, screaming, only to find themselves landing upon a plant built entirely of feathers, which made falling onto it feel rather like sinking into a mattress.

The twins stood up shakily and came face-to-face with something large and fur-covered and incredibly sharp-toothed. It looked like a panther, only its fur was gold.

Fibber grabbed Fox by the arms and pushed her in front of him. "Eat her first!"

The golden panther had paws the size of dinner plates, each one fringed with giant claws, and eyes that were as dark and deep as a well. It narrowed those eyes at Fox.

Panicking, Fox pointed up at Iggy. "Or you could start with him?"

The golden panther opened its cavernous mouth and the twins shook with fear, but to their surprise and relief, the animal didn't eat anyone. Instead, it spoke—a female voice that was low and coated in a growl.

"Children from the Faraway?" The panther blinked. "*Can it be?*"

The twins edged backward until they were pressed up against a large tree. The panther took another step closer to them. Fox could feel the creature's breath—hot and heavy—on her cheeks. But the animal didn't growl or flash her teeth. In fact, she didn't look hungry at all. Her large dark eyes seemed curious and perhaps a little bit hopeful.

The panther dipped her head. "I am Goldpaw, one of the four Lofty Husks that rule the kingdom of Jungledrop. The rest of my kind are patrolling the rainforest to ward off Morg's

Midnights—Brightfur to the west in the Blazing Ridges, Spark to the east in the Elderwood, and Deepglint up north in the Bonelands, but I know I speak for all of them when I say that you are a most welcome sight."

"So, just to confirm," Fibber said, clutching his briefcase to his chest, "you like growling, but you're *not* going to eat us because you're in charge here?"

"It is never a good idea to eat heroes at the start of their quest," Goldpaw said. "That sort of behavior gets everyone into a dreadful muddle."

The panther watched the twins carefully as if weighing up what sort of children they might be. Fox was used to being weighed up by her parents—their eyes were always judging and looking disappointed—but somehow it wasn't the same with Goldpaw. Her eyes blazed with belief, and it made Fox feel, for the very first time in her life, ever so slightly less useless than usual. And, once again, she found herself imagining what it would be like to be the hero who saved the world. But, once again, she found herself remembering Casper Tock and his poky little shop, so she managed to blot the thought out before she got carried away.

Goldpaw frowned. "I did not hear a dragon roar to fulfil the candletree prophecy that help was, at last, on its way."

"I did!" Iggy cried from the Hustleway. "The Snaggletooth Cave roared because the Here and There Express charged out of it, puffing steam and carrying these two heroes from the Faraway, and the whole thing looked *just* like a dragon roaring!" He paused and then bit his lip. "I know I was out-of-bounds after curfew and I shouldn't have been, but Heckle flew off again . . . and really it all worked out for the best."

Goldpaw drew back from the twins and turned her attention to Iggy. Fox was surprised to see that she listened as if she actually cared—as if small, irritating children like Iggy might in fact matter after all. "The parrot that follows you around, repeating everyone's feelings? You strayed beyond the boundary to find her?" she asked.

Heckle, who had been taking a nap inside Iggy's hair, shuffled out onto his shoulder again. She preened her feathers and looked around, but before she had time to pluck out Goldpaw's innermost thoughts, Iggy cut in.

"Yes. I couldn't leave Heckle out there alone. But . . . what I was really trying to say was that, well, maybe if I hadn't found the heroes and got them up onto the Hustleway, they'd be over in the Bonelands by now—with Morg . . ."

"You risked your own life looking after our guests, Iggy," Goldpaw said. "You have done the kingdom a great service—at a time when it needs it most—and so, under the circumstances, you are forgiven for trespassing outside the Boundary for Safe Keeping."

"Looking after us?" Fox scoffed. "I'd hardly call a frantic dash through the jungle being looked after!"

Fox glanced at Fibber, expecting him to say something equally unpleasant about their escapade. But he didn't. He just stood there in his suit, looking small and afraid and decidedly less impressive than usual. Something about the panther, it seemed, was making him behave almost politely.

Goldpaw's whiskers twitched and when she spoke to Fox, there was an unmistakable edge to her growled words. "I imagine what you are trying, very unsuccessfully, to say is: *Thank you, Iggy.*"

Fox, who had never thanked another person in her life, looked blankly up at Goldpaw and then at Iggy.

Heckle shifted on Iggy's shoulder. "The girl with the red hair is wishing Iggy and his annoying parrot—*Oh! What rudeness!*—would just clear off."

Goldpaw tilted her head at Fox, then she looked back up at

Iggy. "Hurry home now—your parents will be worried about your whereabouts. I will take things from here with our guests."

"Heroes," Fox prompted. She had grown rather fond of the term after hearing Iggy use it.

"We'll see," Goldpaw said quietly.

Fox felt an uneasiness slide under her skin. The Lofty Husk wasn't throwing her weight around or being rude and yet it still very much felt as if the panther was in control of this conversation. There was a wild kind of power that seemed to ripple beneath Goldpaw's fur.

"Good luck," Iggy said to the twins as he turned to leave. "It was . . . *quite* nice to meet you both."

Fox made it a rule not to care what other people thought of her, but she could tell that Iggy's faith in her and Fibber had dimmed in just the short time they had known each other. And she was a little miffed because it had felt pretty good having someone believe in her for once. As she watched Iggy dismount his unicycle, swing down between the branches, and scamper through the glowing undergrowth, she felt disappointed that being adored had only lasted such a short while.

Fox turned back to Goldpaw and was met by two dark, disapproving eyes.

"I will say this once and once only: manners matter, especially out here in the jungle. Should you forget to say 'excuse me' when passing a tantrum tree, you may well get walloped to death. Should you forget to say 'please' to a whitegrump when asking for a favor, you may well get gorged through the heart. And, should you forget to say 'thank you' to an Unmapper who helps you, you may well find that the next time you are in a pickle, they do not help at all."

Fox turned to Fibber, hoping he would say something, but her brother was listening obediently. Fox guessed he was still rattled by their fall from the Hustleway, but *she* wasn't going to let a little tumble get in the way of her businesslike approach.

She channeled her most purposeful voice and followed it up with a glare in Goldpaw's direction that she instantly regretted because it made her eyeballs wobble.

"You are very much *not* what I was expecting," the panther said. And then, after a pause, she added: "But, then again, apparently Casper Tock did not look like much, and he went on to save the Unmapped Kingdoms and the Faraway from doom. So let us hope, for everyone's sake, that you improve upon first impressions."

Goldpaw began to walk, her enormous paws soft and silent

as they picked their way through luminous blue plants with bells for flowers and shimmering purple ones dusted with glitter. The twins followed, bickering away to themselves as they left Timbernook behind.

"Names if you please," Goldpaw said. "We don't have much time."

Fibber muscled past Fox to draw level with the Lofty Husk, and Fox could sense a renewed sense of purpose to him now that the quest seemed to be about to start in earnest.

"I'm Fibber Petty-Squabble," he said. "The clever, organized one who's going to find the Forever Fern." He jabbed a thumb in Fox's direction. "And that's my sister, Fox. I have no idea why she's here."

Fox edged past a prickly red plant and scowled at her brother. "Shut it, Fibber. I'm far more likely to find the fern. All you'll do is—"

"You will find it together," Goldpaw said sternly. "Your chances against Morg and her Midnights will be greater if there are two of you."

The twins exchanged an appalled look.

"What are these Midnights?" Fox asked. "What are we up against, really?"

The clanking of the tree frogs rattled through the jungle as Goldpaw led them on into a tunnel of shrubs that folded over them and were dotted with glow-in-the-dark flowers.

"Monkeys," Goldpaw said.

Fibber blinked. "Monkeys? Is that all?"

Goldpaw growled and the flowers in the tunnel trembled. "Morg's monkeys are creatures filled with such terrible darkness that the whole jungle falls silent with terror when they approach."

Fox frowned. "So you've seen these monkeys, then?"

The panther nodded. "Seen *and* injured them. But we cannot seem to kill them. They find their way back to the Bonelands after every raid, and when they return here, they are just as strong as before. There is something unnatural about these monkeys, mark my words; the very darkest magic is keeping them alive."

Fox raised an eyebrow as she followed Goldpaw through the tunnel. How dangerous could a *monkey* really be?

But had Fox seen what was unfolding back in Timbernook at that very moment, had she seen the troop of dark shapes edging—for the very first time—into the heart of Jungledrop because Morg's power had, finally, grown to the point of breaking the phoenix protection charms, had she seen the Midnights snatch Iggy before he made it to his home, had she seen them gag him and bundle him away toward the Bonelands, Fox would not have spoken so lightly of monkeys carved from dark magic.

Chapter 7

Goldpaw pressed on through the shimmering tunnel until it opened out and a large turquoise lagoon sparkled before them. Trees surrounded the water, their branches lined with flickering candles and dripping with wax, and Fox wondered whether these were the trees that spelled out prophecies to the Unmappers.

There was a bridge, made of vines, that led over the lagoon to a beautiful temple fronted by a flight of paint-splashed steps and guarded on either side by what looked like two stone unicorns. A waterfall rumbled into the night on the far side of the lagoon, and beside that was an enormous tree with windows of all shapes and sizes, large pipes leading out into the waterfall itself, and a sign above the door carved into its trunk, which read: THE BUSTLING GIANT.

"Doodler's Haven," Goldpaw told them. "This lagoon was once the busiest place in the kingdom. It was where we made the ink for the rain scrolls. Dashers would return from the jungle with satchels crammed full of thunderberries and they would be mixed with marvels—droplets of rain in its purest form collected in Rumblestar and carried here by dragons—by Dunkers to make ink. Finally, the ink would rush through those pipes into the waterfall and down into this lagoon. Then Doodlers would scoop it up into jars and use it to paint the rain scrolls on the steps leading up to the temple."

Goldpaw smiled sadly. "I wish you could have seen a rain scroll on a Doodler's easel. The hidden magic behind your rain. They were paintings so majestic they made you gasp in wonder."

"Paintings can be that powerful?" Fibber murmured, more to himself than to anyone else.

Goldpaw nodded. "The rain scrolls are carried with the sun scrolls from Crackledawn and the snow scrolls from Silvercrag into your world every sunrise by our dragons so that you have your weather." She paused. "Or at least they were before Morg came to Jungledrop."

Fox glanced at Fibber. He was listening to the panther with

a look of awe on his face. The hardness that had been buried inside him had begun to thaw, as Fox had noticed, and although it still came out now and again (when he was scared or worried or when Fox wound him up because a lifetime of regarding someone as a rival is hard to shake), Fibber had been softening nonetheless. And this was because he had a secret.

It had all begun when his teacher, Mrs. Scribble, noticed something in him last term that everybody else had missed. And when a child who has been overlooked by their parents and almost everyone else in the world *is* finally noticed, they often turn out to be a very different person. Prior to his sessions with Mrs. Scribble, Fibber would have scoffed at Goldpaw's words, but in discovering Fibber's hidden talent and nurturing it, Mrs. Scribble had also taught him to look at the world in a different way. And gradually Fibber's tongue had become less sharp and his heart less thorny. But then he had heard about the Forever Fern on the train and seen the determination in his sister's face and a familiar panic had set in. If Fox presented his parents with an immortalizing fern, which was guaranteed to make millions, he'd be the one sent away. So just like his sister, Fibber had concluded that finding it was the only option open to him.

And yet now, as he stood before a place like Doodler's Haven in the presence of a mighty Lofty Husk, he was overwhelmed by wonder. Suddenly he realized that the quest for the Forever Fern was about something far bigger than beating Fox and impressing his parents. It was about saving Jungledrop and the Faraway and all the people who lived there. And somewhere, deep down, he thought that perhaps it was about saving a sibling, too—about trying to patch up a relationship that, until now, Fibber had pretty much given up on. Maybe this was a chance to work *with* his sister, as Goldpaw had told them, rather than against her, and to come out the other end as friends rather than rivals.

Fox, meanwhile, was experiencing no such revelations. She was simply feeling impatient with the Lofty Husk. "I've never seen any of these magical rain scrolls back home, or a sun or snow scroll for that matter," she said curtly. "Talking isn't going to make the Forever Fern appear. I need weapons and a map." Her tummy rumbled. "And dinner."

She huffed. Being a businesswoman with a proper plan in place was proving exhausting work, and she would have to remind herself to eat more on this quest. Her lunch back in the Neverwrinkle Hotel seemed a long time ago.

Fox thought of her parents again and the look on their faces when she came bounding back to the hotel with an immortalizing fern that would save the family fortune! She tried to imagine the scene. Perhaps a little podium would be nice for when she announced her news. And maybe there could be an orchestra playing some sort of triumphant music in the background—Fox figured musicians were probably quite easy to hire when you were a billionaire-in-the-making. And then there would be the way her parents treated her. Maybe they'd hold her hand when walking down the street or offer to read her a story before bedtime or even remember her birthday. Fox's heart swelled at the possibilities.

But Goldpaw's voice, which was level and strong and said nothing at all about dinner, brought Fox back to reality with a bump. "You have never seen a rain scroll because magic does not bang a gong when it arrives. It comes secretly and silently, without fuss or pomp. Dragons leave the scrolls in the overlooked parts of your world—deep inside caves, tucked into mountain crags, high up in trees—and within moments they vanish and you are none the wiser, though you have the weather your world needs to survive."

The Lofty Husk strode over to a nearby tree, stopped before

it, then opened her mouth. Fox flinched at the rows of bone-bright teeth, but the panther simply breathed upon the bark and golden dust poured from her mouth.

A satchel appeared at the foot of the tree. Fox blinked. Had it been there all along, camouflaged, or had the Lofty Husk conjured it out of thin air?

"The greatest explorers in this kingdom have tried to find the Forever Fern—and failed," Goldpaw said. "I tried and so did the other three Lofty Husks. But we failed, too. Then the prophecy told us that *only* those from far-off shores can unearth the fern's whereabouts, and your arrival here leads me to believe that it is speaking of you two. But you will only survive if you listen to me."

The panther sat back on her hind legs, her large tail curled round her, and looked the twins square in the eye. "Don't get lost, don't get tricked, and be careful what you eat."

She breathed more golden dust that fell about the twins, making Fox sneeze, before it vanished completely. "That breath will protect you from the sun's glare and from the sticklebugs' bites," Goldpaw said. "The objects inside this satchel will help with everything else."

Fox eyed the crumpled leather bag. "Why is there only one satchel? There are two of us."

"As I said before," Goldpaw replied, "you must work together."

Fox threw Fibber a filthy look and snatched up the satchel. She unbuckled it and shook out the contents: a blank piece of parchment, a small mirror, and—most disappointing of all—a spoon.

"You're sending us off into the jungle armed with a SPOON?!" she cried.

Beside her, Fibber was looking increasingly worried. "What about spears and stuff? And maps?"

"The parchment *is* a map," Goldpaw answered. "An indescribably rare one called a flickertug map. It is impossible for Lofty Husks or Unmappers to cross from kingdom to kingdom, but the rulers of Jungledrop, Rumblestar, Crackledawn, and Silvercrag can communicate with one another through enchanted mirror rings, and I have it on good authority from my peers that this flickertug map is, in fact, the last of its kind in *all* the Unmapped Kingdoms."

Fox picked the map up and then jumped as a strange silver glitter shimmered across the surface of the parchment. But no places or words appeared.

"You have to tell the flickertug map where you want to go,"

Goldpaw said. "It would not yield the whereabouts of Morg's stronghold or the Forever Fern when asked, but that might simply be because the wrong people have been asking. . . ."

Fox felt an unexpected shiver of excitement fizz through her.

"And the mirror?" Fibber asked, turning it over in his hands. "What's that for?"

"The jungle is full of tricksters," Goldpaw replied. "Its magical creatures, animals, and plants survive because they are masters of disguise: they can hide in exposed places; they can dissolve before your eyes; they can disappear without trace. But, with a doubleskin mirror, *you* can compete. Just hold the mirror up to your surroundings and your skin, hair, and clothes will adopt the exact colors and patterns of your setting: your ear might resemble a leaf, your nose a twig, your tunic the trunk of a tree. Remember, though, that the doubleskin's magic only lasts a few minutes and you can only use it once before its powers vanish altogether—so you *must* make it count."

Fox eyed the mirror mistrustfully. "I'll believe it when I see it."

"And, finally, the fablespoon," Goldpaw said. "Hold it above a plant and the details of that plant will flash up inside the head of the spoon: its name, its character, and whether it is food or poison." She paused and looked at Fox. "But it only works if you say 'please.' Keep these items safe and—"

The panther's ears swiveled back toward the tunnel. She stood up quickly, her fur on end.

Fibber spun round. "What—what's happening?"

Footsteps sounded in the tunnel and then out rushed an Unmapper—a man this time, with a leaf-tousled beard, raindrop tattoos on his ears and fear plastered across his face. "It's Iggy," he panted. "He's gone!"

"*Gone?*" Goldpaw growled. "I sent him home and watched him leave for Timbernook."

The Unmapper shook his head. "He never arrived. His parents are scouring Timbernook as we speak, but"—he looked down—"there are monkey tracks near his house. They don't look like the tracks the silvermonkeys leave. These ones are bigger, and spiked where claws might be. And they lead north. Toward the Bonelands . . ."

Goldpaw paced back and forth by the edge of the lagoon. "We always feared that Morg would, eventually, turn her attention to Unmappers, hoping to steal more magic from them than she can from thunderberries and animals. And now it seems that terrible day has come. Oh, poor Iggy! The terror he must be feeling. And it was on *my* watch. But for Morg's Midnights to have broken through the phoenix magic into the heart of the jungle." She shook her head. "That means the harpy's power is reaching its height. She will be on the move from the Bonelands soon, so it is not weeks we have left before Jungledrop falls but *days*!"

For a second, Fox felt a surge of guilt. It was because of her and Fibber that Iggy had been late making his way home. But then she remembered that feeling sorry for people was a sign of weakness and she fought hard to bury her feelings.

The Unmapper took a step closer to Goldpaw. "Deepglint is in the Bonelands, you said; he'll find Iggy and bring him home. Won't he?"

Goldpaw hung her head. "There has been no word from Deepglint for a month now."

The Unmapper's face paled.

"But that does not mean that he is lost to us," Goldpaw added hastily. "Deepglint might have found Morg's stronghold and be making plans to seize it. It could be too risky to make contact."

It was the first time that Fox had detected fear, and unease, in the Lofty Husk's voice, and it made her shuffle a little closer to her brother.

"I'll send word via the fireflies to Spark in the Elderwood and ask him to patrol Fool's Leap. We must get Iggy back before Morg's Midnights cross over that ravine into the Bonelands."

Goldpaw turned to the twins. "I will stay here and conjure the strongest spells I know to make the boundary safe for the Unmappers again. You should leave immediately. If Morg's power is nearing its peak, she may be very close to finding the fern. You *must* find it before she does and plant the pearl so Morg will never be able to harm Jungledrop again. If she swallows that pearl and takes the fern's immortality for herself, the Faraway will die and so will the Unmapped Kingdoms as we know them. Then Morg will steal all the Unmapped magic and create a new world with the power of the elements on her side."

"Yes, *yes*, all very tragic," Fox replied. "Now, where will I find shoes and a change of clothes for this quest? My blazer is in quite a state."

Goldpaw shook her head in disbelief, but it was clear that she didn't have time to discipline rude children. "You will find shoes, clothes, and flasks of fresh water in the Bustling Giant." She bounded off toward the tunnel with the Unmapper hot on her heels. "Now, go!" she called over her shoulder. "There is not a moment to lose!"

The twins made their way round the lagoon toward the Bustling Giant, and once inside the great hollowed hallway of the tree, which was lit by dozens of raindrop-shaped lanterns, they got changed into the clothes hanging up on the hooks there. Fibber put on a pair of patchwork-leaf shorts and a feather waistcoat. Fox chose a short feather tunic but kept her tie because it made her feel more strategic and businesslike. (It was a strange look, especially when coupled with the moccasin boots the twins found.) They glanced briefly into a few of the rooms leading off from the hallway, which were filled with vast cauldrons, twisting pipes, and staircases that wound higher and higher up the tree, then they grabbed two flasks of water and made their way outside again.

Fox laid the flickertug map down beside the lagoon and knelt before it. The waterfall roared on, the parchment glimmered silver beneath the candletrees, and even Fibber, whose gaze had kept wandering to the temple in the middle of the lagoon earlier, watched the map eagerly.

"Where is the Forever Fern?" Fox whispered to the parchment.

At first nothing happened. The map simply carried on glistening in the night.

"I knew we shouldn't have bothered listening to that crackpot panther," Fox muttered.

She wondered whether the time was coming for her to see if the phoenix tear could somehow lead her to the fern. But then the map's magic flickered into life and silver words curled out onto the parchment.

SEEK THE CONSTANT WHINGE

Fibber frowned. "Who or what is the Constant Whinge? What kind of map doesn't even show locations!"

Fox gave the map a short, sharp jab with her finger in case showing it who was boss prompted more information. But no new words, or indeed places, appeared. It was only when Fox lifted the map up again that she realized the flickertug's magic wasn't finished with them yet.

"Argh!" she cried as she stumbled forward. "The map's alive! It's—it's dragging me along!"

Fibber shook his head in disbelief. "Flicker*tug*," he murmured, running a hand over it. "Maybe the map will *tug* us in the right direction!"

Instinctively, Fibber reached out to grab the map. Years of trying to keep one step ahead of his sister were hard to shake, even though he knew that none of that mattered anymore. Fox grabbed back and Fibber took a deep breath. He thought of Goldpaw's words about working *with* his sister and reluctantly let Fox yank the map away from him.

"*I'll* lead the way," she snapped. And, with that, she hefted the satchel onto her shoulder with her spare arm and allowed herself to be pulled toward the waterfall spilling into the lagoon.

Fibber followed close behind, still clutching his briefcase.

"Do you really want to cart that briefcase through the jungle with you?" Fox called over her shoulder.

Fibber glanced at the Doodlers' temple again and Fox followed his gaze. What *was* it about the building that intrigued her brother so much?

"The briefcase is coming with me whether you like it or not," Fibber panted. "I've spent too long working on what's inside to abandon it altogether."

Fox didn't have time to remain curious because the map was

pulling her through a gap between the rock face and the thundering water. Then she and Fibber were both running behind the waterfall itself, the sound of it pounding in their ears.

Fox had expected it to be dark behind the waterfall, but there was a strange glow coming from the shelf of rock above them that the water careered off. Fox squinted. Hundreds of tiny bats were clinging to it. She had seen bats before—black ones with jagged wings and grating screeches that tore out of cathedral ruins—but these ones were bright white, like light bulbs, and they hung silently, watchfully, from the rock above the twins as the flickertug map led them on.

The sight was so utterly magical that, for the briefest of moments, Fox and Fibber exchanged glances full of wonder. And in that moment, the competition was forgotten because here they were, being led through the light of a thousand luminous bats by an enchanted map, a map that had not even shown the most legendary explorers or the rulers of this kingdom the location of the Forever Fern.

Fox felt an unexpected thrill at the thought of the map choosing *her*, and being unique—special, chosen—was enough to make her forget, just for a second, that she was unworthy of being loved.

The twins scampered out from behind the waterfall into the knotted undergrowth to find a yellow parrot perched on a low-hanging branch in front of them. They knew, at once, that this was Heckle because the bird took one look at Fibber's briefcase and started muttering about handbags.

"Scoot!" Fibber hissed at the parrot. "This is an important mission."

But Heckle stayed exactly where she was, her yellow feathers lit up by the glow-in-the-dark plants beneath.

Fox glowered at the bird. Seeing her brought back thoughts of Iggy and a prickle of guilt, which she quickly tried to squash. "Clear off, Heckle!" she barked.

Heckle fixed the twins with beady eyes. "The girl and the boy are feeling ever so slightly guilty about my beloved Iggy going missing."

"Shut it, feather-mouth," Fox snarled.

Heckle squawked indignantly, but the flickertug map, it appeared, didn't have time for conversations, because it hauled Fox on again, past an orange plant with clam-like petals that sprang open as Fox brushed past them, then spat out a cluster of spotted frogs that had been sleeping inside. Fibber hastened after Fox, and Heckle followed.

Fox threw a glance over her shoulder. "That parrot is *not* coming on this quest."

Fibber nodded. "I'd rather face Morg than spend any more time with that bird."

But Heckle—who harbored a wild hope that the twins might find Iggy as well as the Forever Fern—had decided that she very much *was* going with them.

Chapter 8

The flickertug map led Fox on into the jungle. At first the trees looked exactly like those she had seen in documentaries about rainforests at school: evergreens, banana trees, cathedral figs, and giant cedars. The only obvious difference was that they were all linked by the Hustleway high up in the understory. Fox took in the vast network of turquoise creepers that zig-zagged through the trees, connecting them all and providing a path through the knotted jungle. But there were no unicycles zipping back and forth, and Fox found it hard to imagine a time when countless Dashers would have been racing along the creepers with satchels full of thunderberries.

Very soon the trees began to change, growing stranger and wilder with every step the twins took. One had hundreds of leaves that seemed to be blank sheets of paper. Another grew a single sock from its uppermost branch. The next one had small silver buds that Fox realized were silver-foil wrappers, only when the twins opened a few up, they saw there were no sweets inside.

Heckle wheeled above the children. "The girl and the boy are puzzled by the trees in the Elderwood, but Heckle is used to such sorry sights. The leaves of the chapterbarks are now blank pages when they used to be filled with unpublishable stories. The left-behinders only grow one forgotten object a year when they used to grow everything from odd socks to house keys and reading glasses. And the gobblequick trees only produce sweets when you beg for several hours. Years ago, you just had to drift past one and it would shower you with toffees."

But now that they were outside the Boundary for Safe Keeping, Fox had noticed something altogether more sinister. Beyond the trees around them, vast stretches of rainforest had been flattened, and plants and shrubs looked as if they'd been burned to the ground. Fibber, too, had seen the black undergrowth and the twins exchanged nervous glances. Morg's dark magic had been in these parts, so what was to say her Midnights weren't still here, looking for the twins?

The parrot flapped on above the children. "Heckle is missing Iggy dreadfully. It was that little Unmapper, after all, who found Heckle in the Elderwood a few months ago, unconscious after a tussle with Morg's Midnights. He nursed Heckle back to health."

Fibber groaned. "I didn't realize the parrot would share her *own* thoughts as well as other people's."

Heckle flicked her tail feathers proudly. "Since her encounter with the Midnights, Heckle began repeating feelings instead of squawks and now she can relate the thoughts of all sorts of Unmappers, animals, magical creatures, and, it would seem"—she gave the twins a hard look—"rude children from the Faraway. The only minds that Heckle cannot read are those of wild beasts or those twisted by dark magic."

The parrot swooped down toward Fox. "Heckle is tired and emotionally overwrought and is hoping she might be able to perch on the grumpy girl's shoulder for a bit. It's the least the girl can do after getting Iggy kidnapped. . . ."

Fox batted Heckle away. "Shoulders are for barging, not perching on. And my *name* is Fox and that's Fibber, so you can drop all the stupid chitchat about grumps and handbags."

Heckle flapped back upward, then said cagily: "The tantrum

tree ahead is considering which of you to wallop first. And Heckle doesn't blame it."

Fox's ears pricked up. *Tantrum tree.* Hadn't Goldpaw said something about navigating one of those?

The map led her closer and closer to a tall tree with thick, spiked branches that grew in large, swooping arcs. It was a bit like the monkey puzzle tree that grew in the park near Bickery Towers back home, only this tree seemed to be bristling—despite the lack of wind—as if it might be slightly *more alive* than an ordinary tree.

Fox gave the first branch a wide berth and then—*WHOOOOOMPH!* A very spiky one above unfurled and took a swipe at her, and had she not sidestepped in the nick of time, she would have been clobbered over the head.

Heckle let out a squawk, which, to Fox, sounded suspiciously like a laugh. "The tantrum tree is feeling the need to express itself. It isn't happy with such impolite behavior."

"SHUT UP!" Fox yelled as the tree thumped its branches down left, right, and center until there was such a maze of prickles surrounding the twins that they couldn't get away.

The tree had them trapped, and it was only a matter of time before one of its swipes would knock them clean out. Fibber flattened himself to the ground as two branches thumped down either side of him. Then Fox found herself remembering what Goldpaw had said about tantrum trees.

"Fibber!" she panted. "We have to *say* something to this tree for it to let us past! Something polite, only I can't remember what!" She yelped as a branch smashed down just beyond her, spraying soil and leaves everywhere. "What do you say when you want to get past someone? MOVE?! BOG OFF?!"

The tree didn't move or bog off. It simply ramped up the walloping.

And it was only when Fibber staggered up and screamed: "*Excuse me!*" that the branches of the tantrum tree stalled for a second.

Fox cottoned on straightaway. "Excuse me! Excuse me! EXCUSE ME!" she roared.

The words felt strange in her mouth, as if they didn't quite fit, but she and Fibber kept yelling them over and over again because the tantrum tree was now winding in its branches, like a retreating tide, until it stood quietly as if it hadn't, seconds before, very nearly knocked them out.

The twins edged away, and Fox gasped as the tree lowered a branch one last time. But it didn't try to wallop either of them.

It simply patted Fibber on the back, then tucked itself back into place again.

Fox lingered for a second below this branch, in case it decided to stoop down and pat her, too, but it remained where it was. After all, it had been Fibber who had remembered the words "excuse me." Not her. For a second, Fox felt a familiar jealousy burn inside her, but then she consoled herself with the realization that leading businesswomen probably didn't hang around waiting for hugs. They probably just carried on stamping their way to the top.

Fibber looked at Fox, and she thought he was going to give her one of his horribly smug grins, but then his face changed completely and he laughed. "That was close, wasn't it? I'm not sure Goldpaw would've been too impressed if we'd been flattened by a tantrum tree this early on in the quest!"

Unsure quite how to respond to this, Fox huffed. Then the flickertug map pulled her on once more, and abandoning all thoughts of a conversation, the twins hurried forward again. Heckle flew above them and this time neither Fox nor Fibber shouted at the parrot. Heckle had, through her insistence on speaking the tantrum tree's feelings aloud, reminded Fox about Goldpaw's words. And perhaps, if the twins could manage not to throttle the parrot as they journeyed on, they could use her as a guide on their quest.

As they made their way through the Elderwood, Heckle sobbed every time they passed a drained riverbed, a blackened patch of rainforest, or a drooping tree: she couldn't bear it that the phoenix magic keeping Jungledrop alive was now slipping away and that those responsible were holding Iggy captive. But Fox blotted out the parrot's weeping, focusing instead on moving as quickly as possible. She didn't want to be stuck in this creepy place a moment longer than necessary. After a while, though, she slowed. She had a stitch, she was badly out of breath, and she knew that if she didn't eat something soon, she'd probably keel over and faint. She glanced up at the tiny gaps between the trees to see glimpses of dark sky. They'd have to think about finding shelter for the night if they didn't reach the Constant Whinge soon.

Finally, the map eased its tugging until it came to a stop altogether at the foot of a tree whose branches were laden with fruits the size and shape of apples but the color of plums. Fox lifted the fablespoon out of her satchel, said "*please*" (having been reminded to do so by Heckle) and held it up to one of the purple fruits. Words started to form inside the head of the spoon:

NAME: OMNIFRUIT TREE
CHARACTER: SAFE, STEADY, AND SATISFYING
RISKS UPON EATING AN OMNIFRUIT: NONE

Fox reached out to pick one, but before she could, Fibber blurted, "You know I don't like heights, but we need to climb this tree and get up onto those unicycles on the Hustleway—*now*."

Fox glanced up. She'd been so focused on the fruits, she hadn't noticed that the flickertug map had led them to transport, too. She looked at Fibber. "Why? What have you seen?"

"A whole bunch of trunklets"—he pointed into the distance—"and I'm not confident we can outrun them in moccasin boots."

Fox thought back to the trunklets on the train who, Tedious Niggle had said, could chew through stone. Chewing through eleven-year-olds was probably not beyond them. "Do you think they've spotted us?"

Fibber shook his head. "They seem very focused on what they're doing."

Fox craned her neck to get a better look, but her brother was taller than her and he could see more. "Which is?"

Fibber shuddered. "Biting trees." He glanced at the

fablespoon in Fox's hand. "We can eat up in the branches. Come on. Let's go."

He lifted an elbow to barge Fox out of the way, then seemed to think better of it and hung back, even though it was clear he was terrified of the trunklets nearby.

Fox climbed on up the tree, her eyes peeled for Morg's dreaded monkeys. Although she said nothing in reply to Fibber, she couldn't help noticing that he was now talking as if he and Fox were on this quest together. Before meeting Goldpaw, she reckoned Fibber would have charged up the tree without warning her of the trunklets. It was almost as if he'd taken the panther's words about working together to heart. . . . But then maybe he was only being nice because he realized that facing down jungle threats would be easier alongside another person. Fox felt sure that as soon as the Forever Fern was in sight, her brother would be looking for a way to ditch her, so she shouldn't let her guard down.

There were two unicycles perched on the Hustleway in the uppermost branches of the tree, and Heckle flopped down onto the saddle of one of them as the twins climbed up to join her. "Fox is wondering whether climbing trees features on the agendas of most successful businesswomen," she clucked. "And Fibber is wondering whether he and Fox might become—"

"That's enough, Heckle," Fibber snapped, his cheeks reddening.

But Fox wasn't listening to the parrot or her brother; she was much more focused on finding something to eat. A quick brandish of the fablespoon showed her that the vines growing round the branches here, laden with green, grape-like fruits, were not to be eaten:

NAME: ICKLESCRATCH VINE
CHARACTER: SLY AND STEALTHY
RISKS UPON EATING AN ICKLEFLUMP FRUIT: ITCHY EARLOBES, THEN, 33 MINUTES LATER, CERTAIN DEATH

So she reached for an omnifruit instead and took a bite. Fox wasn't sure what she was expecting—she only knew that she was incredibly hungry. But the omnifruit was more delicious than anything Frau Longsüffer, the Petty-Squabbles' personal chef, had ever rustled up. And more unusual. The first few bites were savory rather than sweet, almost like munching on a deliciously warm and juicy burger topped with bacon and cheese. Fox carried on eating until she was nearing the end of the fruit. Why, this was banoffee pie now, her favorite dessert! Mouthful after mouthful of crumbled cookies, toffee, bananas, and cream.

Fibber ate ravenously too. Fox was curious as to whether his omnifruit tasted like hers or whether it was crammed full of his own favorite flavors, but she was too proud to ask. Which was a shame because, had she looked over at Fibber, she would have seen that again and again he tried to catch her eye as if, perhaps, he was on the brink of asking her the very same thing but was too nervous to make the first move.

When the twins had finished eating, the map urged Fox closer to the unicycles. So she clambered up onto the branch where they were, mounted one, and then—before she could give it a command—the flickertug map was off again. So strong was the magic hidden inside it that it pulled the unicycle full steam ahead along the Hustleway.

Fibber threw himself onto the second unicycle, yelled, "Follow that girl!" to it, and hastened after his sister.

The Hustleway wound on through the trees as the jungle grew denser, darker, and wilder still. Fox's eyes darted this way and that. Were the Midnights close? Could they sense that she and Fibber were racing through the Elderwood? There were still no Unmappers in sight—they were all safely back at Timbernook at this time of night—but even though many of the trees around the Hustleway had collapsed and numerous plants had been destroyed by the Midnights, there were glimpses of life still. Fox saw a snake with mirrored skin curled round a tree, a gecko with a jewel-studded tail scamper along a branch, and down on the rainforest floor, several junglespooks clad in loincloths having an animated discussion about sensible bedtimes.

The trees around them thinned even more until large gaps appeared in the canopy. Fox gasped as she gazed at the clouds hanging in the midnight-blue sky: Nestled into them were the swiftwings. Their horse-like bodies gleamed in the moonlight, and their tails hung down over the edge of the clouds.

On seeing the sleeping creatures, Fox realized just how tired she was. So, when the map slowed its tugging and a small tree house came into view, wedged between the boughs of the tree ahead, she felt relieved that the map seemed to be guiding them to another stop. At first she hoped this might be the Constant Whinge, but when they reached the tree house and she stepped inside, Fox realized this wasn't the case.

There were no Unmappers or magical creatures inside. Just a bunk bed carved out of the tree itself, a trunk laden with blankets, and a table with two chairs. Perhaps this was where Dashers used to sleep over when they were out collecting thunderberries? Whatever it had been used for, it was clear they should take advantage of the shelter because they weren't going to find the Forever Fern that night.

Fibber grabbed a blanket from the trunk, then, parking his briefcase under the bed, he threw himself down on the bottom bunk. Heckle fluttered round the tree house a few times, muttering about missing Iggy, then made herself comfortable on the windowsill.

Fox took another blanket from the trunk and dragged her weary legs up to the top bunk. Then she snuggled down, the satchel tucked beneath her pillow for safekeeping from her brother. The quiet of the night was broken only by the clanking of the tree frogs, and Fox found her mind wandering to Morg and her Midnights. Was it safe to go to sleep? Or would she wake surrounded by monkeys conjured from dark magic or face-to-face with the harpy herself? Fox shivered at the thought and then told herself she was being stupid. How dangerous could these monkeys *really* be, and surely Morg would leave the Midnights to deal with the twins while she sought out the Forever Fern?

Heckle tucked her beak under her wing, although she

couldn't resist one last revelation of feelings before she nodded off to sleep. "Everyone in this tree house is feeling a little scared and very glad of each other's company."

"SHUT UP!" the twins chorused.

But the parrot was right. Fox may have been trying to work out a plan to get rid of her brother as soon as she found the Forever Fern, but right now she felt glad that she wasn't alone here in this strange world in the dead of night. She rolled over on her bunk and saw that a small branch had wound its way in through the window. It ran all the way along the ceiling before finishing, in a cluster of small, round nuts, above her bed.

Fox eased the fablespoon out of her satchel. The tree certainly felt safe, and the Unmappers had even built a tree house in it branches, but who was to say that it didn't have secret magical properties that might catch her off guard in her sleep? She whispered, "*please*," very, very quietly, then held the spoon up to one of the nuts and read the following words inside it:

NAME: SNOOZENUT TREE
CHARACTER: LAZY
RISKS UPON EATING A SNOOZENUT: IN MOST CASES, SENDS CONSUMER INTO AN ENCHANTED SLEEP FOR ONE MONTH. IN RARE CASES

"What are you doing up there?" Fibber asked.

His voice wasn't cross and challenging, as it so often was. If anything, it sounded like he might just be making conversation. But Fox couldn't find it in herself to trust her brother. He had lied to their mother back in the Neverwrinkle Hotel as calmly as if he'd been talking about the weather, so she knew how good he was at deceiving people if he needed to.

Fox shoved the fablespoon back into her satchel. "Nothing," she snapped. "Mind your own business."

And just like that the conversation was closed.

Fox tucked the satchel back under her pillow and pretended to go to sleep. But what she was really doing was waiting. Waiting for Fibber to drift off so that she could pluck a snoozenut from the branch. An idea had formed in her mind. She would use Fibber to help her find the Forever Fern and then, when the fern was in sight, she'd give her brother a snoozenut to eat and he'd fall into an enchanted sleep. Then the Forever Fern would be hers alone to bring back to their parents! Fibber would follow her back home, when he eventually woke up, but by then Fox would have handed the fern over and it would be Fibber off to Antarctica, not her!

The plan was genius and so excited was Fox by its potential

that when she did, eventually, pluck the snoozenut from the branch above her, and tuck it inside her satchel, she forgot that she hadn't read the full description of the risks involved in eating it. She settled down to sleep, her fist closed round the flickertug map, smug in the knowledge that she had a snoozenut *and* a phoenix tear in her satchel now and the Forever Fern would soon be hers.

Chapter 9

Fox and Fibber might have been fast asleep, but beyond the Elderwood—over Fool's Leap, through a grove of nightcreaks, and up past a rotten swamp—in the heart of the Bonelands, a harpy was very much awake.

Morg sat on a crumbling throne in the antechamber of a long-forgotten temple. Her new wings, built from a shadow-spell that had taken nearly two thousand years to conjure in Everdark, after Casper Tock had destroyed her original pair, were folded by her sides. They had done what Morg had hoped they would: carry her from Everdark to Jungledrop. But that had been a long journey—she had crossed worlds to make it.

The harpy's strength was now restored and you could see it in the black feathers that covered her body and glistened like oil; in her eyes, which burned yellow through the sockets of the phoenix skull she wore over her head; and in her talons, which shone like polished bone. All this was thanks to Jungledrop's thunderberries and the tears of the animals her Midnights brought her.

But Morg's wings were paper-thin and ragged, like scraps of burned paper. It would take more than berries and animal tears to restore them to their former glory. Her hopes rested on the Forever Fern renewing their power and, because a harpy's wings hold her darkest magic, Morg vowed to stop at nothing until she found this fern.

Finding it, though, was proving harder than she had bargained for.

"Bring me the girl and the boy who have come from the Faraway," the harpy spat. "I cannot risk them finding the Forever Fern before me."

It wasn't immediately clear who Morg was talking to. The ruined antechamber no longer had a roof, so the night's darkness fell about it, filling every corner and covering the vines and weeds that grew over the flagstones.

But at Morg's words, a shape shifted in the shadows and a gravelly voice answered. "I will send more Midnights over

Fool's Leap to hunt for the children." There was a pause. "But, if you listen now, you might be able to hear from our latest arrival down in the crypt, an arrival who, I hope, might provide you with even more power."

Beneath the flagstones, and the silence, the faintest sound could be heard: a rattling, clanking noise—that of two little fists shaking prison bars—and then sobbing as the child behind those bars begged again and again to be set free.

"Your increase in strength has allowed the Midnights to break through the Lofty Husks' protection charms *and* the ancient phoenix magic into Timbernook," the gravelly voice went on. "And now we have an Unmapper boy whose tears may possess even more magic than Jungledrop's animals."

Morg leaned forward. "Bring me the child Unmapper's tears. For if I am to kill the Faraway children *and* find the Forever Fern, then my wings must contain some dark magic before the fern restores them to their full power."

The shape in the shadows shifted again and then it walked on two dark, furred legs out of the antechamber and down a flight of stone steps into the crypt. And when the giant ape—for that is what this creature was—came back up, minutes later, a small glass bottle tucked into its palm, Morg's wings twitched.

She rose up on her talons, her wings outstretched, then she snatched the little bottle containing Iggy's tears and swallowed the liquid in one greedy gulp. The harpy sat back in her throne and smiled darkly. She could feel the magic of the Unmapper coursing through her veins.

"Bring me more Unmappers, Screech." Morg's wings shimmered as they drank in Iggy's magic. "Bring me more."

Chapter 10

A cry from Fibber startled Fox awake.

There was a trunklet in the tree house. Or the arm of one, at least. And it was wriggling closer and closer to Fibber's briefcase.

"Oh, no you don't!" Fibber cried, seizing his briefcase and leaping up from his bunk.

The trunklet snatched back its arm, stuck out its tongue, then scampered away down the tree. Which is when the twins noticed what Heckle was up to. The parrot must have risen earlier than the children because she was now perched on the table, placing an omnifruit before each chair.

"Heckle is still very cross with Fox and Fibber because of Iggy's kidnapping, but she is hoping tempers might improve if Faraway folk are fed first thing."

Fibber sat down at the table. "Er—thanks, Heckle," he said, biting into one of the fruits.

Fox blinked. Had she misheard or had she just witnessed a Petty-Squabble saying "thank you"? Fox studied her brother. He seemed to be turning into a completely different person out here in Jungledrop! He'd been terrified on the Hustleway with Iggy; he'd very nearly fainted upon meeting Goldpaw; he wasn't snapping at Fox half as much as usual; and he'd taken to saying "excuse me" to trees and "thank you" to parrots. What had happened to the ruthlessly composed brother she'd known her whole life?

Fox wondered whether she was missing something important in how she was going about her mission and that maybe Fibber had found a better way of doing things. But Fibber's strategy seemed to involve being kind, and that meant being weak, and being weak meant letting the wall around her heart down. Fox was far from ready to start dismantling walls. She thought of the snoozenut in her bag. She had a plan and she needed to pursue it with a clear head.

So she sat down at the table and ate the omnifruit—pancakes, with maple syrup followed by a few yummy mouthfuls of blueberry porridge—in stony silence, refusing to thank Heckle for her efforts in providing it.

A short while later, Fox opened the door of the tree house and peeked outside. Down on the ground, the rainforest was a wasteland of dead thunderberry bushes and shriveled undergrowth. Nowhere, it seemed, was safe from Morg's Midnights. But the understory around the Hustleway here was stubbornly refusing to die: lining the branches were blue orchids, monkeybrush vines with flaming orange flowers, and red, spotted rafflesias. And in among this burst of color, bees buzzed, hornbills squawked, snakes (wearing sun hats) hissed, and a gibbon (holding a walking stick) barked.

Fox stepped out of the tree house, followed closely by her brother. In an instant, everything seemed to freeze. Leaves stiffened, ears flicked, eyes darted. Even the noise subsided. This was a rainforest living in fear. And it was only when the twins mounted their unicycles and sped off along the Hustleway that the animals and plants realized they meant no harm and came back to life.

With the map guiding Fox, the twins cycled on and on through the trees until eventually they came to a river that had not yet been drained of magic by the Midnights. It snaked through the jungle below, blue-green from the plants and trees lining it. For a while, the map spurred Fox further along the

Hustleway above the water, and she gasped as a pod of pink dolphins broke the surface, one after the other, before disappearing from sight. Then the Hustleway veered away from the river and the map slowed its tugging as they made their way down toward the banks of the water. And Fox knew what that meant: It was time to return to the jungle floor.

She and Fibber dismounted their unicycles and climbed down the tantrum tree the map had paused at, muttering "*excuse me*" all the way. Then they resumed their quest for the Forever Fern on foot. They hurried along by the river, now and again catching sight of some strange fish or eel gliding through the water. But, when they came to a purple plant on the riverbank in the shape of an umbrella with dozens of newspapers hanging down from inside it, Fox slowed a fraction. These seemed to be newspapers recalling events in her own world!

She read the headline of the newspaper closest to her aloud: "DROUGHTS, DEATH, AND DOOM!" Then beneath this: "No hope for the Faraway unless rain falls imminently."

Fox's stomach twisted as she let the map pull her on. This time, she couldn't seem to shake the guilt off. Her world was in chaos, Jungledrop was dying, and *she* might be able to do something about it. . . . But her chances of being loved by her parents depended on finding the Forever Fern, and she couldn't, no matter how guilty she felt, let go of that hope.

Burying her doubts as best she could, Fox ran on and on. She'd had no idea that being a successful businesswoman would involve so much rushing about. Perhaps she'd need to factor in hiring a secretary when she got home.

The river widened into a little pool, surrounded by trees so that the sunlight that fell through the gaps in the branches dappled the water—a pocket of the rainforest not yet claimed by the Midnights. And here the map stopped pulling. Fox looked around for a person or a building, but there was just the river, drifting aimlessly on, and the crowded trees bordering it.

Fox frowned. "The map must've stopped here for a reason."

"There!" Fibber cried. "In the river!"

Fox squinted into the sunlight to see that Fibber was pointing at something small, blue-skinned, and pointy-eared that appeared to be swimming through the water toward them. Fox staggered backward as the creature emerged onto the banks of the river and then darted, on webbed feet, behind a plant. It looked very much like a trunklet, only it was blue not green.

"Bash it with your boot!" Fox hissed at Fibber. "Or whack it with your briefcase!"

The creature peeked out from behind the plant it was hiding behind, then scuttled back into its leaves again. It did this three more times.

Heckle flapped down from a branch and squawked, "Heckle thinks that the boglet is trying to tell us something."

"Well, why doesn't it just spit it out?" Fox barked.

"Remember what Iggy said," Fibber told her. "Magical creatures can't speak."

And to Fox's surprise, her brother bent down, almost gently, in front of the boglet. He didn't say anything to the little creature. He just crouched before it—and watched.

Fox drummed her boot on the ground. "We haven't got all day."

"The boglet is feeling terribly overwhelmed by the arrival of the Faraway heroes," Heckle explained, "so picking out its thoughts is proving quite difficult."

The boglet stood, looking at Fibber, water dripping from its pointed ears, then it scurried back behind the plant. It popped out seconds later and then hid once more. Again and again it did this. The more it repeated the action, the more Fox wondered whether it was, in fact, trying to communicate with them, as Heckle had said.

"Do you know something about the Constant Whinge?" Fibber said quietly, tentatively, in a voice that showed he hadn't had much practice at being gentle, but was keen to try all the same.

The boglet peeped out from behind the plant and nodded. Then it hid again.

Heckle parked herself on the ground beside Fibber. "The boglet's thoughts are less of a jumble now, and Heckle believes it wants you to know that you have *arrived* at the Constant Whinge."

Fox threw her hands up in the air. "We haven't arrived at our destination! Look—there's nothing here!"

Fibber looked around, frowning. But he didn't raise his voice at the boglet. He spoke calmly, quietly, so as not to frighten it away, in a manner so unlike him that Fox had to rub her own ears to make sure that it really was her brother speaking. Why was he being *nice* again?

Fibber watched the boglet a while longer, then his eyes lit up. "The Constant Whinge is invisible," he said slowly. "That's what you were trying to tell us by hiding one minute, then appearing the next, wasn't it?"

The boglet nodded.

Fox frowned. She had always been told by her parents that being nice was a waste of time and yet here was Fibber being nice *and* getting the information they needed. She tried to follow his example and threw the boglet a grateful smile, if only to urge it to reveal a little more, but her face wasn't used to such an expression and she ended up grimacing at the creature instead. The boglet shrieked under Fox's scowl and she felt embarrassed and cross and jealous all at the same time. Fibber was better than her at everything! Even communicating with magical creatures . . .

"How are we meant to find something if it's invisible?" she grumbled.

Fibber turned to her. "I don't know, but I think we've got to trust the magical creatures here. We won't survive otherwise."

Fox snorted. "You're a fine one to be talking about trust. You're always tricking people and telling lies."

Fibber seemed about to say something, then he noticed that the boglet was shuffling away toward the river again. "Hey!" he called.

The boglet turned.

"I just"—he paused—"wanted to . . . thank you for your help."

The boglet grinned at Fibber's words, as if it knew something the twins and Heckle didn't. Then it hopped back into the river and vanished from sight, but as it did so, a very strange thing happened. The sunshine streaming down between the branches hanging over the river seemed to shiver and blur. It was almost like watching a mirage, only eventually mirages give way to obvious, predictable things. But there was nothing obvious or predictable about what was left in the wake of this one.

A ramshackle wooden hut appeared out of thin air, balanced on stilts over the water. There were wooden steps leading up from the riverbank toward it and a sign hammered over the closed front door, which read:

THE CONSTANT WHINGE

JUNGLE APOTHECARY

Fox gazed at the window beside the door. Behind the glass she could see a row of bottles, all shapes and sizes, filled with berries, leaves, and powdered bark. She couldn't believe that she was moments away from victory! But just as she was about to rush up the steps to claim the fern, there was a short, sharp bang and something green and glittery exploded out of the window, sending shards of glass flying.

"I thought I had been quite clear on this, boglets," a voice inside the hut muttered. "I do *not* wish to be disturbed."

Ignoring this outburst, Heckle fluttered onto the step before the door. The twins followed carefully, watchfully, their eyes glued to the window in case the owner of the voice should step into view.

But their eyes were not the only ones fixed on the Constant Whinge. There were others watching from the surrounding trees too. And had Heckle and the twins not been so excited by the appearance of the shack, they might have noticed that the jungle had fallen quiet and there was a strange ticking noise eating into the hush.

Three monkeys looked on from the shelter of the understory. But they had nothing in common with the silvermonkeys Fox and Fibber had seen leaping through the branches the day before. These monkeys were blacker than night and their orange eyes, which moved eerily from Fox to Fibber and back again, gleamed with terrible menace.

Chapter 11

"Fox is wishing Fibber would do the knocking," Heckle declared, "and Fibber is wishing Fox would do it."

"Fox is wishing the parrot would keep other people's thoughts to itself," Fox muttered.

That said, as they halted before the door of the Constant Whinge, Fox *was* surprised that Fibber—usually so confident—wasn't striding ahead into the shack to claim the fern for himself. In fact, he looked very much as he had done upon first setting foot in Jungledrop: scared.

"Fine," Fox said. "I'll do it." She reached out a shaking hand (for deep down she was frightened too) and knocked on the door. She waited, heart thudding. Whoever was inside the hut hadn't sounded pleased to be disturbed.

"If you've come about a runny nose," the voice snapped, "I'm all out of neverdrip salts." It was a male voice and it sounded old and tired. "If it's earache you're worried about, then you'll have to wait until November to be cured: I can only make eavesdrops when the eaves plants are in season. And, if you're here with gout, maybe it's time you stopped drinking so much junglejuice."

"We—we don't have runny noses or earache or, um, gout," Fibber said. "We—"

"*We*," the voice groaned. "There's more than one of you?"

"Three, if you include the parrot," Fibber said nervously.

"How incredibly tiresome."

There was a shuffling inside the hut. The twins waited hopefully for the person behind the voice to appear, but instead there came a clank of bottles, a fizzing noise, and another short, sharp bang followed by more green glitter bursting out of the window.

"Bother," the voice mumbled. "It looks like the Constant Whinge is here to stay for a while. . . ."

There was a pause and then footsteps, slow and shuffling, advanced toward the door.

Fox held her breath. Fibber clutched his briefcase to his

chest. Heckle muttered something about universal fear. The door opened.

In its frame stood a very old man. From his feather waistcoat, patchwork-leaf shorts, and the raindrop tattoos on his ears, Fox supposed he was an Unmapper. But he looked far wilder, older, and grumpier than the others she had seen. For a start, there were short tufts of weeds sprouting out of his ears, and his long white beard was intertwined with leaves and twigs. There were even clumps of moss growing between his bare toes.

"What do you wa—" he began, but stopped short as he took in the two children who stood before him. "So the candletree prophecy has finally come true. The Faraway folk have arrived. . . ."

Heckle cocked her head. "The old man had thought, after what happened to Ethel some years ago, that his work as an apothecary was finished, but now—"

"Careful, parrot," the apothecary said. "I have a buttonshut potion in here that permanently closes all manners of things: doors, hearts, mouths, *and beaks*."

Heckle shut hers immediately.

The old man turned to the twins. "Eight years ago, I cast

a charm on the Constant Whinge to make it invisible. I vowed that this shack should only reappear if the boglets who live along the riverbank felt it absolutely necessary. Over the years, the boglets have summoned it for several distinctly unimportant things. Like when the youngest of their kind got incurable hiccups and then when his grandmother started burping bubbles. And each time I successfully conjured a junglespit explosion to make the Constant Whinge invisible again."

He eyed the broken glass outside his window. "Until today." He took a deep breath. "You are the Faraway folk the prophecy promised—here, I presume, to rid the kingdom of Morg. So why, may I ask, are you skulking round my shack?"

"The Forever Fern," Fox said eagerly. "Do you have it inside?"

"Goldpaw gave us a flickertug map," Fibber explained, "and when we asked where the Forever Fern was, it led us to you."

The old man was silent for a moment. "There was a time when I collected plants, ferns, and berries from across the kingdom to cure almost every imaginable ailment." He paused. "But I have never come across the Forever Fern."

Fox felt her hopes clatter down and she scowled at the apothecary. "Then the map's stupid and the fern's stupid and you're probably stupi—"

Fibber cut in. "The map must have led us here for a reason. Maybe you've got something else inside that can help us?"

The man sighed. "I don't dish out potions anymore. Not since . . ." His voice trailed off. "You're wasting your time here."

He went to close the door, but Fox stuck out her boot to prevent it from shutting. "Listen up, moss-foot. We're on a very important quest here and we're not leaving until you cough up some leads on this fern." She barged past the old man into his shack. "So, what can you give us that might help, hmmmmm?"

"Are all Faraway folk this rude?" the old man muttered to Fibber. "Or just the under-eighteens?"

"My sister's not so much rude as"—Fibber paused—"*keen*. There's a lot at stake. We have to find the fern, you see."

The apothecary sighed. "Since the fate of the world is hanging in the balance, I suppose you'd better come in. Not that I harbor any sort of hope that I'll be able to help you."

As Fibber and Heckle followed the man inside, Fox scoured the shack, looking for anything that might be of use to her. There were shelves and glass-fronted cabinets lining the walls and every single one held row upon row of glass bottles, pots, goblets, and jars all with strange-looking contents and labels:

SIFTED SUNBLOSSOM: CURES BALDNESS (APPLY DAILY)

GOBBLEQUICK RESIN: CURES FUSSY EATERS (CONSUME BEFORE MEALTIMES)

MUDDLED STINKHORN: RADICALLY REDUCES LATENESS (APPLY IMMEDIATELY BEFORE TRAVELING)

DRIED MILKWEED: CURES BAD DREAMS (PLACE UNDER PILLOW BEFORE GOING TO SLEEP)

WRIGGLEWORT LEAVES: CURES STIFF JOINTS (MASSAGE INTO FEET AFTER STRENUOUS EXERCISE)

"Got anything to summon up lost things?" Fox asked.

The apothecary closed the door, then sat down at the table in the middle of the shack. And it was only then that Fox noticed the state of the objects strewn across the table's surface: crusty test tubes, a broken magnifying glass, weighing scales clogged with cobwebs. It was as if the apothecary had started an experiment years ago, then abandoned it halfway through and left it to rot.

Fibber looked around. "Or maybe you have something in here to kill a harpy?"

"Even if I did, I couldn't promise it would work," the old man said gloomily. "I used to be legendary. Unmappers and magical creatures would come from across the kingdom for cures from the Constant Whinge. 'Doogie Herbalsneeze will sort you out,' they'd say. 'He's the best there is.' But what's the use of helping everybody else when you can't help the one you love?"

The old man held two wrinkled hands over his face and, to Fox's horror, she realized that he was crying. She watched, aghast. She'd never seen a grown-up cry before and she found it deeply unnerving, like watching the edges of the universe break apart.

"Make him stop," she hissed to Fibber. "Immediately."

But when Fibber reached out a hand toward the apothecary, he only sobbed louder.

At which point, Heckle took it upon herself to reveal some innermost thoughts. "The old man is feeling both pain and relief in crying and—"

The apothecary wailed even louder.

"Thank you, Heckle," Fibber said firmly. "That's enough for now."

When Doogie Herbalsneeze's words did come, they tumbled out in a rush of tears. "I searched the kingdom for the most powerful plants and mixed thousands of potions when my dear wife, Ethel, fell ill eight years ago after trying to protect a thunderberry bush from Morg's Midnights."

The old man wiped his nose with a handkerchief. "But the dark magic of those monkeys had already seeped into her and nothing made any difference in the end." He looked up at the twins. "I couldn't save her, so there's no way I can help you rescue the whole kingdom."

Fox drew out the flickertug map from her satchel and looked at the silver words, THE CONSTANT WHINGE, glumly. It had brought them all the way here. For nothing. She held the map out now in case it wanted to tug her on again, but it lay limp in her hands.

She turned to Fibber. "Now what?"

Fibber sat down at the table; it seemed he wasn't ready to give up quite yet. "I'm sorry about your wife," he said to the apothecary. And then, after a pause: "Sometimes, no matter how hard you try at something, it just doesn't work out. But I don't think that makes you a failure. Maybe it means that all the trying is leading toward something else."

Fox stared at her brother. She could just about cope with Fibber being nice to the boglet. That behavior had, after all, made the Constant Whinge appear. But apologizing for another person's pain was a step too far. What on earth was he up to?

"You may have closed yourself off from the rest of the kingdom," Fibber went on, "but if the map led us to you, it has to be for a reason. It must think that somehow *something* here can help us in our quest for the Forever Fern. Jungledrop needs you, Doogie Herbalsneeze. You have a part to play in defeating Morg."

The apothecary was silent for a while and then he let out a loud sniff. "This is the problem with letting children into your workplace: they start teaching you to hope all over again."

Fox looked around at the shelves. "But how can a bunch of useless plants help?"

Doogie wiped his eyes. "Plants are never useless," he told Fox firmly. "They can regrow even after they've been eaten. They can sprout up in pockets of the jungle where it's too dark to see. They can live off air and mist. They can reproduce without moving. They possess more than twenty senses. They absorb carbon dioxide and release oxygen from their leaves, which people and animals need to breathe." There was an energy to the old man's voice now that hadn't been there before. "Plants are not just decorative furniture; they keep your world and mine *alive*."

"But there won't be a Jungledrop or a Faraway if we don't

find the Forever Fern," Fibber said quietly. "You said you were a legendary apothecary, so you must know of something that can help us. *Please?*"

Fox slumped down into a chair opposite Fibber. He seemed to be getting very good at being nice. And it was starting to make Fox wonder whether maybe her brother wasn't just trying to outwit her on this quest, that he actually meant what he was saying. But this would be going against everything their parents had taught them. . . .

"I suppose there is *something*," Doogie said after a while. "When I was trying to save Ethel, I realized that the puckleberries should be seedless *before* being added to the crushed smidgeroot for them to be fully effective. My Ethel was too ill by the time I made the discovery. I—I was too late. . . . But if consumed early on after an onslaught of dark magic, I think this cure could just be powerful enough to save a life."

He hobbled over to a shelf, pulled off a few dusty books, an egg cup full of moss, and several silver fir cones, then picked up a small, cork-stoppered bottle filled with purple liquid. Its label read: PUCKLESMIDGE SYRUP: RESTORES HEALTH IF CONSUMED ASAP AFTER EXPOSURE TO DARK MAGIC.

The flickertug map tingled suddenly in Fox's hands, as if

acknowledging that *this* was the reason it had led them to the Constant Whinge.

"Pucklesmidge will be your best bet against the Midnights and indeed Morg," Doogie said. "If anything can save you from dark magic, it'll be this syrup."

Fox reached out a hand to grab the bottle from Doogie, but the apothecary held it back from her and gave it to Fibber instead. "Thank you, boy, for awakening something inside me that I had thought was long dead."

Fox started. Fibber was even being rewarded with life-saving potions because of his niceness now. She straightened her tie and tried to make herself look as likable as possible. But the apothecary didn't thank her or hand over an extra bottle of the life-saving cure.

Instead, he glanced down at the map in her hands, then fixed his wise old eyes upon her. "A flickertug map senses the journey the heart needs to make to reach a destination, not the feet. It *will* eventually lead you to the Forever Fern, of that I have no doubt, but remember: The things you search for are often much closer than you think."

Fox nodded stiffly. She had no idea what the Unmapper was talking about, but there was something in the way he spoke, and in the way that he looked at her, that made the wall around her heart quiver. The apothecary might have entrusted her brother with the cure, but he was telling Fox that *she* would be the one to find the Forever Fern. And that confidence in her—that blind faith—reached out into the most hidden and precious parts of Fox.

She smiled shyly, a real smile this time, and when she looked up at Fibber, she saw that he was smiling too, as if—just possibly—the years of loathing that had passed between them didn't matter quite as much as they'd thought. Fox blushed and looked away. It was a rare thing to find herself exchanging a real smile with a family member, and she wasn't altogether sure what it meant.

Heckle cooed from her perch on the back of an empty chair. "Fox is feeling a little less cross than she was before, Fibber is feeling a little less scared, Doogie Herbalsneeze is feeling a little less sad, and Heckle is feeling a little more confident about finding Iggy. Oh, Heckle does so love it when a quest lifts people's spirits like this." She paused. "Perhaps a spot of food would cement the positive atmosphere?"

The apothecary smiled, then reached inside a store cupboard and rustled up two vegetable wraps that the twins—and

Heckle—ate quickly. When she'd finished, Fox looked up at the front door and noticed that it was open. Just a crack. And yet she had distinctly remembered Doogie Herbalsneeze closing it after Fibber walked in. Fox watched the door with narrowed eyes. Perhaps it had been pushed open by the breeze?

But when a fist wrapped itself round the edge of the door—a fist fringed with black, jagged claws—Fox knew that there was no breeze outside the Constant Whinge.

Chapter 12

Everyone saw the monkey's claw at the same time, but it was Doogie Herbalsneeze who spoke first, his voice an urgent whisper as he spun round and pointed at a cabinet in the corner of the shack. "Quick! It's a secret door out of here! Leave—now—and don't turn back!"

The front door continued to creak open.

"But *you*?" Fibber whispered, before turning to follow Fox to the cabinet.

The apothecary reached for several potions and emptied them into a bowl on the table. They began to bubble and hiss. "It's as you said, my boy: All the trying was leading to something else."

What happened next happened fast. At the precise moment

the door opened fully to reveal the dark silhouette of a monkey, two more monkeys appeared at the window, carefully stepping over the broken glass, and the mixture in the apothecary's bowl exploded. Thick blue steam immediately filled the shack so that it was impossible to see who was where or what was what. But Fox, Fibber, and Heckle blundered on, scrabbling for the handle of the corner cabinet and dragging themselves inside while the shack behind them erupted with noise: chairs toppled, glass smashed, monkeys screeched—a sound so shrill and terrible it was as if Hell itself had opened up.

The cabinet was roomier than expected inside and Fox crawled further into it, pausing just once when she heard the apothecary cry out in pain.

"Keep going!" Fibber panted. "I don't want to leave him either, but everything will have been for nothing if we're captured now!"

Fox hurried on. What was wrong with her? Worrying about a man she'd only just met! She crawled toward the back of the cabinet, then pushed it open and sunlight flooded in. They found themselves on a jetty leading away from the shack over the river. And tearing away from the far bank was a herd of swiftwings who had been drinking, just moments before, at the water's edge. Fox whirled round to see blue smoke pouring out of the shack—from the chimney, the window, and the door—then there was an explosion of purple, followed by clouds of yellow and red. It looked like Doogie Herbalsneeze was throwing everything he had at the Midnights and, for now, it seemed to be working.

"We need to get out of here!" Fibber cried.

Fox could feel the map's magic stirring in her pocket, so she brought it out into the open again and looked down to find a new word sparkling in silver on the parchment:

SHADOWFALL

The map seemed to be tugging upward, not enough to lift Fox off her feet, but very much insisting that *that* was the way it wanted her to go.

"I—I don't understand," Fox stammered. "Shadowfall sounds like a place, but why is the map pulling us *up*? We can't fly!"

There was a thunder of footsteps behind them and Fox tensed. She spun round once more to see the monkeys had found the secret passageway and were now pouring out of it. They raced down the jetty, their orange eyes fixed on the twins, their razor-sharp teeth glinting in the sunlight, and behind them crawled the battered apothecary.

Heckle squawked in terror.

"What do we do?" Fibber cried.

But at the very moment the first of the monkeys should have set its claws and teeth into Fox, there was a swooshing sound. Suddenly the twins were swept from the jetty, hoisted onto the back of something large and brown and very unstable, and whisked up into the sky.

The monkeys hissed and screeched below, but the twins were out of their grasp now. Fox clung onto a feathered neck while two large brown wings beat either side of her. It was a swiftwing. It had stayed behind to help them while all the rest of its herd had rushed off. And from the way it flew—clumsily and with a great deal of panting—Fox was in no doubt about which swiftwing this was.

Total Shambles.

She gulped as she remembered his faulty takeoff the day before and yet here he was, risking his life to save them. With the map still urging them onward, following the river just beneath the overhanging trees, it was as if the enchanted parchment had known that a swiftwing was the only way the twins would escape from the Constant Whinge alive.

Heckle settled herself in Fox's lap, and the girl was too pre-occupied with what was happening below to nudge the parrot off. The monkeys were dragging Doogie Herbalsneeze away from the shack. Were they taking him to the Bonelands to face Morg all because he'd tried to protect Fox and Fibber? Or did Morg want Unmappers like Doogie and Iggy for other reasons?

Fox glanced over her shoulder at Fibber. He was terrified of heights, so without thinking, he had wrapped his arms round his sister's waist. And though Fox would never have admitted it, there was something solid and comforting about the way her brother clung to her. But as the twins locked eyes, Fibber seemed to realize how unnatural and awkward it was for the two of them to be in such close contact. He hastily moved his hands to the swiftwing's back and curled his legs tighter round its sides.

Fox made a point of shuddering dramatically to show her brother that she hadn't liked the clinging on any more than he had. Then, quite unexpectedly, she found herself asking: "Do you think Doogie will be all right?"

"If we find the Forever Fern, he might be," Fibber replied.

And Fox wondered then if maybe Fibber was actually hoping to find the fern to save Jungledrop and their own world rather than himself. Back on the Here and There Express, he had said that, like her, he saw the plant as his chance to secure his place as a Petty-Squabble. However, given his odd behavior since their arrival here, Fox wondered if he might now have other motives. Something had been changing inside her brother for some time and that something had been awakened even more in Jungledrop. Fox looked again at Fibber's briefcase. What, really, had her brother been pouring his heart and soul into back home? Because the longer this quest went on, the more Fox felt sure that it wasn't being a ruthless businessman that fired him up. It was something else entirely.

Panting hard, Total Shambles flew on over tumbling waterfalls and remote lagoons, then he ramped up the heavy breathing and, with a triumphant squawk, charged up through the branches that arched over the river. The twins bent down over him to avoid a mouthful of leaves and then they were soaring—or, more accurately, flapping strenuously but still airborne—above the canopy.

"Jungledrop—it's—it's *huge!*" Fox stammered.

She had felt small down on the jungle floor, but up here, where the treetops spread out into the distance for as far as the eye could see, Fox felt absolutely tiny. And only now did she realize just how much of the kingdom had been drained of magic. Now and again there were patches of greenery in the canopy, but for the most part the jungle had been sucked of color and life. Fox spotted a more ordered ring of trees, still alive and standing some way south of them, and she supposed that must be Timbernook. But now that the Midnights had broken through the phoenix magic that protected the Unmappers' homes, who knew how long it would be before Timbernook fell into Morg's hands too?

Fox cast her eyes over the destruction. Somewhere, in all this chaos, she had to find the Forever Fern. She clutched the flickertug map tighter. It was still urging them on, toward wherever Shadowfall was, and Total Shambles seemed to follow its course as if he could sense the magic bound up in the parchment. And Fox knew that, whatever happened, she mustn't lose this map. Finding the fern without it would be impossible.

The afternoon sun was low in the sky now, catching the clouds that hung above the canopy and wrapping them in gold. Fox ducked as Total Shambles flew through a low-hanging cloud, ruffled his feathers to shake off the moisture, then carried on flying above the sprawl of trees.

Fox had never ridden a horse before or, in fact, a bike. Bernard and Gertrude Petty-Squabble had said that activities outside school should be focused solely on formulating plans to make money and there wasn't, as far as they could see, anything profitable about galloping around on a horse or charging about on a bicycle. Hobbies were a waste of time in their eyes.

Fox wondered if her parents would have changed their mind if it had been a swiftwing or a unicycle powered by junglespit in question. For although Fox knew she mustn't lose sight of the important business implications of this quest, she couldn't deny that magical methods of transport were just a tiny bit thrilling. They made her want to whoop and giggle, two activities that were, predictably, frowned upon as a Petty-Squabble.

Fox watched as the sun set beyond the furthest trees, leaving a flame-orange sky in its wake, and she thought of their journey so far. A lot of people had been surprisingly helpful: Tedious Niggle and the Here and There Express had got them to Jungledrop; Iggy had kept them safe from Morg's Midnights; Goldpaw had given them a satchel full of magical objects; the boglet had helped conjure the Constant Whinge; Doogie Herbalsneeze had given them pucklesmidge syrup; Total Shambles had whisked them to safety in the nick of time; even Heckle had proved useful with the tantrum tree and the omnifruits.

Fox had always been told that great things were achieved by individuals stamping on and jostling others out of the way, but that had not proved to be the case here in Jungledrop. Perhaps, Fox thought, it would be worth mentioning a few of the Jungledrop inhabitants in her victory speech to the press, which she would deliver from the penthouse suite of the Neverwrinkle Hotel while holding a glass of whatever extremely successful people drank when celebrating (bubbling wine?) and with her proud parents looking on.

Heckle twitched in her lap. "Heckle is a little nervous that we are heading so far north, but hopes we are getting closer to Iggy?"

At the mention of the north, Fox shifted. Didn't the Bonelands lie in the north of the kingdom? Surely the flickertug map wasn't demanding they go *there*?

From behind her, Fibber said: "Goldpaw told us a Lofty Husk called Spark would be patrolling the ravine that separates the Bonelands from the rest of Jungledrop. So even if that is where we need to go to find the fern, we'll be fine as there'll be a Lofty Husk nearby." Fibber paused. "Right?"

"Yes," Fox replied, though deep down she wasn't sure. She remembered Goldpaw also saying that there had been another Lofty Husk patrolling the Bonelands beyond the ravine, but that he hadn't been heard from for a month. Perhaps Morg's Midnights had seized him. . . . So what was to say that the Lofty Husk patrolling the ravine hadn't been set upon by the Midnights too?

Total Shambles flew on. The sky was darker now, poked with stars, and in the far distance, there were large birds soaring above the treetops. They were just silhouettes against the moon, but even from their outline Fox could tell what they were.

Vultures.

And everyone knew that vultures usually only hovered over one thing: dead bodies.

It was too dark to make out much of what lay ahead, but at the sight of the vultures, Heckle gave a little squeak. "Heckle is now feeling extremely queasy and worried."

And it seemed that Total Shambles was suddenly in agreement. The map was still urging them onward, but the swiftwing was heading down now as if he'd decided that this was as far as he would go.

Fox shut her eyes and held her breath as Total Shambles plunged toward the canopy of trees, hurtling through a narrow gap in the branches. Fox had been expecting a few glow-in-the-dark plants and magical trees still standing below, just as there had been in other parts of the rainforest, but what she saw instead made her stomach lurch.

The swiftwing wasn't dropping down because he wanted to stop; instead, they were careering over a ravine, a plunging drop flanked either side by towering rocks that seemed to stretch on for miles and miles in both directions. There was a rickety bridge crossing the divide. And on the far side of the ravine—no glowing plants or glittering Hustleway—was the dark shape of a forest full of dead trees.

Chapter 13

"Fool's Leap!" the parrot screamed. "Heckle thinks we should change course! Immediately!"

"Turn back!" Fox yelled at Total Shambles. "Turn back!"

The map was desperately tugging Fox's arm upward. It had seemed to want to cross over into the Bonelands, but it had also been very insistent about them keeping above the jungle canopy. It was obviously not happy that Total Shambles had decided to approach things another way. And there was something different in how the swiftwing was flying now too. He seemed out of control and not in the same slightly shambolic way as earlier. He was wobbling from side to side and his wingbeats were slowing down. He screeched as the ground grew closer and then, only by a whisker, he cleared the ravine and crash-landed in the Bonelands.

The twins tumbled off Total Shambles's back and glanced around fearfully. They could feel the full weight of dark magic here. Not a single tree crowding round them had managed to cling on to a leaf, orchid, or vine as some back on the other side of Fool's Leap had done. These trees were like old husks—bare-branched, withered, and throttled by fungi. And the plants dotted here and there in the undergrowth were horribly creepy: bushes sprouting bulging eyeballs; shrubs shrouded in thick, sticky cobwebs; a cluster of flowers with toenails for petals.

Fox's shoulders bunched in fear and she shot a panicked look at Total Shambles. "You idiot!" she hissed. "Why did you land down here?! Morg's Midnights are bound to be close!"

The swiftwing tried to get up, but his legs buckled beneath him and he rolled onto his side and gasped.

"He's hurt!" Fibber cried.

And when Fox took a closer look, she saw that her brother was right. There were claw marks on Total Shambles's hind leg, three deep gashes oozing blood.

"The monkeys must have lashed out just as we took off," Fibber said. "All this time Total Shambles has been flying, he's been in pain. No wonder he crash-landed! He couldn't go any farther." He looked at his sister. "He would have kept going, following the pull of the flickertug map, if he'd been well enough. I'm sure of it!"

Fox looked down at the parchment in her hand. It flopped uselessly, any spark of magic seemingly gone.

"How are we going to get to Shadowfall?" she cried. "The map didn't want us to come down here. It wanted us to stay above the canopy, and now it's not doing anything at all! Crash-landing in the Bonelands was *not* part of its plan!"

"Maybe not," Fibber said, "but Total Shambles is injured. What if the map is pausing, like it did yesterday when we had to stop for food and shelter, because it knows we need to help the swiftwing?"

"*Help him?*" Fox spluttered. "But—but we could be ambushed by the Midnights! Or attacked by Morg herself!"

She glanced at the injured swiftwing and tried to steel herself against feeling sorry for him, which was hard because Total Shambles was now whimpering and shivering, and it took everything in Fox not to rush to his side and give him a pat. Fox braced herself against such drastic action. Businesswomen didn't do patting when the going got tough; they did stamping. "We haven't got time for this. We need to get going." Fox shuddered at the plants around them. "*Now!*"

Ignoring his sister, Fibber reached inside the pocket of his shorts and drew out the little bottle of pucklesmidge syrup.

Fox shook her head. "No. Absolutely not, Fibber. We went all the way to the Constant Whinge to get that, and it's the only thing that will keep us alive if Morg's Midnights close in!"

"We'd be dead already if Total Shambles hadn't saved us," Fibber said quietly. "Now we need to save him."

Heckle, who was lying facedown on the ground with her head under her wing, said in a muffled voice, "Heckle is feeling very afraid of the nightcreaks."

Fox spun round. "N-nightcreaks? What are they?"

And then her pulse quickened as it became very clear what Heckle was referring to. Now that the twins were quiet, and Total Shambles's whimpering had dropped to a shaky breath, Fox heard another noise in the silence. A creaking sound, like the bones of someone very old cricking into life.

Fox glanced at the trees around them and her eyes widened. The branches were dead and yet they were, unmistakably, moving. They weren't thrashing about like the boughs of the tantrum tree had done, but the very tips, which ended in clusters of straggled twigs, were moving nonetheless with tiny, creaking actions. Fox gasped as she realized that these twigs looked uncannily like thin, bone-like fingers waking up and reaching out to the twins.

"We need to find Spark—if he or she is even still alive!" Fox cried. "We don't stand a chance here without a Lofty Husk's protection!"

Fibber shook his head stubbornly. "I'm not going anywhere until Total Shambles is healed."

And though the nightcreaks were reaching ever nearer and the flickertug map definitely hadn't advised they hurtle down into the Bonelands, Fibber pulled the cork off the bottle anyway. He ducked as a nightcreak reached out its clawed hands for him and poured the syrup over the wounds. Total Shambles winced in pain.

Fox yelped and scuttled backward as another nightcreak swiped at her, its twig fingers bristling excitedly at the prospect of a new catch. Fox rolled out of its reach, scurried a little distance away, and then glanced over the edge of Fool's Leap. Her stomach lurched. The drop was vast, a sheer face of rock plunging down into the shadows, but there was something else down in that ravine too. Something that made Fox's blood chill.

Sprawled on a ledge of rock jutting out a few meters down was a panther. And, in the moonlight, Fox could see that its once-golden fur was blotched with red. She swallowed. This had to be a Lofty Husk and she could tell by the way it lay—its neck twisted, its eyes open and empty—that it was no longer alive.

Shaking with fear, Fox hurried back to Fibber. The nightcreaks were swiping left, right and center with their straggled claws, but Fibber was keeping ahead of them, twisting this way and that every time they dipped close so that he could pour the last of the precious cure over the swiftwing's leg.

"The Midnights—they—they killed the Lofty Husk patrolling Fool's Leap," Fox stammered. "Spark. He's down in the ravine, I'm sure of it! And if Goldpaw hasn't heard from the other Lofty Husk who's been patrolling the Bonelands, I think we can safely say that one has been killed too!" She jumped to the side to avoid a nightcreak's grasp, then glanced at the empty bottle in Fibber's hands. "We don't even have any pucklesmidge syrup to save us when things go wrong now! We're on our own in the Bonelands!"

Total Shambles struggled to his feet.

"Not quite alone," Fibber said, leaping back to avoid a branch. "The syrup has closed Total Shambles's wounds. I doubt he'll be able to fly tonight, but he may be stronger tomorrow." He looked ahead, into the Bonelands. "We should keep moving. Get away from the nightcreaks."

And as if the flickertug map could tell that Fibber's work here was now done, it sparked into life, pulling Fox between two grasping branches. Fibber followed with Total Shambles limping on behind and Heckle fluttering nervously above. Then the map, despite a few close shaves, led them out of the nightcreaks and into a part of the forest where the undergrowth had risen up so high it was almost impossible to see the trees.

Strangler vines wrapped themselves round hollowed trunks, cobwebs hung like veils, fungi spread out like a rotten carpet, and everywhere there were brambles. The thorns were larger than any Fox had seen back home, and their whiteness made them look more like fangs than thorns. But the map was tugging her on toward what looked like an opening in the brambles. A tunnel of sorts.

"There," Fox pointed. "We should be safe inside that tunnel. For tonight, at least."

Fibber nodded. "It'll give us somewhere to rest out of sight until Total Shambles has recovered."

The tunnel was almost the size of a large car, and tall enough that Total Shambles could, when he hung his head, limp inside. Moonlight trickled through the gaps in the brambles, falling about them in spiked shadows, and Fox noticed that there were little nuts, not unlike the snoozenut in her satchel, growing on a shrub that had become entangled with the brambles. She lifted the fablespoon out, whispered "*please*," and held it up to one of the nuts.

NAME: DUSKNUT BUSH
CHARACTER: PERSISTENT, THRIVES WITH VERY LITTLE SUNLIGHT
RISKS UPON EATING: NONE, THOUGH BITTER AFTERTASTE

Fox picked one and bit into it. It wasn't nearly as tasty as an omnifruit, and the bitter aftertaste really was unpleasant, but it was food nonetheless. She was too frightened to feel properly hungry, but she knew that they should eat every chance they got because who knew what dangers lay ahead? So Fox, Fibber, Heckle, and even Total Shambles chewed on the nuts—right up until the point they noticed the firefly approach the tunnel. It hovered at the entrance, a beacon of light in the tangled forest.

"Goldpaw talked of the Lofty Husks sending messages through fireflies," Fox whispered, a glimmer of hope sparking inside her.

Fibber's eyes lit up. "Perhaps this is a message from Goldpaw saying that she's on her way to help us?"

The twins watched, spellbound, as the firefly moved back and forth. So bright was its light that it left its glowing movements hanging in the dark as words, like the way a sparkler does when you wave it at night. Fox read the message aloud:

"Dear Fox and Fibber,
It is Goldpaw here. Wherever you are in Jungledrop, I hope that you are safe.

Since Iggy's kidnapping, more Unmappers have been taken by the Midnights, so I have instructed everyone to remain in Timbernook, where the protection charms are strongest. But in staying here, we have limited access to food and water. So the survival of everyone and everything in Jungledrop depends upon your finding the Forever Fern in the next few days—before Morg's dark magic closes in on us for good. . . .

Trust in the flickertug map. It will guide you well, and I have faith that your time in Jungledrop will show you that quests are more easily won and foes more likely beaten when you have someone by your side. Know that Brightfur and I believe in you and that, while you search for the fern, we will do all that we can to protect Timbernook and Doodler's Haven from Morg's dark magic so that there is a chance, in all of this, for us to send rain on to the Faraway in the end.

You are all our only hope now.

Goldpaw."

The firefly melted into the night and, as the darkness returned, Total Shambles hobbled to the entrance of the tunnel, perhaps to keep guard.

Fibber watched him. "He may not be that graceful, but he's a noble swiftwing all the same."

Fox scoffed. "What use will an injured swiftwing be against Morg's dark magic?"

Fibber thought about this. "Maybe it's a bit like what Goldpaw said in his message: *foes are more likely beaten when you have someone by your side.*"

And such was the way that Fibber said those words that Fox wondered whether her brother was just talking about Total Shambles.

The swiftwing rested his head on his front legs while Heckle nestled herself on top of Fox's satchel.

Fox lay down in the dark too, but she couldn't sleep. "What was the point of Goldpaw's message?" she said sulkily. "Apart from saying that more Unmappers have been kidnapped and time is running out, it didn't tell us anything we don't already know."

Fibber was turned away from her, his body curled protectively round his briefcase, but he was listening all the same. "Maybe there doesn't always have to be a point to a message," he said after a while. "Maybe Goldpaw just wanted us to know that we're not alone. That she and Brightfur are rooting for us."

Fox said nothing. Nobody had ever rooted for her. The very idea seemed extraordinary.

They fell silent again. And the Bonelands was silent too. An eerie stillness hung over everything. Eventually, Fibber spoke, his voice just a whisper in the dark.

"I'm tired, Fox."

Fox was about to reply that she was incredibly tired too, but that she was sure it was par for the course when being a successful businesswoman, so really this was quite good training. But then she hesitated because there was something about the tone of her brother's voice again that made her wonder whether there was more than one meaning to his words.

"I'm tired of doing things for Mum and Dad that I don't want to do," Fibber said quietly. "Tired of competing against you. Tired of being told by Mum and Dad, every single day, that I don't measure up to you—that you'll be the one to save the Petty-Squabble empire because you're better than me." He paused. "And I'm tired of waking up each morning, pretending I'm someone I'm not."

Fox could scarcely believe what she was hearing. All her life *she* had been told by her parents that Fibber was the superior twin. That he was cleverer than her. That he was a better liar than her. That he was, ultimately, far more talented and that he would save the family fortune. She had grown up believing herself to be the talentless, unlovable one. Yet if Fibber was telling the truth now, then, unbeknown to her, *he* had been told that *she* was the one her parents had the most faith in.

Fox stared into the darkness of the tunnel. She knew her parents thought rivalry inspired greatness, but had they really been pitting her and her brother so obviously against each other all their lives only to save the Petty-Squabble empire? How could she and Fibber have fallen for such a trap? Anger boiled inside her. She had always known her parents withheld their love for her, but could it be that the same was true for Fibber, too? Then another thought made its way through the anger. . . . If all this was true, then maybe there was a chance for her and Fibber to be allies rather than rivals.

Fox felt an almost uncontrollable urge to pour out her most secret thoughts to her brother: to tell him that she was tired too—of stamping all over other people, of the pressure from her parents, of the feeling that she was never good enough. But the wall around her heart was still high and sturdy, and although she could feel the words forming inside her mouth, she found herself trapped in silence. For it is hard for someone who has been lied to their entire life to start over and trust again. And because the world had always seemed to Fox to be pitted against her, she didn't recognize kindness and truth when they did, finally, come along.

"I know I've spent most of my life lying and scheming," Fibber continued, as if he could read his sister's thoughts. "To you, to Mum and Dad, to everyone, really. But I lied because I was too afraid of telling the truth—of Mum and Dad finding out that I'm no businessman-in-the-making, that I don't have any profit-soaring strategies up my sleeve, that I'm never going to be the one who saves the Petty-Squabble fortune. That really, deep down, I don't want to be."

Fox listened, hardly daring to hope that Fibber was, at last, telling her the truth. She had always felt worlds apart from her brother, despite the fact that she had never known a day without him. And yet could it be that they weren't so different after all?

"I've been wondering"—Fibber paused—"ever since I saw Doodler's Haven, whether maybe there's a place for me in this kingdom after the quest finishes. Out in Jungledrop, I could do what I'm good at, what I enjoy. I'd be happy."

Fox frowned. Fibber had been terrified when he'd stepped off the Here and There Express, and now he was saying he wanted to *stay* in Jungledrop? What had he seen in Doodler's Haven that had changed his mind? Her thoughts whirred with possibilities. But because, for so many years, Fibber had imagined Fox to be secretly sly, and through her behavior tonight she had given him no reason to question this, Fibber interpreted his sister's silence as scorn.

So, with a sigh, he moved the conversation on. "We need to take Goldpaw's advice and work together to find the Forever Fern. And we need to do it for Jungledrop and all those suffering in the Faraway because otherwise there won't be a world for you to go back to."

Fox wished she could see Fibber's face so she could search it for the telltale sign of a lie. Although she wanted, with every fiber inside her, to believe him, she couldn't shake the years of lying and competition. And surely that's what all this was now. Another trick—Fibber's greatest yet—to pull the wool over her eyes, to make her think he was on her side when really he was planning to double-cross her in his own devious way as soon as they found the Forever Fern.

Fox listened as Fibber fiddled with the buckles on his briefcase. She thought of the contents bitterly. Her brother had a backup plan in there. One Mrs. Scribble believed in. And Fox *only* had the Forever Fern. Everything—finally being loved and cherished and not being sent away—hinged on her beating Fibber and being the one to take home the fern to their parents.

"What's in your briefcase?" Fox asked guardedly.

Fibber stopped fiddling with the buckles immediately, but he didn't turn round.

"You heard me: What's inside it?"

Fibber sighed. "I've been trying to be honest, Fox. I've told you exactly how I feel for once, but you've given nothing back.

You just listened in silence and now *you've* brought up the briefcase again. I'm not going to say what's inside *it* unless *you* tell me what's inside *you*."

Again, Fox felt words forming on the tip of her tongue. An opportunity had opened up unexpectedly. And the weight of such a thing hovered between the twins like a small, invisible bridge in the dark. Fox wanted to say that her deepest longing was for a brother who she could talk to on the way to school, who she could hang out with on weekends, who she could laugh with on holiday. But the thought of everything she might lose if she let herself wish things were different swelled inside her and mingled with the fear of opening up only to be double-crossed by Fibber. So the wall around her heart stood firm.

Heckle's voice slipped into the darkness. "Trust is like a shoelace," she said quietly. "It takes *two* hands to tie it into something worthwhile."

Fox wasn't sure whose thoughts the parrot was revealing—perhaps simply her own—but she knew that she couldn't give in now. There were years of feeling unloved standing in the way of this moment and, no matter how much she wanted to believe Fibber, she couldn't.

Silence surrounded them once again.

Finally, Fibber sighed. "Goodnight, Fox."

There was a pause and then Fox mumbled, "Night."

After a while, Fox noticed her brother's breathing grow deeper and slower. She waited a while longer to be absolutely sure that Fibber, and indeed Heckle, were asleep, then she took a deep breath. Important businesswomen focused on agendas and targets; they didn't spend time messing around with emotions and trickster brothers who had suddenly decided to be nice. She stood up quietly and tiptoed over to Total Shambles.

It wasn't that Fox had it in for the swiftwing, though she *was* pretty cross that Fibber had used all the pucklesmidge syrup on the creature. It was more that Total Shambles seemed a threat when paired with her brother and she was jealous of the bond they seemed to share.

What if, when Fox had gone to look over Fool's Leap earlier, Fibber and the swiftwing had been plotting something together? If Total Shambles's leg did make a full recovery, he could just whisk Fibber into the sky and leave Fox in the Bonelands to be finished off by Morg. She couldn't take the risk of having him around, and her fear and suspicion now swallowed any thoughts of patching things up with her brother. Besides, Total Shambles wasn't even of use as protection against dark magic; he still couldn't fly. It was time for her to take action and outwit her brother before he did the same to her.

Fox leaned in close to the swiftwing's ear and whispered: "I know Fibber might seem all decent and good, but he's the best liar in the Faraway. He's won medals and trophies for his trickery." She winced at the embellishment. "So it's my bet that all those nice things he was saying earlier about staying to heal your leg weren't true. He might have given you the pucklesmidge syrup, but it's only because he plans to use you to get closer to the Forever Fern. He'll ditch you, the first chance he gets, as soon as he thinks you're no use anymore."

Total Shambles cocked his head at Fox and his eyes grew sad.

"If I were you," Fox whispered, "I'd head back across the bridge over Fool's Leap to where you belong, and where it's safer, before Fibber lands you in all sorts of trouble over here."

The swiftwing looked from Fox to the sleeping Fibber, then back again at Fox, as if hesitating for a moment, then he picked himself up, his head hung low. He seemed to want to stay. Perhaps he genuinely thought he might be able to protect the twins, despite the risks in it for him and the fact that he was now lame. Fox felt a stab of doubt that she was doing the right thing. But then she imagined what it would feel like to be double-crossed by Fibber and the swiftwing and left alone in the Bonelands.

"Go!" she hissed. "Head home."

Total Shambles limped quietly out of the tunnel, and Fox watched as he padded away into the night.

And so it was that Fox and Fibber lost an ally that night. An ally they were much in need of. Because in the Bonelands, Morg's Midnights were not just monkeys. She had other creatures bound to do her bidding here, too. Like the pit of hog-nosed vipers not so far from the bramble tunnel the twins hid in. They had sensed the arrival of the Faraway children and they were stirring now, their fangs drenched in poison.

Chapter 14

Fox woke at sunrise. At least she assumed it was sunrise. It was lighter than it had been the night before, but dawn in the Bonelands looked very different to how it had been on the other side of Fool's Leap. Back there, shards of golden light had beamed down through the gaps in the canopy, but here, what light managed to reach the forest floor was a watery gray. Rain pattered beyond the entrance of the bramble tunnel and Fox's thoughts turned to Total Shambles. Had he limped over the bridge and begun his journey back to Timbernook? Or had Morg's Midnights found him? Guilt wavered inside her.

Fibber sat up and rubbed his eyes. "Where's Total Shambles?"

Fox shrugged and tried to look innocent. "Must've wandered off."

Fibber scrabbled to the tunnel entrance and peered out. "Total Shambles?" he whispered. "Are you there?"

The rain pattered on in the silence.

Fibber waited and waited until it became clear the swiftwing had gone. Then he rounded on his sister. "You said something to him, didn't you? Something that made him leave!"

There was an awkward squawk. "Heckle is finding the tension inside the bramble tunnel a bit uncomfortable."

Fox gripped the map, which had begun tugging her toward the entrance of the tunnel, and pretended not to hear her brother or the parrot.

Fibber grabbed his sister's shoulders and shook them. "What have you done, Fox? Total Shambles was our friend! He saved us outside the Constant Whinge! He would've helped protect us in the Bonelands!"

Fox shook Fibber off. "Helped *you*, perhaps! But I'm not stupid, Fibber. Both of you would have left me as soon as you found the Forever Fern. You were in it together! So I'm sorry if I spoiled your plans!"

Fibber threw his hands in the air. "What's it going to take for you to believe me, Fox? I was telling the truth last night, but you're so stubborn and closed up you don't want to hear it! I've been trying to work *with* you on this quest, hoping we might get along a little better *and* save Jungledrop at the same time, but all *you* seem to want to do is ruin things! It'll be *your* fault if Jungledrop and the Faraway are destroyed! Weren't you listening to Goldpaw when she was talking about the rain scrolls and all the Unmapped magic bubbling away over here without any of us back home even knowing? This isn't some stupid race to rescue a family fortune. You've *got* to see the bigger picture: Finding the Forever Fern is about saving the world and everyone in it!"

He yanked the flickertug map from his sister's hands. "I can't let you get in the way anymore. From now on, *I'm* in charge!"

Fox's face flushed with rage. How dare Fibber speak to her like that! She knew she was right not to trust his sudden change of heart. This proved that her brother wasn't so different from before because here he was—once again—thinking he knew better than her.

"You most certainly are *not* going to be in charge!" Fox cried. "Goldpaw gave *me* the map!" She reached out, grabbed the map, and pulled—hard. There was a loud, sharp rip. Fox glanced down. In her hand was one half of the flickertug map. And in Fibber's was the other.

"You—you ripped it!" Fibber gasped, his eyes wide with shock.

Fox's heart thumped. "It wouldn't have happened if *you* hadn't snatched it from me in the first place!"

She looked at the two pieces of parchment. They no longer glistened silver or bore the word "Shadowfall" or tugged in any sort of direction whatsoever. They were just blank pieces of parchment. Whatever enchantment had fizzed away inside the map before was now gone.

Heckle hung her head.

"That was our *only* way to find the Forever Fern!" Fox cried.

She glanced at Fibber's briefcase. Despite what he had said about the quest being about the "bigger picture," and not the family fortune, here he was all smug in the knowledge that he had something of value inside that briefcase should they fail to find the Forever Fern. As always, Fibber had come out on top.

Tears rose up inside Fox and then she remembered the contents of her satchel. Fibber wasn't the only one with a backup plan, after all . . . She reached a hand inside and felt for the phoenix tear. Would the little marble tingle or flicker when she brought it out into the open, as it had done back in the Faraway? It was the only option she had left now. Then her fingers brushed against the snoozenut. . . . And so furious was she with Fibber for tearing the flickertug map and ruining its magic that she didn't think twice about the consequences of what she was about to do. She didn't stop to think that if her brother fell into an enchanted sleep, she'd be alone in the Bonelands. She didn't stop to think that he might be telling the truth about them needing to save the world and work together. She didn't stop to think that maybe she was making a colossal mistake. Fox was angry and she simply wanted to eliminate her competitor once and for all.

She waited for Fibber to look away, lifted out the snoozenut, then began tugging the dusknuts from the shrub next to her. She thrust a handful at her brother, with the snoozenut tucked in among them. The nuts were almost identical so there was no way of telling the dangerous one hidden in their midst.

"If we don't eat," she snapped, "we're as good as dead anyway."

"Fine," Fibber grunted. "But then we need to make a plan—fast—because it won't be long before Morg's Midnights find us."

Fibber ate the handful of nuts begrudgingly, and Fox watched, her heart quickening. Would the magic of the snoozenut work immediately? Would her brother simply slump over and start snoring, then wake a month later, by which time—hopefully—she would have found the Forever Fern and made it home to claim victory?

Fox held her breath as Fibber yawned, shook himself, and then yawned again.

"It's the strangest thing," he said, blinking to keep his eyes open. "I just can't seem to"—he yawned again—"stay awa—"

Before he could finish his sentence, a strange blue glitter spilled out of his mouth and danced round him.

Heckle began clucking. "Heckle is suddenly feeling very worried!"

"What's—what's happening?" Fibber cried, clawing at his mouth.

The glitter thickened and swirled round Fibber. Fox's pulse drummed. Her brother, who had been so solid and real before, suddenly looked wispy and faint behind the blur of blue, and his voice was nothing more than a muffled cry. And then, in a moment of terrible clarity, Fox remembered that in the tree house she had only read *half* of the fablespoon's explanation about the snoozenut. *In most cases, sends consumer into an enchanted sleep for one month*, it had said. But there had been more words after that:

In rare cases . . . Only she had stopped reading because Fibber had interrupted her. Fox felt her chest tighten as the blue glitter spun round her brother, holding him prisoner in its whirl of magic. Fox bit her lip. What had she done?

There was a sudden *POOF*, like a clump of soot tumbling down a chimney and landing in a fireplace, which flung the buckles of Fibber's briefcase open and sent the flurry of papers inside dancing about the tunnel. Then the swirl of blue seemed to unravel and Fox watched, in horror, as the shape of her brother changed. He grew smaller, much smaller, and decidedly more hairy, until he wasn't a boy at all.

He was a little, brown, shaggy-haired sloth.

And had this sloth not been looking at her with Fibber's big dark eyes, now ringed with black and surrounded by fur, Fox would have insisted that the snoozenut had done away with her brother altogether.

Heckle blinked. The sloth blinked. And Fox raised two hands to her mouth in horror.

The sloth surveyed his tubby belly before turning his clawed paws over as if he, like Fox and Heckle, could scarcely believe what had just happened. Then he looked at the contents of the briefcase scattered about the tunnel. And when

Fox glanced at these papers, her eyes widened in surprise. The pages weren't filled with numbers and graphs and complicated spreadsheets correlating with some magnificent business plan, as she had expected. They were filled with *paintings*. And these paintings weren't just good. They were incredible.

There were watercolors of places: the view over the River Isar from Fibber's bedroom back in Bickery Towers; the avenue of trees lining the driveway to their school; the interior of the penthouse suite at the Neverwrinkle Hotel. There were oil paintings of fruit bowls, furniture, and sunsets. And there were charcoal sketches of people: an elderly couple walking a dog in the park; the man who ran the bakery near their home kneading bread; and—Fox gulped—there was one of her and Fibber together. They were walking over Wittelsbacher Bridge in Munich, and they weren't wearing matching business suits and scowls. They were in jeans and sweaters and they were smiling, possibly even laughing, together. The wall around Fox's heart wobbled.

Fibber tried to speak, but a sound halfway between a squeak and a bleat came out instead. A single tear smudged down his furry cheek.

And Fox knew then that Fibber had been telling the truth

the night before after all. He *was* tired of fighting with her and trying to be someone he wasn't. And now it was as if, through his paintings, Fox was able to see her brother properly for the first time. He was an artist-in-the-making! Perhaps Fibber had hoped, one day, that he might make a living out of his art, but he'd followed Fox onto the Here and There Express because he'd known, deep down, that the paintings in his briefcase probably wouldn't sell for much and he couldn't return to the Neverwrinkle Hotel without a proper fortune-saving plan in place, otherwise he'd be packed off to Antarctica. So, all this time, Fox had been worried that Fibber's briefcase held a backup plan to trump her at the last minute, but really he'd just been keeping the things he loved close at hand, quietly pursuing his passion and hoping hard that no one discovered his secret.

Now everything was starting to make sense. Fox thought of the snuggler chair back on the train. A park bench had appeared for Fibber because it was the perfect place to sketch and watch the world and its people drift on by. And then there had been Fibber's fascination when Goldpaw showed them Doodler's Haven and his words the night before about wanting to stay in Jungledrop, to "*do what I'm good at.*" Here there were Unmappers who painted for a living—no wonder Fibber had felt there might be a place for him! All the signs had been there, but Fox had been so convinced that her brother was out to get her that she hadn't seen them.

She thought back bitterly to all the nights she'd cried herself to sleep because her parents had made her feel that Fibber was better than her, more lovable than her, when really, just down the corridor in the same house, her brother had been worrying about the very same thing. And neither of them had ever known. Until now.

Fox knelt down in front of the little sloth and picked up the drawing of her and Fibber. Her own eyes blurred with tears and the wall around her heart, which had seemed so indestructible before, trembled again. Fox had cried many times back home into her pillow, alone, but as she wept now, she felt the world as she'd known it sway. Fibber's heart had been filled with longing, just like hers—for the chance to follow his passions, be loved by his parents, and laugh with his sister. All the secret things that Fox had yearned for year after year, too, but had been too proud and scared to admit.

"What have I done?" she sobbed. "Oh, what have I done?"

Fox looked at her brother and her world shifted. Everything

she had felt was so important before seemed to unravel and she saw their quest for what it really was, for what Fibber had known it was ever since meeting Goldpaw. Not a petty search to secure a family fortune and somehow win their parents' love, but an odds-defying mission to save the world. Because, despite what her parents had led her to believe, all those people back home suffering as a result of the terrible droughts mattered. And everyone here at the mercy of Morg mattered, too. At the end of the day, stamping all over other people didn't get you anywhere except stuck in a bramble tunnel with a brother you'd just turned into a sloth.

And it was then that the wall around Fox's heart finally crumbled, piece by jolting piece, until her heart was out in the open, aching and bruised and brimming with regret. She cried and cried, wishing she could take back what she'd done to Fibber, but not knowing how. The sloth cried too, and Heckle had the good sense not to go trumpeting everyone's feelings out loud because it was very obvious what the mood in the tunnel was just then.

"I'm so sorry, Fibber," Fox sniffed. "I was cross with you, so I gave you a magical nut to eat. It was meant to send you into an enchanted sleep while I went off to find the Forever Fern. But there must have been a side effect that turned you into a . . ." Her voice trailed off. "I should've believed you, only—only there was so much standing in the way. And the reason I didn't tell you that I'm tired and miserable too, was because I thought you were trying to trick me. I should have trusted you!"

The words spilled out. It was easier, strangely, talking to a sloth rather than a human. The fur seemed to soften things a little. And the fact that the sloth couldn't speak back—that helped too.

"You always seem so confident, so sure of yourself and your plans," Fox said with a sob.

The sloth sighed and Heckle, sensing this might be a good moment to help, hopped onto Fox's shoulder. "Fibber is thinking that he's far from sure of himself. He wishes you knew how scared and lonely he's been."

Fox swallowed as she looked at the little animal. "Mum and Dad have always told me that *you* are the one who's going to save the family fortune. But it seems they've been telling you it's going to be me. All along, they've been playing us, Fibber."

The sloth's eyes filled with more tears.

"Maybe you're not as sure of yourself as you seem," Fox said to her brother after a while, "but you're talented, Fibber."

She looked around at his paintings. "Really talented. Unlike me. All I'm good at is messing things up."

The sloth laid a sad little paw on Fox's knee. Fox flinched at his touch. It felt unnatural to have her brother, even if he was a sloth, reaching out a comforting hand. And yet there was something kind and hopeful in the way his paw rested on her knee.

Heckle leaned close to Fox's ear. "Fibber is trying to tell you that, despite everything, he's not going to leave you. He still believes you're in this together and you need to work *with* each other to find the Forever Fern." The parrot drew herself up and said, in a louder voice: "Much as Heckle is rather fond of outbursts of remorse and grand scenes of reconciliation, she really thinks we should be making a move to find the fern, and Iggy, now."

Fox thought about the task ahead. They had no map—and Spark and Deepglint weren't going to come to their aid—but there was still the phoenix tear, a glimmer of hope in the face of the impossible. Fox drew it out of her satchel and the sloth squinted at it in surprise.

"We can use *this* to find the Forever Fern, Fibber," Fox said eagerly. "I lied back on the Hustleway. I didn't lose the phoenix tear. I've had it in my satchel all along! And if the fern is as powerful as everybody says, maybe we can use it to change you back into a boy as well as to save the world and set everything right."

Fox held the phoenix tear up. But it didn't tingle or flicker like it had done back in the Faraway. And it didn't tug her in a certain direction as the map had done. She waited for a few more moments, just in case, but nothing happened. In fact, the marble simply sat there in her hand, looking distinctly unmagical.

Fox's shoulders slumped. How could they save the world when she didn't have an ounce of talent inside her and they didn't, it appeared, even have a grain of magic left on their side? She thought of the news coverage she'd seen back home: of stick-thin children in Third World countries gathered round empty wells; of parched savannahs empty of animals; of villages torn apart by war. She'd blanked all that out before. She'd hardened her heart because she'd been stupid enough to assume that she was above it, that being a Petty-Squabble meant you didn't have to care about those less fortunate than yourself.

And yet everything and everyone was connected, really. Doogie Herbalsneeze had known it about plants when he told the twins they kept kingdoms and worlds alive. Goldpaw had known it about Jungledrop's magical creatures when she insisted the twins treat them with respect. Fibber had discovered it on their quest when he had urged Fox to work with him for the sake of everyone suffering at the hands of Morg.

And now, as Fox realized it too, fresh tears trickled down her cheeks and splashed onto her satchel. She turned to her companions. The sloth was looking very forlorn indeed, and even Heckle seemed nervous about stepping outside the tunnel, despite her words about pressing on. Fox did her best to wipe away her tears. She had always been taught that success came to pushy individuals, not motley crews made up of parrots and sloths, but now, like most other things she'd been told by her parents, she needed to prove that theory wrong.

Fox took a deep breath. "So somehow we've got to save the world. And all we own is a doubleskin mirror and a fablespoon."

The sloth nodded. Heckle did the same.

"I feel like I should have a sword or something," Fox said. "Or at the very least some kneepads or a mouthguard." She looked at the sloth. "How are we going to do this, Fibber? We need to find Shadowfall, but we don't have a clue where to start. . . ."

The sloth stared at Fox with shining eyes, and she couldn't

help feeling that he was trying to tell her something. Thankfully, Heckle stepped in at exactly the right moment.

"Fibber is thinking that you should press on north, further into the Bonelands, because the flickertug map seemed to suggest the Forever Fern was in that direction. And that you should stay alert for Morg's Midnights, but offer kindness, rather than stamping, to any creatures you might meet who are on Jungledrop's side." There was a pause. "Fibber also thinks you should let Heckle perch on your shoulder from time to time when she gets tired of flying."

The sloth raised a skeptical eyebrow as if to say there might have been some elaborating on the parrot's part.

Fox managed a weak smile. "You can perch on me whenever you're tired, Heckle."

The parrot ruffled her feathers in delight, and Fox scooped Fibber's drawings into her satchel with the phoenix tear, the mirror, and the fablespoon. Then she yanked off her tie and tossed it into the tunnel—she hadn't been altogether convinced it had really worked with the feather tunic anyway. She crawled toward the entrance of the tunnel and tried to think clearly. She was no longer a businesswoman, but she was a woman with a purpose nonetheless. So she would have to try, for the sake of the world and everyone in it, not to mess this up.

Mist hung about the trees outside, low and thick and brooding. And there was a strange hissing noise not so far away that made the hairs on Fox's arms prickle. But when she strained her ears again to listen, the forest seemed unnaturally quiet. She turned to see that Heckle had hopped after her, but Fibber was—unsurprisingly—moving at the pace of a sloth, and a pygmy one at that. Slowly. So slowly, it was hard to tell if he was moving at all.

Fox hesitated for a moment before picking the sloth up. She'd never really held hands with or hugged her brother, or anyone for that matter, before. But she knew that if she didn't help Fibber now, there would be no way he'd keep up. And so, carefully, shyly, Fox lifted the little sloth in her arms. He looked up at Fox hopefully, and she had to fight everything inside her to stop bursting into tears again. Having her heart out in the open and trying to be kind meant that the slightest thing seemed to set her off.

She scooped her brother onto her back, and Fibber wrapped his furry arms round her neck, his small, clawed paws closing in a knot under her chin. Fox smiled at the brush of fur against her skin; it wasn't exactly a hug, but it felt as warm and as safe as she imagined hugs might feel.

And, though Fox had made a number of mistakes out in Jungledrop, she knew she'd got one thing right as she stepped out into the mist. She'd teamed up with her brother. And she hoped that having a sibling on her side, or on her back as was the case now, could make the difference between winning and losing in a forest full of dark magic.

Chapter 15

Fox walked deeper into the Bonelands, picking a path through the withered trees and rotten plants while Heckle flew on a few meters ahead. So thick was the mist that now and again Fox wondered whether the parrot had flown off completely, but she always reappeared in the end, a jolt of color against the gloom. Eventually, the mist thickened so much that Fox couldn't even see the ground beneath her feet. She felt the sloth tighten his paws round her neck.

"Heckle," Fox whispered. "Where are *you*?"

The reply that came was not a squawk but a hiss. A long, rasping hiss that needled its way through the mist.

Fox leapt back. The hiss came again. It was close. So close it seemed to scratch the insides of her ear, and at the sound of it,

Fox scuttled sideways, which, it turned out, was exactly what the hissing creatures wanted.

The ground beneath Fox's feet fell away, and she shot downward with a scream. The only reason she didn't fall any further was because she managed to grab two fistfuls of weeds, but now she was dangling above a large, soily pit. She clung to the weeds on the rim, and the sloth clung to her for all he was worth.

And then the hissing sounded again.

Fox forced herself to glance down, then immediately wished she hadn't. Beneath her the pit was full of vipers. And there were so many of them they wove in and out of each other, all patterned scales and flickering tongues, like a heap of slithering chains. But what sent a rush of fear right through Fox was the realization that the snakes were, one by one, raising their heads, and their black fangs were getting closer and closer to her feet.

Fox tried to haul herself out of the pit, but the weeds she clung to were wet and rotten and, every time she gained a few centimeters, a handful would snap off and she'd have to reach for another clump to stop herself tumbling into the pit.

"Heckle!" she gasped. "I need your help! Where *are* you?!"

But the parrot was nowhere to be seen. Perhaps the bird had gone so far ahead she hadn't even heard Fox scream.

Fox scrabbled for a firmer hold as the snake tongues got nearer still, but no matter how hard she tried to pull herself out, she just couldn't. The hissing grew louder and panic seized Fox's body so that all she could do was cling on, her eyes bulging with fear. And had it not been for the little sloth hugging her tight, she might well have given up then and let herself fall to her doom. But she clung on, even when the first of the vipers raked at the skin of her ankle with its fang.

Fox cried out. Not from pain but from the deadening sensation that was now spreading through her leg. The snake's fangs were coated in poison, that much was clear, and it was a poison that seemed to be turning her foot to—Fox glanced down—*stone*!

It was then that Heckle came to the rescue. She *had* heard Fox scream when she fell and she *had* heard her scream again when the first of the vipers attacked. She had been gaining height, climbing up through the sky as high as she dared, to lend her ambush speed and force, so that when she did, finally, come hurtling down from the canopy, she was a fury of talons and feathers.

The parrot squawked and screeched as she batted at the snakes with her wings, tore at their scales with her talons and pecked as hard as she could with her beak. Thankfully, whatever curse the viper's poison had laid on Fox's leg hadn't had time to set in for good because, as she looked down, she saw it was returning to normal, no longer stone but skin. And having Heckle come to her rescue spurred Fox on to try to haul herself out of the pit again.

She pulled with renewed strength, buoyed by the knowledge that the jungle's most emotionally intrusive parrot was battling for her, as if she actually mattered and was worth fighting for.

Fox yanked herself free of the pit and ran blindly on. Heckle followed. The parrot was missing several feathers, but she was alive and free from the vipers. And with the sloth still clinging to Fox's back, the three of them tore through the forest, away from the pit as fast as they could. Fox didn't even stop when she felt a paw pinching her cheek.

"Ouch," Fox panted as she leapt over a fallen tree and ran on. "What did you do that for, Fibber?"

It was Heckle who replied. "Fibber is trying to remind you to thank Heckle for her marvelous rescue back there."

Fox bit her lip. There was so much to remember when saving the world: staying alive, running fast, thanking others for saving you.

"Thank you, Heckle," Fox added. "You really were magnificent in that pit. Iggy would have been so proud."

Fox wasn't familiar with expressing gratitude, but surprisingly, saying "thank you" had actually felt quite nice and not at all like a weakness as she'd thought it might. And had she not been running for her life, she wondered whether this might have been an opportunity for a high five or perhaps a handshake or even a hug? She'd have to remember that next time someone charged in and saved her life.

Heckle seemed delighted at the praise, though, and she twirled in delight before flying on ahead. Fox hurried through the undergrowth, deeper into the Bonelands, and though it was a bit cumbersome running with a sloth *and* a satchel on her back, she was glad of her brother's presence. It made the quest a little less lonely and frightening.

The snakes didn't follow them, as Fox had feared, but she heard them send their hiss out into the mist. It coiled round her before moving on, and she realized that there were words in the sound and they were intended for someone else entirely:

"We send this hiss out to our queen
To tell her just what we have seen.
A Faraway girl is in our home:
It's time now, Morg; time to roam."

Fox put her hands over her ears and ran on through the trees. "They're telling Morg to come after me, aren't they?"

Heckle fluttered level with her, but didn't say anything, and Fox didn't bat her away. Both the girl and the parrot knew that Morg would be after them soon and they had to stick together at all costs.

Fox kept running, but the doubts were spinning inside her now. She didn't have a plan—not a proper one anyway—so what hope did she and her companions have of finding the Forever Fern? She remembered Goldpaw's words back in Doodler's Haven with dismay: "Don't get lost, don't get tricked, and be careful what you eat." She'd already been careless about what she'd given Fibber to eat, and now it was becoming dreadfully clear that she was getting very lost indeed. The mist curled through the trees in great bands of white, masking the way ahead and behind and around her. Fox felt almost dizzy. How long had she been running and had she made any progress at all?

"We could be going in circles for all I know!" Fox cried out to Heckle.

The sloth nuzzled into her neck, as if to urge his sister on, and Fox kept running because the alternative—waiting for Morg and her Midnights to come and finish them off—didn't bear thinking about. The mist thinned a little and Fox found that she could see the lay of the land a bit better now. She was on a path of sorts, which led through an avenue of bare-branched trees that loomed over her like the bars of a cage. And nailed to the trunks of these trees were gilt-framed mirrors.

Fox jumped at the reflection she saw in the one she was hastening past. It showed her face, her fear unable to hide itself, only Fox was older in the mirror. Much older. Her skin was gray and sagging, her back hunched, and her hair straggly and gray. Fox grabbed her braid and pulled it forward. She breathed a sigh of relief to see that it was still thick and red. The mirrors were lying, obviously goading passersby into thinking they'd been lost in the mist for years and years. Fox shuddered and hurried on past the last of the mirrors.

There were stones around the trunks of the trees now, and they rose up out of the soil in rigid gray blocks. Fox peered closer. The stones were rectangular with words carved upon them.

"Gravestones," she murmured.

Heckle swooped down onto Fox's shoulder and shivered. "Heckle does not think it wise to read the inscriptions on the unhappy ending plants."

But Fox couldn't tear her eyes away because there, in front of her, was a gravestone that bore her name:

IN UNLOVING MEMORY OF
FOX PETTY-SQUABBLE.
WHO DIED, ON THIS DAY
CHEWED APART BY GLOOMBEETLES
UTTERLY UNLOVED AND ALONE AND
USELESS.

Fox whimpered. "Even the plants know I'm good for nothing and are predicting I'll die rather than find the Forever Fern." Then she gasped, and the sloth around her neck stiffened, as they spotted the gravestone next to hers:

RIP,
FIBBER PETTY-SQUABBLE.
WHO DIED, ON THIS DAY

MUNCHED BY A MIDNIGHT
AND STUCK, IN THE UNDERWORLD,
AS A SLOTH FOR ALL ETERNITY.

Fox reached up a hand to clutch the sloth's paw. "They think I've no hope of changing you back into a boy!" she cried.

Heckle tutted. "Heckle knows never to trust dark magic or to take it personally."

But when they passed the next gravestone—

UNLOVINGLY REMEMBERED
PARROT CALLED HECKLE.
WHO DIED, ON THIS DAY
SAVAGED BY A WITCHCROC
HAVING FAILED HER BEST FRIEND,
IGGY, WHO REMAINED LOST
FOREVER.

The parrot dissolved into a gibbering wreck. "Dying without finding Iggy?!" she wailed. "Oh, just the thought of it breaks my feathery heart!"

Fox quickened her pace, despite her own anxiety, to prevent

Heckle losing it altogether. They carried on through the trees, and Fox tried not to dwell on the fact that instead of buds or leaves dangling from the branches, there were now tiny, clinking skulls. She looked down at her feet, to steady her nerves, which was when she noticed that the path was about to fork. She craned her neck to see that a little way ahead the path split again, then doubled back on itself. She scoured the trees and saw that there were dozens of paths all leading off in different directions. This was a maze of options and she no longer had any idea which path was the right one.

Heckle, still perched on Fox's shoulder, twisted her head closer to the sloth. "Please think a little louder, Fibber. It might help us."

Fox waited on the path and Heckle waited on her shoulder. Then the parrot said: "Fibber can't help us with a way out of this maze, but he wants you to remember all the people who believe in you, Fox. My dear Iggy, Goldpaw, Doogie Herbalsneeze—not to mention Fibber himself and Jungledrop's most impressive parrot. So have faith in yourself and choose a path."

Fox thought back to meeting Iggy, of how full of hope and excitement he'd been when he'd met Fox and Fibber on their arrival in Jungledrop. She thought of Goldpaw's message through the fireflies saying that she and Brightfur believed in her. She thought of Doogie telling her she'd find the Forever Fern in the end. She thought of the way her brother had shown her he wasn't going to leave her by putting his paw on her knee in the bramble tunnel and the way the parrot had saved her from the vipers. And she felt just a tiny bit braver than she had done before.

Fox blew out through her lips, then she took the path she hoped would lead north. But the further down it they went, the more the mist thickened and the more her doubts grew.

"I think we're going south again!" Fox cried. "It's impossible to know which way is north!"

She stopped dead in her tracks. There was a sound close by. A frantic, fluttering sound followed by short, sharp clinks. Fox tucked herself behind a tree, then she and Heckle peered out. Fox frowned. Hanging down into the screen of mist, from the branches of a rotten tree, were dozens of cages, each one the size of a shoebox. The bars of these cages were small and incredibly close together. They had to be because the prisoners inside were butterflies. Hundreds of glass-winged creatures who seemed to be desperately trying to break free.

Fox watched them beating their wings against the bars of the cages, again and again, but unable to get out.

"Heckle has seen glasswing butterflies in the past on their migrations through Jungledrop, but never before has she seen them trapped by dark magic." She lowered her voice. "It is a sin in this kingdom to imprison winged things."

The butterflies flung themselves again and again at the bars.

"Perhaps this is what Morg's Midnights do to creatures who stray into the Bonelands," Fox whispered. "Trap them before taking them to wherever Morg is hiding so that she can somehow steal their magic. . . ."

Fox knew that she needed to press on with her quest, but something deep inside made her hesitate. Something that wouldn't have stirred within her at all had the wall around her heart not come crashing down earlier that day.

"We need to free the butterflies," Fox said to Heckle and Fibber.

Despite their fear, the parrot and the sloth nodded.

Fox was terrified, too. All she really wanted to do was find another bramble tunnel and hide. But the butterflies needed her help, and being on this quest, Fibber had specifically said, meant working *with* Jungledrop's creatures.

She tiptoed out from behind the tree and although it was a fiddly task, and her fingers were shaking with fear, she pushed back the little bolts that secured the doors until one by one the butterflies flitted out into the open. Their glass wings were magnificent, like slivers of moonlight against the gloom, but the creatures didn't disappear on being released. Instead, they massed round Fox and she felt a gentle ripple of air against her skin as they beat their wings. Then the butterflies flew, all together, in the same direction over one specific path.

At first Fox assumed they must be heading back toward Fool's Leap, but when they kept stopping and turning, as if they were checking to see whether Fox was following, she wondered if the butterflies were actually showing her a way through this misty maze. Did they know, as the boglet and the swiftwing had done, that Fox and her companions were on a mission and needed all the help they could muster to nudge them closer to the Forever Fern?

She ran, almost giddily, after the butterflies with Heckle, trying not to resent the increasing weight of the sloth and the satchel on her back. After all, it was *her* fault she was carrying a sloth in the first place. . . . The butterflies turned this way and that, gliding over fallen trees and swooping under hanging creepers, until eventually the mist was all but gone and Fox found herself at the edge of a very large swamp.

The water was gray and mirror-still now the rain had stopped. Fox looked up. The sky above her was shrouded with clouds so that everything seemed to be in black and white even though it could only have been midday. But being in the open once more made her feel as if she could breathe again. She turned her eyes back to the swamp. It was oval in shape and so large Fox couldn't see where it ended on either side of her, but ahead, on the far bank, the forest seemed to rise up into tree-covered mountains.

"You led us north," Fox whispered to the butterflies. "Thank you."

Again, the situation didn't seem quite right for high fives, or indeed handshakes and hugs, but saying "thank you" made Fox feel unexpectedly warm inside, and she hoped the butterflies knew how grateful she was. She never would have found her way out of the mist without them or—she reached up and patted the sloth—without her brother's quiet faith in her.

There was a clattering sound and Fox watched as a cluster of flamingos, a burst of pink against the murky scene, launched themselves out of the water to her left, then soared over to the far side of the swamp. The glasswing butterflies melted into the trees, no doubt back toward Fool's Leap and safety. But Fox knew she had to stay and cross the swamp and then make her way toward where the land grew steeper. Because that direction, clearly, was north and if she trusted what her brother had said, through Heckle, about the flickertug map trying to lead her there, then that was where she'd go.

"How do we cross this swamp?" Fox said to Heckle, who was waddling toward the bank of the river. "Because if there are pits of snakes beneath the soil of the jungle in the Bonelands, I dread to think what's lurking under the surface of that water."

The parrot cocked her head, then scuttled backward a few steps. "Heckle is wondering what that shape gliding toward us is."

The sloth craned his furry head round Fox's neck to get a better view, and Fox peered into the distance. Her eyes widened because there, skimming over the surface of the water toward them—as if the departing flamingos had summoned it—was a boat.

Chapter 16

It was a small vessel, about the size of a rowing boat, but it was scooped up at the front as if it had been carved into a specific shape. There was a cloaked figure sitting in the boat who, every now and again, dipped a wooden staff into the water to ease the vessel across the swamp.

Fox didn't cower away. And neither did Heckle or the sloth. The glasswing butterflies had led them here, which meant that the Forever Fern was probably somewhere beyond this swamp, and now it seemed there might be a way to cross the water, after all.

The boat was halfway across now, and Fox saw that it was painted white and the prow was actually carved into the elegant neck and head of a flamingo.

"I come in peace," the figure in the boat said. It was a

woman's voice, lilting and strong, though Fox couldn't tell whether it belonged to someone young or old. "I am the last Unmapper left in these parts," the woman called. "I have been hiding out over here and waiting for you."

Fox took a very small step backward and Heckle fluttered up onto her shoulder. Goldpaw hadn't mentioned any Unmappers living in the Bonelands.

"I am here to help you cross the swamp and continue your search for the Forever Fern," the woman went on.

The boat was a stone's throw away now, but still the figure didn't lift her cloak back from her face. She kept her body completely hidden.

Fox couldn't help wondering *how* the woman had known that she would come this way. Even Fox herself hadn't known she'd end up at the swamp until a few moments ago. The sloth tightened his grip round Fox's neck, which made Fox take another tiny step backward.

Heckle stiffened on her shoulder. "Heckle is feeling worried because she can't read the Unmapper's thoughts. . . ."

The boat was approaching the shore now, and overhead Fox noticed that the flamingos were flying back toward them too. She could hear that their wings were beating with an unusual sound: a *clattering* rather than a *whrum.* With one final push, the cloaked figure let the vessel glide right up to the wooden jetty in front of Fox. The Unmapper stretched out a hand to pull herself up onto the pontoon, and the air turned suddenly cold.

The Unmapper had fingers, but where skin should have been at her wrist, there were feathers. Black ones that shone like oil.

She stood on the pontoon and though the hood of her cloak was still draped over her head, Fox caught a glimpse of a yellow eye that burned with malice. And as soon as Fox locked eyes with the figure, the magic that had been holding the whole scene together—the magic that had made Fox feel like the boat had come to help her—vanished.

This boat *had* come for Fox, but not in the way she had hoped.

The boat's planks transformed into bones. And when Fox looked up, she saw that the flamingos soaring toward them were now vultures that looked also to be made entirely of bones. Creatures stirred in the swamp around the boat, too, and Fox's eyes widened as the heads of several large black crocodiles broke the surface of the water.

But most terrifying of all was the figure on the pontoon. No longer feeling the need to hide, it threw back its cloak and Fox screamed at what she saw: the body of a woman, but a woman covered in black feathers, with talons for feet, a long pointed skull over her head, and two shining black wings tucked in at her sides. Heckle hadn't been able to read the Unmapper's thoughts because this was no Unmapper. This was a creature filled with dark magic.

This—Fox realized—was the harpy, Morg.

"And so, girl from the Faraway, we meet at last," Morg sneered.

Fox didn't wait to hear any more. She turned and ran, legs pounding, arms pumping, with the frightened sloth bouncing on her back and Heckle flapping in front as together they rounded the swamp. It was too late for the doubleskin mirror: Morg's eyes were pinned on Fox so she couldn't melt into the forest unseen. She fled, the crocodiles following her every move, skulking through the water with teeth bared, while up above the vultures trailed her on skeleton wings.

And down on the forest floor, scuttling round the bank of the swamp like a large, deformed beetle, came Morg. Her wings were bristling with dark magic now, which she had put to use by disguising the flamingos and the boat, and which she planned to use again as soon as she closed in on the troublesome girl. But those wings were not yet strong enough to grant the harpy flight. Instead she scuttled over the ground because she'd let a Faraway child escape once before and she wasn't going to make the same mistake twice.

"Give up, little wretch," the harpy crooned. "There is no one left in the Bonelands to help you now!"

Fox threw a look over her shoulder to see Morg churning up the reeds with her talons and tearing round the swamp after her. She was gaining on Fox, no matter how fast she ran, and though the weight of the sloth and the satchel were slowing Fox down, she refused to part with either.

So frightened was Fox by the harpy on her tail that she didn't see the vulture that was dive-bombing toward her. The first she knew of the attack was a punch to her shoulder as the bird rammed its weight into her. Fox stumbled backward, then tripped over a log but forced herself up and carried on running. Another vulture was making a beeline for her now, and though Heckle tried her best to ward it off, the bigger bird batted the parrot aside, charged on toward Fox, and pinned the girl to the ground.

The harpy laughed. "You see? There is no escaping my dark magic in the end!"

Fox pushed and shoved, Heckle pulled and tore, but the vulture's hold was firm and Morg was drawing closer and closer. Then the sloth, still clinging round Fox's neck, bit the vulture, attacking the joint that held its wing to its body. The bird's hold slackened for a second, and Fox seized her chance to wriggle free. She sprang up, blundering on, ducking and sidestepping when the next vulture hurtled down toward her.

The swamp seemed to go on forever, and Fox could feel tears burning behind her eyes. She was tired now. She couldn't outrun the harpy and she knew it. Morg had dark magic on her side, and sooner or later she'd close in.

Heckle flapped on, puffing hard. "Heckle wants the girl to know she won't leave her. And nor will Fibber."

The sloth leaned against Fox's cheek, then squeezed her hard, and Fox tried not to let her tears fall. She made one last attempt to focus on escaping, despite knowing that this was where her quest ended. Where *everything* ended. With no one to stop her, Morg would find the Forever Fern, and then the Unmapped Kingdoms and the Faraway would crumble. And yet still Fox kept running because sometimes the very last thing to leave you is hope.

Then Fox felt a cold and leathery hand thump down on her neck and she felt even that tiny kernel of hope shrivel.

"Silly girl." The harpy's breath was a rasp. "You really thought that someone as pitiful as you could find the Forever Fern and save the world? You actually believed that you could make a difference?"

Morg stood upright now, towering over Fox like a giant bat, while Heckle twisted away from the vultures massing round her in the sky.

Fox stopped struggling and sobbed in fear.

"Look at you," Morg spat. "Worlds are built by people of power, not by insignificant little girls."

The words may have been spoken by a harpy, but they made Fox think of her parents and the things she had been told her whole life: that stamping on others and being more powerful than everyone else was the only way to get to the top. And now that all seemed lost, Fox wondered whether they'd been right. Perhaps being kind and helping others only ever led to being trampled on. Maybe hearts were safest if shut behind very high walls.

Then the sloth on her back nuzzled his head against Fox. And the warmth of that gesture, the affection bound up in it, made her realize that, despite how everything had panned out, her parents and Morg were wrong. Fox would have traded all the money in the world, and all the power that came with it, to have even the smallest of chances to save the Unmapped Kingdoms and the Faraway—and to love and be loved by her brother.

The harpy kept her hold on Fox, opening her wings wide to perform a curse that would snuff the light out of the Faraway child in an instant. Fox quivered as Morg threw back her head and laughed. Then black smoke hissed out from her wings.

But, at the very moment the smoke was about to seep inside Fox's mouth and snatch her life clean away, something large and strong barreled into the harpy and knocked her to the ground.

For a second, Fox wondered whether Total Shambles had come back. But what she saw on twisting round was not a swiftwing.

It was a panther, with a roar that rattled the leaves on the trees and fur that was unmistakably gold.

Chapter 17

Fox's first thought was that Goldpaw had come to their rescue, but this panther was bigger and the fur on one of its legs had been ripped away. Was this Brightfur, then, sent by Goldpaw to help?

The panther moved fast, kneeling in front of Fox and nudging the girl and the sloth onto its back, before the harpy had even had time to stagger to her feet.

"*You?*" Morg spat. "But you were bitten by Screech and stripped of your—"

Fox didn't hear any more. She grabbed a fistful of fur at the panther's neck as Heckle shot down into her lap beside the sloth. And then they were off, bounding round the swamp at breakneck speed, as the panther tore away from Morg.

"After them!" the harpy shrieked. "After them!"

The vultures clattered ahead, and the crocodiles patrolled the water should the golden panther make the slightest mistake and slip. But the creature's footing was perfect, each stride landing with precision and power as it pounded on. And though Fox was like a jumble of sticks on its back, not yet attuned to its rhythms and its ways, she held on for all she was worth.

Morg was hot on their heels, scrabbling over the bank of the swamp as fast as her talons would go. But the panther was stronger and seemed to know the lay of the land in a way that suggested it had been here for quite some time—and that made Fox question whether this was Brightfur after all. This panther knew when to jump over sinkholes, when to swerve inland when the ground became marshy, and when to run, flat out, because there were no obstacles in its way.

And little by little it broke away from the harpy. It left the swamp behind too, as it surged on north. Into the part of the Bonelands, Fox had seen across the water, where the land rose up into foothills covered by dark, brooding trees.

Fox, Heckle, and the sloth clung on, hardly daring to believe what was happening. They'd made it past the swamp, and as the trees closed in around them, they lost sight of the vultures, and Fox was sure that even Morg couldn't find a way through the forest like this panther could. It charged on, leaping over fallen trunks as if they were twigs and swerving left then right round jutting branches as if it could sense a way on with just its whiskers, as if it knew—in this wild nightmare of a forest—exactly where it wanted to go.

From far behind them, Fox heard an anguished screech. Morg realized that she had lost them now and Fox knew it too, because this panther was bristling with strength and speed. It moved like water through the forest, deeper and deeper as the land rose and fell and they entered the heart of the Bonelands.

At the point where the land climbed upward again, Fox expected the creature to shoot on up through the trees, but instead it ran, fast, toward the rock face in front of them. Fox held her breath. Surely the panther was going to swerve? Couldn't it see that the route ahead was a dead end? But the panther carried on toward the rock, and just when Fox felt sure they'd career straight into it, she noticed a small gap. A gap that she imagined anybody else who came this way would have missed.

The panther slid inside and then, finally, it stopped running.

It shook Fox, Heckle, and the sloth off its back with a grunt, and Fox's mouth fell open as she took in her surroundings.

They were in a cave, but not some poky space dimmed by shadows. This was a vast atrium that spread out before them like an entirely different world from the rest of the Bonelands. One untouched by Morg's dark magic . . .

Glowworms lit the cavern, clinging to the roof like thousands of crystals. Greenery sprouted between the slabs of rock that formed the cave floor, a burst of life amidst a forest of death. And right at the back of the cave, so far away Fox had to squint to see it, there was a waterfall pouring down into a lagoon and slipping away as a stream through some hidden crack.

"All this," Fox murmured, "lying hidden in the Bonelands."

The panther grunted again, then it stalked off deeper into the cave. It moved with less precision now that it knew they were safe, dragging its paws and with its tail swinging low. It was tired, Fox realized, and she watched as it slumped down on a shelf of rock that jutted out over the lagoon.

Fox scooped up the sloth, hoisting him onto her back once more, then looked at Heckle, who was cocking her head at a green plant with thousands of intricate swirls on each frond.

"Heckle is, for once, almost speechless." And yet the parrot went on and spoke anyway because she just couldn't help herself. "Heckle thinks we are in Cragheart, the cave that legend says holds every Unmapper's fingerfern." Her eyes brightened. "Maybe Iggy's fern is somewhere in here."

At the mention of the word "fern," Fox stooped to look at the green plant beside Heckle. Each frond was coated in silver markings that looked exactly like fingerprints.

"Heckle has heard the stories," the parrot went on. "When an Unmapper is born, a fingerfern sprouts in Cragheart, but no one has ever reported finding this cave except the legendary explorer, Mildred Amblefar."

Mildred Amblefar . . . Fox remembered the book she'd read on the Here and There Express. It was only three days ago, and yet so much had happened since then. She looked about the cave and saw that, though at a glance the ferns all looked the same, on closer inspection each one had a distinct pattern. *Might the Forever Fern be here, too?* Fox wondered. But then surely the Forever Fern would look slightly different from all these fingerferns. Surely its magic would single it out?

She glanced at the panther resting on the rock. This was a Lofty Husk, she was sure of it, because ordinary panthers were black not gold. And yet it hadn't spoken as Goldpaw had. It hadn't carried itself with the same authority either. This panther seemed bound by its own rules.

"That can't be Spark," Fox whispered over her shoulder to her brother. "Goldpaw said she was at Fool's Leap and I definitely saw a Lofty Husk down in the ravine. But what about the other one, the Lofty Husk sent to patrol the Bonelands to find Morg's stronghold? Maybe that one isn't dead, as Goldpaw feared?"

Heckle hopped closer to Fox and the sloth. "Heckle assumes you are referring to Deepglint. He's Jungledrop's only male Lofty Husk left now that Spark has fallen."

Fox turned to the sloth again. "Do you reckon this is Deepglint?"

The sloth watched the panther for a few moments and then he nodded.

"I think so too," Fox said. She placed a hand on the strap of her satchel to steady her nerves, then glanced at Heckle. "Should I just go up to him and start talking? Only he doesn't seem very interested in us now that we're away from Morg. . . ."

Fox hadn't had much experience in making new friends, and she wasn't altogether sure what the protocol was. But it mattered. Greatly. Because the stakes in this particular situation could turn out to be rather high: become friends or get eaten if the panther wasn't, in fact, a Lofty Husk after all.

"Heckle thinks sharing thoughts is always a good way to begin a friendship."

"Yes, well, you would say that, wouldn't you?" Fox murmured.

She walked further into the cave, glad of both the sloth and the parrot's company. The glowworm light fell on the three of them, bright and blue and glittering with promise, and the waterfall was so brilliant close up—a shower of water that fell into a crystal-clear lagoon before winding out of the cave—that Fox almost forgot to speak to the panther at all as she looked about in awe.

Heckle settled on her shoulder, then hissed in her ear: "Heckle is just double-checking Fox will do thanking first and ordering about second."

Fox nodded. She was, despite the trauma of the last few hours, gradually learning the importance of manners on world-saving quests. But it was useful having Heckle onside to remind her all the same.

Fox cleared her throat and spoke to the panther. "Thank you for rescuing us."

The animal's head was turned away from Fox, so that it was facing the waterfall, and when it didn't react, Fox wondered whether it had heard her over the roar of the water.

She tried again, a little louder this time. "It was very kind." Once more, it didn't seem to be the right moment for high fives, handshakes, or hugs, so instead Fox added: "We'd definitely be dead if you hadn't shown up so . . . thank you."

The panther swung its large head round and fixed Fox with deep dark eyes. But it didn't get up. And it didn't speak. Instead, it looked at Fox silently for a very long time and, worrying this was some sort of test, Fox brushed the hair back from her face, straightened up, and tried to look as likable as possible. Failing tests at this stage of the quest would not do at all.

The panther kept staring, its gaze cool and distant.

"Are you Deepglint?" Fox asked. "One of Jungledrop's mighty Lofty Husks?"

At the name, there was a slight but noticeable shift in the panther's expression. Its whiskers twitched and its ears, which had been pinned back before, swiveled forward. But it didn't speak or nod.

And then Fox felt Heckle's grip on her shoulder tighten and the parrot's voice, when it came, was a whisper in her ear: "Heckle told you once that she can read almost everyone's thoughts, but not those minds filled with dark magic or beasts who are fully wild." She paused. "This panther saved us from dark magic, so it must mean it's not one of Morg's followers, but Heckle still can't read its thoughts, which means it could be—"

"—fully wild." Fox swallowed.

The panther's ears were still pricked, and it was watching its visitors intently. Fox's glance slid to the pile of bones in the corner of the cave, and she felt a rush of panic. If this was a wild panther and not a Lofty Husk, had it whisked her off solely for its dinner? Although it wasn't drooling, which seemed like a good sign to Fox. And when it did open its mouth, which sent Fox edging back a few steps, it only did so to lick the patch on its leg where there wasn't any fur.

Even so, the parrot's guard was now up. "Heckle thinks we should leave," the bird hissed, "at the first chance we get. It's not safe here."

But there was something about this panther, something Fox couldn't quite explain, that made her want to stay. She thought back to what Morg had said to it by the swamp. She'd only caught the first part—*you were bitten by Screech and stripped of your*—but the words echoed in her head now.

Heckle, who was clearly not getting very far rummaging through the panther's thoughts, was now rummaging through Fox's instead.

"Heckle is confused as to why Fox is still trying to understand the panther. We should be making plans to leave. To find the Forever Fern *and* Iggy. Perhaps when the beast falls asleep?"

"But what if me and Fibber are right, Heckle?" Fox murmured. "What if this panther *is* a Lofty Husk? What if this is Deepglint himself, only stripped of the magic that makes him a ruler: his voice, his responsibilities, his memories, his reason for being in the Bonelands at all? Maybe that's why he's hiding out here in Cragheart."

The panther stood up suddenly and sloped down the rocks until it was standing before Fox. It was huge, and solid, and Fox felt as if she was in the presence of a golden boulder, but she tried her best not to move or shake or reveal the fact that she was totally talentless and unqualified for this quest. The panther circled the girl, and when it came to her satchel, it paused and sniffed it. A look—half recognition, half wonder—seemed to flick across its eyes as if it was remembering something. . . . The expression vanished as swiftly as it had appeared, but it made Fox think.

"The phoenix magic inside the satchel," she said to Heckle and her brother. "I think the panther can sense it. Maybe *that's* why it came to our rescue with Morg. It felt the call of the ancient magic that it was once bound to."

Heckle hopped to the ground, and Fox tugged the satchel over the sloth and off her shoulder, glad to be free of its weight. She dug around inside. There was a surprising amount of debris within the satchel following the chase through the forest—soil, leaves, torn paper—but Fox pushed it all aside and found the phoenix tear. She drew it out, and though it didn't glow as it had done back in the antiques shop, something in the panther's expression changed as it locked its eyes on it. A moment later, it growled and its face hardened once more.

But Fox made a decision deep inside Cragheart then. She knew now that the only reason her world existed was because of phoenix magic. The only reason she had found a way through to Jungledrop was because of phoenix magic. And the reaction of the panther to the tear made her sure that the only reason he had rushed down to the swamp was because he had felt the pull of the phoenix magic inside Fox's satchel. Since arriving in Jungledrop, she'd made mistake after mistake because she had failed to trust and so now, whatever Heckle said, Fox decided that she would trust in this panther and in the magic of the phoenix tear.

The flickertug map may have stopped working, but Doogie Herbalsneeze had told her it would sense the journey of her heart, not her feet. And now that the wall around Fox's heart had crumbled, she was learning, at last, to listen to it.

Chapter 18

Fox tucked the phoenix tear back into her satchel and tried, once again, to speak to the panther. "We're on a quest to find the Forever Fern—"

"—*and* Iggy," Heckle prompted.

"—so that we can save Jungledrop and the Faraway from Morg," Fox continued. She scuffed her boots against the cave floor, suddenly feeling ridiculous telling a panther who had come to their rescue only moments before that she, a parrot, and a sloth were in charge of saving two worlds and a kidnapped Unmapper. And yet this was the worrying truth of things.

The panther said nothing, and Fox felt a familiar impatience rise up inside her. They didn't have time for silences and secrets. They had a matter of days before Morg found the Forever Fern! So great was Fox's frustration that she very nearly threw a tantrum. But then she remembered what Goldpaw had said about manners. She wasn't altogether sure hurling her hands in the air, kicking the ground, and possibly even shoving the panther would get her very far.

She took a deep breath instead and looked at the animal. "You saved us down by the swamp, and we wondered whether we could ask for *your* help again. Could *you* show us the way to Shadowfall, where we think the Forever Fern is?"

"Heckle is *really* not sure about this. . . ."

But Fox knew that she and her brother were in this together. Fibber thought the panther was Deepglint and that was enough to bolster Fox's hope that it might be too. Certainly the panther looked and acted as if it was wild, but Fox looked incompetent and very often acted it too, and yet enough people had believed in her that she had tried to make a go of this quest. They had made her think she was capable of more than she'd even imagined, just by having faith. So it seemed to make sense that, if *she* believed enough in the panther that stood before her, she might be able to bring Deepglint back to himself, to make *him* remember what he was truly capable of doing.

Fox spoke again. "We were following a clue from a flickertug map, but I went and tore it because I was going about the quest like a maniac, so now we have no idea how to get to Shadowfall."

The panther listened quietly, as if it was following what Fox said, but still it didn't speak.

And this time Fox couldn't stop her frustration spilling out. "Oh, come on," she muttered. "If there is really more to you than what we can see, then wouldn't you rather save the world than fester away inside a cave that nobody ever finds?!"

Fox instantly reddened. She hadn't meant to be quite so blunt, but when the weight of the world is heaped on your shoulders and you're used to bossing others about to get what you want, old habits die hard. Fox wedged her fists into the pockets of her tunic, just in case they accidentally shot out and punched the panther in the face, and mumbled an apology.

The panther snorted and then—to Fox's surprise—it turned away from her, walked back down the length of the cave, and vanished through the gap it had come in by.

The parrot tutted. "Heckle really doesn't think there's any point trying to reason with the panther. Even if it was a Lofty Husk, whatever Morg did to it, Heckle doesn't think it can be undone. And if it's gone hunting for food now, we'd better hope it catches something, otherwise"—the parrot winced—"it'll turn to us for its dinner. We need to make a run for it while we have the chance and press on to find the Forever Fern and Iggy."

"But what if we help Deepglint find his way back to his real self, then he leads us to Shadowfall and helps us beat Morg?" Fox replied, for she still couldn't shake the feeling that the panther really was a Lofty Husk.

"Heckle thinks this panther is wild and it very much looks like it's going to stay that way." The parrot paused and glanced at the sloth.

"What's Fibber saying?" Fox asked because she could tell, from the sloth's imploring eyes, that her brother was thinking something that he wanted to share and the parrot had cottoned on.

Heckle sighed. "Fibber is thinking that if people can change, maybe animals can too."

They talked for a while longer, desperately trying to agree on a plan, but before they could, the panther reappeared.

Fox froze at the sight of it. The fur around its mouth was red and wet. There was dirt clogged between its claws. And looking at the animal now, it seemed wilder than ever. Had she been wrong about it after all? Were they about to be its second course?

Heckle shot off to the far end of the cave and rammed herself into a crack in the rocks beside the waterfall, but the sloth stayed curled round Fox's neck, trembling slightly, and Fox herself didn't move a muscle. She watched as the panther walked past her and her brother, back toward the lagoon. It lay down by the water's edge, and Fox, gulping down her fear as she tried her best to trust her heart, followed it.

The panther grunted as Fox approached, and from up in the crags, the parrot whimpered: "Heckle is almost certain that Fox and Fibber are the panther's dessert."

Fox gulped, but she didn't turn away. She knelt down by the lagoon, close enough to the panther for it to know that she was interested, but at a safe enough distance so as not to be mauled with a single stroke of its claws. She wondered whether all friendships, when they first got going, were this tricky to negotiate. Fox looked at the animal and realized it wasn't just resting by the water. It was watching something, its ears pricked forward, whiskers tense, as it looked down into the lagoon.

Fox risked a little peek in the water herself and saw silver-scaled fish darting this way and that. The next thing she knew, the panther had dashed a paw into the water, flipped one of the fish out, then slammed a paw down on top of it until it was limp on the rock in front of Fox.

"For—for me?" she asked cautiously.

Fox felt that being offered a dead fish probably wasn't how most friendships began, but it was the way this one was heading, so she tried to look as grateful as possible.

The parrot cleared her throat. "Heckle recommends you use the fablespoon. The panther could be trying to poison you before it eats you for dessert."

Fox reached for the fablespoon inside her satchel, her eyes still fixed on the panther, but then she noticed him sigh. Her hand hovered over the magical item. If this really was Deepglint and she was going to try and help him find his magic again, she needed him to know that she trusted him.

"Thank you," she said instead, and went to pick up the fish, holding the panther's gaze.

The beast took a deep breath and, for a moment, something like doubt seemed to linger in its eyes, then its gaze softened and the panther breathed out over the fish. Fox's mouth fell open.

The panther's breath was gold, as Goldpaw's had been when she breathed over the candletree back in Doodler's

Haven and the satchel filled with magical objects appeared. Fox watched, entranced, as flames burned round the fish, cooking it through, and shadows danced on the cave walls. And she knew then for sure: This panther was a Lofty Husk. This was Deepglint all right. Even if he no longer knew it.

The fire crackled on, even when the panther nudged the fish out of the flames toward Fox and turned over a stone to reveal dozens of juicy insects beneath for Heckle and the sloth. Heckle didn't fuss and worry about being eaten then. She squawked with delight and flew down to Fox's side because she knew too that Fox and Fibber's hunch had been right. They were in the presence of a Lofty Husk, and if they could help him find a way back to his magic, they wouldn't be facing Morg alone.

They'd have a golden panther on their side.

Chapter 19

Fox rose early the next morning, but not, it seemed, as early as the panther. By the time Fox had rubbed her eyes and sat up, it was clear that Deepglint had already been out on a morning hunt to satisfy his own appetite and brought back berries and nuts for the rest of them. Fox, Heckle, and the sloth ate with no mention of the fablespoon and also no mention of the drool coating the food, which had been carried into the cave inside the panther's mouth.

A little part of Fox had hoped that, on waking, the panther might have remembered, somehow, who he really was. That he would start speaking and lead them on to Shadowfall. But when Fox raised the idea of his coming with them again, the panther stayed where he was, still and silent by the lagoon, as if his golden breath the night before had never happened at all. And Fox had to bury her head in her satchel and breathe deeply for several minutes to stop herself from venting her frustration once more.

"Maybe it's too much to ask you to come," she said, after she had regained her composure. "But we have to go on. The Unmapped Kingdoms and the Faraway are counting on us. So I want you to know, before we go, that I don't believe that what Morg did to you has changed you forever. I think you're still Deepglint inside."

The panther flicked a piece of dirt from between his claws, and Fox watched as the dirt dropped into the lagoon and sank to the bottom. Then she noticed something glistening among the rocks in the deepest part of the lagoon. She peered closer. It wasn't a shoal of fish. They were silver and darting and what she was looking at was gold and still. Fox blinked. It looked like a heap of sunken treasure, and she was surprised that she hadn't noticed it the night before.

The panther stared at it curiously as if, perhaps, this was the first time he had set eyes on it too.

Heckle and the sloth crept a few steps closer, and Fox shifted so that she was at the very edge of the lagoon. Something about the heap of gold seemed to flicker with magic. Then Fox squinted at the treasure and she saw it for what it really was.

A jumble of letters, each one carved out of solid gold. There was an *E* and a *G* and—Fox adjusted her position—was that a *T* and an *L*? She forced her eyes to find a pattern. There was another *E*, a *P*, and an *I*. And then Fox knew, without a flicker of a doubt, what she was looking at, even though she couldn't see the final two letters. She only knew that she had to dive down and get them before they vanished, because so much—finding Shadowfall, beating Morg, and saving the world—depended on it.

Fox kicked off her boots, then, without thinking twice or listening to Heckle's reservations, she jumped into the lagoon. The panther leapt up, alarmed, and the sloth let out a little squeak. But Fox was already kicking down beneath the surface of the water.

She shoveled the letters into her hands, then kicked upward, spluttering water, before bundling herself out onto the rocks that lined the lagoon. She laid the letters out in front of the panther, her heart quickening as they formed the word she knew they would:

DEEPGLINT

The letters sparkled in the cave, but the panther simply grunted and Fox had to fight the urge not to kick him in the shin for being so ungrateful. She had no idea why there were golden letters spelling out the Lofty Husk's name at the bottom of the lagoon, but she felt as if they might be important and the least the panther could do was acknowledge that she'd gotten soaking wet collecting them.

Then the panther looked at the letters more closely, a look that seemed to pass beyond the golden shapes and move to memories of long-forgotten things. And suddenly a golden mist rose up from the Lofty Husk's name, reminding Fox of the panther's breath the night before, and it dried her tunic right through.

Then the mist danced about the panther, a shower of golden light, and he shook himself hard as if waking from a very long sleep. Fox gasped. He looked bigger suddenly, and stronger, but that was not all. He opened his mouth and at long last he *spoke*—in a voice that was low and rumbling and shuddering with strength.

"You—you found my magic," Deepglint said. "Without our names, we Lofty Husks are but wild beasts. And when Morg's curse stole my name, and with it my magic, I all but forgot who I was. But a Lofty Husk's name will never stray far from him, even if it has been stripped away by evil."

Deepglint looked at Fox, and his eyes shone with gratitude. "You saw my name in the lagoon where I did not because you believed in me when I no longer could." He dipped his head. "A heart full of faith and kindness is a rare and powerful thing."

Fox faltered. She had always assumed her heart was filled with dreadful stamping things, but here was a ruler of Jungledrop telling her the opposite.

Deepglint drew himself up, tall and proud. "Kindness has a way of digging what we lose back up, even if what we lost was half buried at the bottom of a lagoon. My voice, my memories, my magic only appeared because of *you*, Fox. Because you were bold enough to trust in me and kind enough to believe that it would make a difference."

Fox glanced at her brother. "The sloth—he believed in you too."

Deepglint smiled. "Then he is a very wise sloth."

Fox looked down. "He's called Fibber, and though he doesn't look like it right now, he's my brother. Only, I turned him into a sloth because I was being awful." She sighed. "I'm hoping the magic of the Forever Fern, if we find it, might turn him back into a boy again."

The panther dipped his head at the sloth and the little creature dipped his head back, and at the same time Heckle muttered something vague and sheepish about *almost* believing in the panther too.

"I will repay all your kindness," Deepglint said, "not simply because it is my duty as a Lofty Husk to protect every good soul who enters Jungledrop, but because it would be an honor to stand alongside you three in this quest."

Fox was having trouble taking everything in. Here was a Lofty Husk treating her as if she mattered, as if she wasn't entirely unlovable and useless, and it looked as if he might be joining them on their quest. Her heart quickened at the thought. "You're coming with us to Shadowfall?"

The panther leapt up onto the ledge above the waterfall and rolled his shoulder muscles back and forth, as if preparing to jump, and when he looked down at them, Fox noticed that his eyes blazed with purpose. And fight.

"I am," he said.

Heckle squawked excitedly and the sloth raised a cheery paw.

"Shadowfall is the name of Morg's stronghold," Deepglint

said, his voice a low growl. "A forgotten temple that she now calls her own several miles north of here."

Fox's face paled. "Why would the flickertug map tell us to go to *Morg* to find the Forever Fern? Surely we should be staying one step ahead of the harpy at all times. And if the Forever Fern is somehow at Shadowfall, then why hasn't she found it and swallowed the pearl to grant her Immortal power?"

Deepglint shook his head. "That I cannot say. Magic rarely makes sense, at the beginning anyway."

Fox thought back to the flickertug map and how it had only yielded the first destination of their quest when the right person asked for it. Which was *her*. Could the same be true for the Forever Fern itself? Could it be up at Shadowfall, within arm's reach of Morg, and yet somehow still hidden because it was Fox who was meant to find it, not the harpy?

Deepglint glanced down at his leg. "I stumbled across Shadowfall almost a month ago now. I stalked right up to the gates before it, but I underestimated the reach of Morg's power. So intent was I on launching myself at the harpy to try and save Jungledrop that I did not see her servant, an ape called Screech, until his jaws snapped down on my leg. Screech wears a key on a piece of string around his neck—I fear it is he who keeps Morg's prisoners locked up—and he is filled with Morg's darkest curses, because the moment I felt his bite, my name and my magic left me. Suddenly I did not know why I was there or who I was. All I knew was that I needed to run, so with the strength I had left inside me, I fled. That was when I found Cragheart and took refuge here. It was weeks later that the phoenix magic in your satchel called me down to the swamp. And now, it seems, we must journey back to Shadowfall together."

Fox steadied herself. "You really think we should try and break into Morg's stronghold, knowing what happened last time you went there, to search for something that Morg may, if she has enough dark magic on her side now, stumble across before us?"

Deepglint nodded, and beside Fox, the parrot ruffled her feathers. "Heckle doesn't like the plan one bit, but she also doesn't like missing Iggy one bit either, and he'll be at Shadowfall, so we must go on even though everyone is terrified."

"If we leave now, we will be there by nightfall," Deepglint said.

Fox hoisted her satchel over her shoulder. It felt heavier than she remembered.

"I've got a doubleskin mirror in here," she said, "although

Goldpaw said it can only be used once. I've also got a fablespoon, a torn flickertug map, a phoenix tear, a flask of water, the rest of the nuts you brought us, and my brother's paintings, which I'm not leaving behind, even if you and Heckle think that's silly. Because they're important. As important as the phoenix tear." She picked the sloth up and wound his arms round her neck.

Deepglint looked from the sloth to the satchel. "Keep the phoenix tear safe; it called me to you and you restored my magic, so perhaps it can help your brother, too, though its magic will happen of its own accord."

The Lofty Husk leapt down from the shelf of rock and walked alongside Fox as Heckle fluttered ahead, back through the cave toward the entrance. Fox's heart was thumping at the thought of the journey ahead, but as she looked at Heckle and Deepglint and felt the warmth of the sloth on her back, she couldn't help feeling that heading out into the unknown, knowing you had people on your side, might be a little like what it felt to be part of a loving family. And the thought made her heart feel a tiny bit fuller.

She tiptoed outside the cave after the panther, her skin tingling with fear. It was midmorning, but the sky was gray and close. There were no tree frogs croaking or birds squawking. The place was quiet, as if holding its breath, and all about them the trees crowded in like crooked giants. Dead creepers hung from branches and moss crawled over everything.

Deepglint turned to Fox. "I will carry you only if it is an emergency. It drains my magic to carry another, and I fear I may need every ounce of it for when we get to Shadowfall. So, for now, I want you to follow me because I will teach you how to run."

Fox frowned. "But I know how to run."

The Lofty Husk grunted. "Not in the wild, you don't."

He slunk beneath a vine dripping with spiders, each one the size of a plate, before skirting round a boulder. Then he quickened his pace up the slope, leaping onto upturned logs and slinking past shrubs fringed with fangs. The panther moved as if he was made of silk, and though Fox felt self-conscious at first as she followed him through the trees, she found that if she moved like him—carefully and watchfully, pouring every ounce of concentration she had into the ground before her—she moved faster. And more quietly, too.

Fox had never been particularly sporty back home, but then again she'd never had anyone to play sports *with*. She'd never kicked a football around with classmates or tried to throw a basketball through a hoop after school with friends. She'd never been on a bike ride with her dad or a jog with her mum. And yet here she was, forging a way through the Bonelands with surprising speed and agility because a panther had taken the time to show her how. She ran on, mirroring his moves, until they climbed to the top of a steep hill where the trees were small enough to peer over.

The Bonelands spread out around them while behind, to the south, Fox could see Jungledrop proper, and in the far, far distance a single speck of greenery. Timbernook was still standing against Morg's magic. But only just . . .

Deepglint shook his head. "If we don't save Jungledrop tonight, Morg's dark magic will swallow the whole kingdom."

To the north of them there were jungled mountains rising far higher than the foothills they stood among now. And cascading down from the largest mountain, a few miles away, there was an enormous waterfall whose water was entirely black.

"Shadowfall," Fox murmured. "Morg's temple is somewhere in there, by the waterfall, isn't it?"

Deepglint nodded. He pressed on through the trees that, once again, grew taller and more mysterious. Fox followed like a shadow, every creaking branch or snapped twig sending shivers down her spine, but she didn't stop. She kept moving through the forest, her footfalls soft but sure, as she, the sloth, and Heckle followed Deepglint ever north toward Shadowfall.

They only stopped when a message from the fireflies, which now reached Deepglint because his magic had returned to him, appeared before them. They read Goldpaw's words about Morg's Midnights kidnapping still more Unmappers, despite the protection charms she and Brightfur had cast, about Jungle-drop being in mourning for Spark, and her plea for Deepglint to answer if he could.

They sent word back to Goldpaw that they were together and would be closing in on the Forever Fern soon. But once the message was sent, Deepglint walked off on his own.

Heckle perched on a branch level with Fox. "The biggest mistake grown-ups make, whether they're people or magical beasts, is thinking that tears must be hidden." The parrot bowed her head. "Crying over the loss of a friend shows the strength, not the frailty, of love. And love, of all things, fares better when it's cradled in the open."

Fox watched as Deepglint returned moments later. He avoided her eye and they ran on in silence for a few more miles until afternoon came and with it rain. And though the forest felt eerie—wind chimes echoed through the trees and plants grew everything from miniature coffins to rat tails and bat wings—nothing jumped out at them.

Goldpaw had implied Jungledrop was swarming with Morg's Midnights, so Fox thought it strange that she hadn't seen a single one since setting foot in the Bonelands. . . . What was Morg's grand plan in all of this? Where were her monkeys? And how long would it be before the harpy used her growing power to find the Forever Fern?

Sometimes, though, it's better not to know all the answers. For if Fox had been able to glimpse inside Shadowfall at that very moment, what she would have seen unfolding before Morg's throne would have chilled her to the bone.

Chapter 20

The light had begun to fade when Deepglint stopped before a stretch of dark, densely packed trees. They had wide trunks that bent forward in a mess of scoops and bulges, and their branches rose up in jagged clusters like crops of unruly hair.

"Eat the rest of the nuts you brought," the Lofty Husk said quietly. "We will need all our strength for the hunchbacks ahead."

Fox grimaced. "Hunchbacks?"

Deepglint nodded toward the trees in front of them. "Like the nightcreaks, these enchanted trees are bidden to do Morg's command. One false move and they will finish us off."

Fox's pulse skittered. The scoops and bulges on the trunks of the hunchbacks were *faces*. Sunken eyes, gnarled noses, and—Fox tensed—wide, gaping mouths.

The parrot hung back in the air. "Heckle is wondering whether there is another way on to Shadowfall?"

Deepglint shook his head. "Hunchbacks line the Bonelands from east to west. You have to go through them to go on. So keep your wits about you, but save the doubleskin mirror for later, Fox. I have a feeling our need for it will be greater if we make it as far as Shadowfall."

And, with that, Deepglint set off toward the trees. Fox followed with Heckle flitting nervously above and the sloth wrapped round her neck. But the minute they stepped beneath the hunchbacks, the trees' dark magic stirred. A wind picked up, slow at first and moving with a moan in its wake. Fox hurried alongside Deepglint, then he broke into a run and Fox ran, too, faster and faster between the trees until the forest was just a blur around them.

But the hunchbacks knew there were visitors in their midst, and the clusters of branches that resembled hair twisted this way and that, like muscles flexing.

And then a terrible howling started. Fox's face drained of color, and the sloth's arms stiffened round her neck. The noise seemed to be coming from the gaping mouths of the hunchbacks, and as it grew louder, the wind gathered pace.

"Keep running!" Deepglint roared. Then he glanced up at Heckle. "And keep flying!"

As Fox pushed on through the trees, she felt glad that Deepglint had taught her how to run in the wild, because the wind was so strong she could feel herself being blown toward the mouths of the hunchbacks, and it was taking every ounce of her concentration and strength to stay on track. But this was no ordinary wind tearing through the forest. It didn't blow; it sucked. Because this was the breath of the hunchbacks and it was gusting round Fox, desperately trying to nudge her closer and closer toward the hungry mouths.

Fox skidded over the undergrowth as a fresh gust snatched her right up to the trunk of a hunchback. The sloth clamped his jaw on the bark, stalling the tree's pull, but the cavernous mouth still loomed before them and little by little the sloth's hold weakened. Then Deepglint was there, yanking Fox away, his teeth gripping her tunic, and Fox ran again, on and on through the trees, with the sloth clinging to her for all he was worth.

Heckle screeched as a tree sucked so hard it pulled a feather from her tail. But still she flew. And still Fox ran. But when a double-trunked hunchback inhaled, yanking Deepglint from his feet and slamming him against its roots, Fox stopped and rushed to his aid.

"Go on!" the Lofty Husk cried as the hunchback sucked and sucked, gradually lifting the panther's body up toward its gaping mouth.

Fox watched, in horror, as the panther's legs were swallowed in the hole until just his head and his scrabbling paws remained.

"I won't go on without *you*!" Fox cried, yanking at the panther's paws and hauling hard.

Deepglint's eyes met hers. "You must go on, Fox! There is too much at stake!"

Fox blocked out his words, never loosening her grip on the panther's paws for a second, and even the sloth dug his claws into the Lofty Husk's fur. But cursed trees have to breathe out eventually. So the moment Fox felt the hunchback release its breath, she pulled with all her weight at the Lofty Husk until she, the sloth, and the panther fell to the ground, a tangle of limbs, fur, and claws. Deepglint was up on his feet first, and before Fox could follow suit, she felt his heavy jaw grip her tunic and haul her up onto his back, then he stooped down for the sloth and yanked him aboard too.

This, the Lofty Husk knew, was an emergency.

Then Deepglint was bounding on through the trees again, even though the wind roared and the branches shook. Fox hung on to the scruff of the panther's neck while the sloth buried himself in her lap and Heckle hurtled down to join him. When Fox had ridden the panther before, she had jiggled about on his back, but now she knew the Lofty Husk a little better. She'd watched how he moved, her eyes glued to his every step, and she felt her way into his stride.

They burst out of the wood, leaving the hunchbacks thrashing with fury behind them, and Fox saw that the forest had come to an end for a reason. Before them stood a river, cutting through the trees, with long, wispy reeds lining its banks.

Fox eyed it nervously in the gathering dusk. The water that flowed sluggishly between its banks was black.

"We're close, aren't we?" she panted. "The water's black because Shadowfall's near?"

Deepglint nodded, but he said nothing for a while as he caught his breath. And then, quietly, he spoke. "If you and Fibber had not stayed and helped me earlier, I would have been swallowed by the hunchback." He padded along next to the river, his footfall silent among the reeds. "Thank you."

"Anyone else would have done the same," Fox said.

Deepglint paused for a moment. "You underestimate what you and your brother are made of, girl."

Fox felt the sloth in her lap puff out his little chest with pride and she smiled. Then Deepglint walked on, hugging the river close, even though its waters glimmered like oil.

The parrot hopped from Fox's lap to her shoulder. "Heckle is wondering what horrors are still to come. An ambush from a river full of crocodiles perhaps? A last-minute hello from Morg's Midnights?"

Fox shuddered but Deepglint kept walking. On the far side of the river there was an avenue of trees. But they weren't nightcreaks or hunchbacks this time. These trees were white because they were made entirely of bones.

Deepglint stopped. "That," he said, nodding at what the avenue of trees led to. "That is what's next."

Fox felt her skin bristle. In the fading light at the far end of the avenue, she saw a tall black gate set between towering walls made of shards of bone. The walls ran in a wide circle so that it was impossible to see the temple inside. But even so, Fox could tell from the black waterfall careering down the mountain behind the bone walls that this, at last, was Shadowfall.

Her eyes returned to the avenue of trees. There were shapes moving among the branches: dark, furred shapes with long, swooping tails. And suddenly it made sense why they hadn't seen any of Morg's Midnights in the Bonelands so far. . . .

They were all here. Hundreds of them, swarming the trees around the gate, clearly placed there by Morg to guard the temple against intruders.

"Whatever the harpy is up to," Deepglint whispered, "it is clear she does not want anyone interrupting."

"Do—do you think she's found the Forever Fern and it's inside the temple?" Fox asked. "And that's why she's got all her Midnights guarding Shadowfall?"

Deepglint shook his head. "If Morg had found the fern, we would know about it. No, I believe it is still here somewhere, just beyond her reach." He paused. "And she has not got *all* of her followers out on guard tonight. There is no sign of the ape called Screech, the one who wears a key around his neck and is in charge of keeping Morg's prisoners locked up."

Fox looked again at the monkeys squatting in the trees. "But still," she murmured, "there are *so* many Midnights here. How will we find a way through the gate?"

Deepglint narrowed his eyes, then slunk low into the reeds so that they were all hidden from sight.

Fox scooped the sloth from her lap and placed him on her back, then slid off the panther and turned to face him. "We can't beat an army of those monkeys. Even Goldpaw said she hadn't found a way to kill them."

The parrot cowered in the reeds beside Fox. "We have to. Somehow. Because Heckle knows that Iggy is inside. And with night approaching, there are only a few hours left to stop Morg before she seizes *all* of Jungledrop's magic."

Deepglint said nothing at first, then his ears pricked forward and he frowned. "Listen," he whispered. "Listen hard."

At first Fox could only hear the river moving darkly through the reeds, but then her ears caught what Deepglint had heard. A strange but distinct ticking sound. Like that of dozens of clocks ticking away in the dusk.

And that's when the beginnings of a plan started to take shape inside Fox.

Back in Doodler's Haven, Goldpaw had said the monkeys went back to the Bonelands after every raid, then when they returned, they were just as strong as they had been before they were injured. The panther had said it was because there was something unnatural about them.

The plan in Fox's mind grew, and sensing that his sister was formulating an idea, the sloth snuggled into her neck as if to urge her on.

"I may be wrong about this," Fox said after a while, "but I think I may know a way we can get past the Midnights and into Shadowfall." Her eyes shone at the possibility. "But we'd all need to play a part. And it would be dangerous. . . ."

The parrot gulped. "Heckle is rather nervous about where Fox's thoughts are heading. . . ."

But Deepglint leaned in. "I am listening. Because nothing, and I mean nothing, is more powerful than a child in possession of a plan."

And those words gave Fox the courage to tell the Lofty Husk hers.

Chapter 21

They crossed the river over a bridge made of bones, and Fox held her breath the whole way, partly because she was terrified one of the bones was going to fall away and she'd plunge into the black water and partly because she was dreading the Midnights hearing the bridge creak as the group made their way across.

But the monkeys didn't hear or see the intruders approach, because Heckle had stayed true to her word. The parrot had flown, unseen, across the river a short while before the others and then, hidden in the undergrowth around the avenue, she had crept behind the trees until she was beyond the Midnights. Then she had squawked loudly. And at the exact moment the monkeys craned their necks toward the disturbance, Fox and Deepglint, together with the sloth, had made their way over the bridge.

Heckle skulked back through the cover of the undergrowth to join the others, who were crouching in the reeds before the avenue of trees. The ticking sound was louder now that they'd crossed the river, and as Fox watched the Midnights, their orange eyes gleaming in the trees, she hoped that her hunch about them was right. Because if it wasn't, this was the beginning of the end.

The group watched and waited, just as they'd said they would, and then, as dusk gave way to night and a full moon rose above the trees, Heckle hopped onto Fox's shoulder and Fox drew the doubleskin mirror from her pocket. She held it up to the china-white avenue of trees and the undergrowth around them. Then, under the moonlight, she looked at her reflection and gasped. Her skin was the same shadowy green as the reeds around them. She, and indeed the sloth around her neck and Heckle on her shoulder, was completely camouflaged by their surroundings.

Now it was Deepglint's time to act. He dipped his head at Fox, as if to wish her luck, then he stood up, stalked into the avenue of trees—and roared.

The Midnights, caught off guard, shrieked in surprise. Then they began jumping up and down on the branches, hissing and squealing with excitement. But they didn't leap down to attack the Lofty Husk because, beyond the bone walls, the panther's roar had summoned another.

Moments later, the gate to Shadowfall creaked open and the Midnights yelped with pleasure as a giant ape swaggered on two legs between the trees. Fox balked as she took in the long, swinging arms that ended in clawed fists, and the glinting eyes—fixed on the Lofty Husk—that sat above a mouth filled with daggered teeth. Hanging round the ape's neck, on a piece of string, was the object Deepglint had spoken of earlier, the object Fox's whole plan hinged on tonight: a key.

Heckle shrank into Fox's hair at the sight of the ape, and the sloth on her back stiffened. Before them was a being capable of stealing a Lofty Husk's magic.

The panther roared again as the ape drew up in front of him. And Fox knew that if she didn't act now, she never would. So, still camouflaged and therefore unseen by the Midnights and Screech and even by Deepglint, Fox shot out of the undergrowth and raced between the trees. She ran past Deepglint, her skin, hair, and clothes the white of the trees one second and the color of night the next. The Lofty Husk only knew Fox had passed him and that their plan was on track so he should stand his ground because the sloth had reached out a paw in the nick of time and brushed it against the panther's fur. Fox took a wider berth round Screech before climbing onto the lowest branch of the tree behind the ape.

"You come again, cat!" Screech threw back his head and laughed. "Did you not learn from last time that your magic is nothing in the face of Morg's? That you—"

He stopped suddenly and wheeled round. Fox froze. The ape must have heard Heckle use her beak to snap off a boned twig a few branches above her. Was their plan foiled, then? Had they wasted the magic of the doubleskin mirror? But Screech looked right through Heckle, Fox, and the sloth as he scanned the branches.

As soon as the ape turned back to Deepglint, the plan was back in action and Heckle passed the twig to the sloth on the branch below, who then slipped down several branches at once and passed it to Fox. Then, as quickly and as silently as she could, which was difficult because of the increasingly cumbersome satchel on her back, Fox slithered to the end of the branch. Holding her breath, she stretched out her hand with the twig clasped in it.

The ape towered above Deepglint, his clawed fists raised, and the Midnights in the trees barked with delight.

Fox reached out the twig toward Screech, trying to steady her shaking hand. She focused intently, blocking out the ticking noise droning from the trees and the hollering of the giant ape. All her attention was on moving the twig toward the string around Screech's neck. Finally, she managed to scoop the twig under the string. Then she yanked hard.

The string and the key flew up into the air, and Fox flung her arm out to catch them. For one fearful moment, it looked like the key would slip through her fingers, but then she felt it firm in her hand. Her fist curled round the metal, and the ticking noise that had filled the trees suddenly stopped.

The monkeys—every single one—dropped from the branches they had been clinging to. As they fell, they began to twist and shrink until all that was left at the foot of the trees were dozens and dozens of mangled black clocks. Even Screech, a tower of brute strength and dark magic, now shuddered on all fours as his body began to dissolve into a pile of black grit.

Fox could hardly believe her eyes. Her hunch had been right: Morg's Midnights weren't ordinary monkeys. They were mon*keys*! Not animals made from flesh and bone, but clockwork creatures controlled by the cursed key Screech had worn around his neck.

And *that's* why the monkeys had kept coming for Jungledrop's thunderberries, animals, and Unmappers, even when injured: because every time they returned to the Bonelands, Screech simply wound them back up again with his key. The only way to kill them was, as Fox had suspected, to steal the master key.

Fox paused in the tree as Screech's voice, the last part of his magic to depart, rose up from the pile of grit.

"You will never enter Shadowfall," he sneered. "The way in looks just like the way out!" He laughed darkly, then his voice grew fainter. "And you will never beat Morg. Her reign is only just beginning. . . ."

The ape's voice ebbed away until, finally, silence fell.

Fox pocketed the key, scooped up the sloth, and with Heckle fluttering excitedly round her, she scrambled down from the tree. Then she ran toward Deepglint. Her plan hadn't turned out to be a total disaster! By working together, they had found a way past Morg's guards.

"We did it!" Fox cried. "We actually did it!"

Deepglint smiled. "But of course we did. Because when individuals come together, worlds can be shaken."

Before Fox could stop herself, she'd flung her arms round the panther's neck and hugged him. The Lofty Husk wrapped a large paw round her waist while the sloth burrowed under her chin and Heckle nestled into her hair. Fox had never been hugged before and now she was being held by a panther, a sloth, *and* a parrot.

Fox had always assumed that hugging meant things moved about on the outside—arms round waists, heads on shoulders—but it also seemed to be about things shifting on the inside. Because hugging was an overlapping of hearts, too, and that, Fox concluded, was what made it so wonderful. Her eyes filled with tears suddenly and she felt very glad that she was still invisible. But when the camouflage wore off a few seconds later and Fox appeared with blurry eyes, no one said anything about it. And Fox made a mental note that crying during a hug didn't mean that everyone ran away from you afterward.

The group eyed the gate between the bone walls. There was a ruined courtyard beyond. A fountain still stood in the middle, but the water had long since run dry and the stonework was covered in algae. There were statues here and there, but most were half crumbled to the ground and tangled in creepers.

"We'd better get going," Heckle said, fluttering up from Fox's shoulder. "Who knows what state Iggy could be in or what

Morg's really up to, but if the Forever Fern is inside Shadowfall, we need to break in and find it before she does. . . ."

Fox laid a hand on the gate. She had presumed it would hold fast, another obstacle steeped in curses to stand in their way, but it swung open, creaking eerily as it did so. Fox felt the sloth shudder on her back, then she and Deepglint walked inside.

Fox looked about her. There was something sad about the courtyard. The statues—carvings of swiftwings, boglets, trunklets, and all manner of magical creatures—might once have been magnificent, but had now been left to decay. A temple reared up against the moon. Perhaps it had been grand before, but now it was draped in moss and much of the stonework had flaked away.

There were steps leading up to a door that was closed and barred with a mesh of vines so thick they looked like chains. This, it seemed, was the only way into the temple, because there were no windows and the bone walls that enclosed Morg's stronghold ran right up to the sides of the temple itself, so there was no space to creep round.

Fox picked her way between the statues until she was standing in front of the huge stone door. She tried pulling at the vines that crisscrossed it, and Heckle also tried clawing and pecking at them, but they clung on with supernatural strength. Even when Deepglint barged into the door with all his weight, it still didn't open.

The Lofty Husk looked at Fox. "I fear we are going about this the wrong way. What was it Screech said just before he died?"

Fox shivered as she recalled his voice hanging between the trees. "*The way in looks just like the way out.*"

The parrot sighed. "Heckle is so confused! Of course a way in looks like a way out! A door is a door—you go in *and* out of it."

"We're missing something, then," Fox said. "We need to think about this completely differently."

She turned away from the door, less sure now that the answer lay there, and began walking between the statues. She paused before the one just inside the gate. It was smothered by ivy and moss, but even so, she could see that it was a unicorn. She felt the sloth shift position on her back and noticed he was craning his neck toward the statue.

Heckle landed at Fox's feet, then cocked her head up at the sloth. "Fibber is thinking it strange that the whitegrump's eyes are glowing."

"Whitegrump?" Fox asked.

"Jungledrop's version of a unicorn," Deepglint explained. "Though decidedly worse tempered."

Fox started to pull the ivy and moss from the head of the whitegrump so that she could get a better look. And when she did, the group gasped.

"Its eyes are mirrors," Deepglint murmured.

The mirrors were smudged with soil, but when Fox looked into one, she could still see her reflection staring back and the gate to the courtyard behind her. "The way in looks just like the way out," she said quietly. "It makes sense now. . . . Clever Fibber for noticing the whitegrump's eyes."

The sloth gave a bashful smile.

Deepglint frowned. "What are you and Fibber suggesting, Fox?"

"This mirror reflects the gate—the way out," Fox replied excitedly. "So, what if the way *in* is somehow through the whitegrump?"

Hastily, Deepglint brushed the rest of the dirt and moss away from the mirrors, then Fox pressed down on them with her fingers. And as she did so, there was a crunching sound, like stone gears slotting into place. Suddenly the statue of the whitegrump lurched backward, like a horse rearing, and a way into Shadowfall opened before them.

Chapter 22

Fox and Deepglint hurried down a flight of stone steps to find themselves in a crypt lit by torches fixed to the walls by iron brackets. Shadows flickered on the stonework and a passageway led on ahead of them. Beneath the domed roof of the crypt, though, tucked into the shadows, were hundreds of cages. And from each one came the sound of someone or something sobbing.

Deepglint leapt off the final step and hastened over to the cages. Here, locked behind bars and starved of sunlight, were all those who had been stolen by Morg's Midnights. There were smaller cages holding featherless birds and emaciated lizards, then bigger ones crammed with limping orangutans and shaking gibbons. Fox's heart filled with sorrow as she looked upon them.

But it was the last row of cages that sent a jolt of guilt through her. Each one held an Unmapper captive, and at the sight of them, Heckle shot off Fox's shoulder and pushed through the bars of the farthest cage, flapping round the Unmapper inside and calling his name over and over again. Fox's breath caught. It was Iggy.

But gone was the boy who had burst out of the understory on a unicycle, full of talk and life. He was thin now—terribly thin—and his eyes were ringed with dark circles.

"Oh, Iggy," Heckle sobbed. "What have they done to you? My poor little Iggy."

The boy held his parrot close. "You came for me," he said, his voice cracked and faint.

"Just as you came for me all those months ago in the Elderwood." The parrot placed a claw on Iggy's hand. "Heckle crossed Fool's Leap and battled through a forest of hunchbacks to find you. She would never, ever abandon you, Iggy."

With shaking arms, the boy cradled the bird to him. "You're the best parrot in Jungledrop, Heckle."

Fox's eyes moved to the cage alongside Iggy, and she saw the old apothecary: bruised and frail, but still somehow hanging on to life.

Deepglint squinted at the cage. "Is that you, Doogie

Herbalsneeze?" he whispered. "After all these years?"

The apothecary's eyes brightened a little at the Lofty Husk's voice. "The very same," he said. "Nudged into making the Constant Whinge visible by the Faraway children." Doogie turned to Iggy in the cage next to him. "I told you help would come," the apothecary croaked. "I knew they wouldn't let us down."

Fox swallowed. Like Iggy, Doogie was only a prisoner here because he'd helped her and Fibber. And while there had been a moment in the Constant Whinge when Fox had softened a little and listened to the apothecary's words, she'd done no such thing with Iggy. So although it was embarrassing to have to apologize now, when the rest of the prisoners were looking up to her—the hero who had swept in to save the day—Fox knew she owed it to the little Unmapper.

She knelt down before Iggy's cage. "I'm so sorry, Iggy," she said. "I was awful to you when we first met and it's my fault you ended up in here." She looked down at the ground. "I've been a terrible hero."

Iggy smiled weakly. "Terrible heroes don't rescue people, but you're here, just like Doogie said you would be. And so is Heckle." He looked around. "Where's your brother?"

The sloth on Fox's back reached out a paw and waved.

Heckle cleared her throat. "The sloth is, in fact, Fibber. Heckle will explain all that later, Iggy. But for now, know that Fibber is feeling very pleased to see you and he's very sorry for acting like an idiot"—the sloth squeaked, and the parrot paused as she listened to the boy's thoughts—"a *total* idiot back when you first met."

Iggy smiled.

Then Deepglint voiced something Fox had been thinking as soon as she set eyes on the prisoners. "Morg has inflicted terrible evil on you all," he growled. "I can sense it in the air, but I can also see it in the way you look. There is something almost ghost-like in your appearance."

Fox glanced at the apothecary. He was still Doogie Herbalsneeze, but he was ever so slightly fainter around the edges as if his very form was only just managing to stay in this world.

Doogie clasped the bars of his cage. "Jungledrop's thunderberries restored Morg's strength. But to increase her power still more, Morg started drinking the tears of the animals and the Unmappers." He looked down. "Each evening, Screech comes to the crypt and steals our tears for the harpy. If the giant ape comes again tonight, I fear for many of us that he'll be draining the last of our magic and, with it, our lives."

Fox shook her head. "Screech won't be coming here again. We saw to that." She felt for the ape's key inside her pocket and drew it out. Screech had been Morg's jailer as well as the master of her Midnights after all.

"Quickly," Deepglint urged. "We don't have a moment to lose. We must free the prisoners and press on to find the Forever Fern and stop Morg!"

Fox set to work on the padlocks dangling from each cage. The locks were all different shapes and sizes, but Screech's key was imbued with a strange kind of magic so it opened the first few cages easily. Fox knew it would take hours—which they didn't have—to unlock *all* the cages in the crypt, though, however fast she worked. But then the key in her hand vanished and with it the dark magic that had kept the cages closed in the first place. One by one the cage doors opened of their own accord and the animals and Unmappers limped out into the crypt.

"Fr-free," Iggy stammered. "Free at last!"

Heckle, now perched on the little Unmapper's shoulder, snuggled against his chin. "And we will right what Morg has done to you," she said. "You'll see." The parrot fluttered from Iggy's shoulder onto Fox's.

"You're—you're leaving me?" Iggy cried. "But we've only just found each other again!"

"Heckle didn't imagine she'd be one for perilous quests," the parrot sighed, "and yet here she is, firm in the knowledge that she has not finished saving Iggy Blether or Jungledrop yet." She cocked her head at the young Unmapper. "Heckle won't rest until she's helped undo what Morg did to you and the rest of the prisoners."

Iggy's face filled with pride as he looked at Heckle.

"Make your way up these stairs, across the courtyard, and out of the gate," Deepglint said to the Unmappers. "Wait for us under the avenue of trees—it is too risky for you to navigate the hunchbacks and the nightcreaks and all the other creatures lurking in the Bonelands on your own."

"But the Midnights!" one of the Unmappers, a young girl, whispered. "We hear them screeching—they'll only drag us back here!"

Deepglint shook his head. "There are no Midnights anymore, so there is nothing to fear. Fox saw to that. Now go. We will come for you as soon as we can."

The Unmappers hastened up the steps out of the crypt, and the animals, sensing the chance to escape, followed.

And then it was just Fox, Deepglint, Heckle, and the sloth in the crypt. They hurried down the passageway, Fox's heart pounding at the thought of facing Morg at every turn, until they came to a dead end.

They skidded to a halt then. Fox pushed hard against the wall of stone, but it didn't move. "The crypt can't just stop! This was the way into Shadowfall—the *only* way in!"

"Shhhh," Heckle hissed. "Your thoughts are buzzing about Heckle's head so loudly she can't hear the trunklet's properly."

At the mention of trunklets, the sloth tightened his grip round Fox's neck.

"The trunklet's?" Fox whispered.

They were silent for a while as Heckle listened. And then the parrot nodded firmly. "There's a trunklet on the other side of this dead end, Heckle thinks. Seems he made a pact with Morg to pull off the biggest prank in trunklet history—to bar the way into the temple with an Impassable Wall—only now that he's sensed the presence of a Lofty Husk on the other side, he's wondering whether he might have taken things a bit far."

Deepglint stalked right up to the stones. "Listen here, you little wretch."

There was a squeak from the other side.

"You had better bite your way through these stones and open up a way for us or"—he took a deep breath—"when I do come face-to-face with you, I shall eat you." He turned to Fox and said, in a whisper, "I never eat magical creatures, but threatening disobedient ones is another matter entirely."

There were a few more squeaks from beyond the wall, then the sound of jaws working furiously and stone crumbling away. A little green head appeared. It stuck out its tongue at Fox, then, on seeing the Lofty Husk, carried on biting away at the stones until eventually a space big enough for Fox and her friends to step through opened up.

They rushed through it, leaving the trunklet grumbling behind them, and ran on down the passageway until, eventually, they came to another stone staircase. Fox took a deep breath, then she climbed on up it with Deepglint by her side.

She didn't know quite what to expect at the top of the steps, but it certainly wasn't what lay before her. They were standing in the corner of what might once have been an antechamber. There was a crumbling throne in the middle and stone walls that towered up on all sides. But there was no roof. Only the night sky, peppered with stars. And because a full moon shone down, Fox could see quite clearly what had taken over this space.

A garden.

Only this was a garden like none Fox had ever seen before because every single plant was black. Vines as thick as snakes and as dark as coal twisted up the walls. Bushes laden with black fruits dripped juice the color of ink. And shrubs with black-stained teeth snapped open and shut. But what made Fox shiver most was the enormous plant in the middle of the hall, the one that grew at the foot of the throne.

It was a fern. Fox recognized its distinctive fronds because she'd been keeping an eye out for them after seeing the finger-ferns in Cragheart. But Fox could tell that it wasn't filled with phoenix magic. Instead, the plant before her seemed to ooze darkness. It was black, like all the other shrubs around it, but its fronds moved—up and down, up and down—as if, just possibly, it might be breathing.

There was no sign of Morg. Only this garden built from curses.

Fox looked on in horror, then, in a tiny whisper, she said: "Could Morg have conjured her own Forever Fern?"

From Fox's shoulder, the parrot narrowed her eyes. "Heckle can see the harpy has conjured *something*, but this is no Forever Fern." The plant pulsed away at the foot of the throne, and

Heckle glanced at the sloth just behind her. "Fibber agrees. He thinks this thing looks like it's drenched in dark magic."

Deepglint growled. "We must destroy it, because with Morg evermore growing in power, who knows what this fern could be capable of?"

Fox eyed the plant nervously. If it *was* filled with curses, she would need all of her strength to wrench it out of the ground. She raised a hand to lift her satchel over the sloth and off her back. It had been feeling heavier and heavier as the journey went on, which now struck Fox as slightly strange because she hadn't added anything extra to it. She shrugged the thought away. There were more pressing things ahead of them now, and she knew she would need all of her energy to pull Morg's fern loose. But when she placed a hand on the strap of her satchel, a terrible silhouette filled the moon. Fox tensed and the sloth on her back shivered.

High up on the far wall stood Morg, her jagged wings outstretched.

"Welcome to my Night Garden," she crooned. "A place full to the brim with dark magic." She tilted her masked face. "I see you have laid eyes upon my Forever Fern."

Deepglint snarled. "That is no Forever Fern."

"Perhaps not in the way that you think," Morg replied. "But it sprang from the deepest of curses. From a seed soaked in poison and wrapped in a strand of the night. And I was only strong enough to perform this curse because I've been swallowing the tears of the Unmappers and creatures of this kingdom. Now, as long as this fern exists and grows, so, too, will my power."

Morg launched off the wall, her wings rippling through the night, and glided down to her throne. As she sat there, breathing in the fern's horrible power, Fox felt the ground beneath her feet tremble.

Fox reached under her chin and clutched the sloth's paws. Then Heckle shifted even closer to Fox's neck, and Fox, in turn, shifted even closer to Deepglint. The flagstones around them broke apart, and a cluster of enormous black roots burst out, spraying soil and stones into the air.

Deepglint gnashed at the roots with his teeth, Fox darted this way and that, the sloth tore with his claws, and Heckle flapped furiously. But the roots grappled through and fastened round the panther, the girl, the sloth, and the parrot and began hauling all four of them through the Night Garden toward the harpy.

Fox dug her nails into whatever she could—plants, vines, soil, and leaves—but this garden and its plants belonged to Morg, and they seemed bent on dragging her victims toward the throne.

"No!" Fox cried. "It can't end this way! Not when we were so close!"

A lump lodged in her throat as she thought of how far they'd come, how much she'd changed and how many people—both here in the Unmapped Kingdoms and back home in the Faraway—she'd be letting down if she lost to Morg now. Not least her brother. Would he stay a sloth forever because she'd failed to stop the harpy in time? Then there were her parents. They had lied to her. They had pitted her against her brother. And yet, despite all that, she still wanted to see them again and to save them from the terrible fate Morg had in store for Fox's world.

The harpy's cackle echoed through the garden. "I told you before: Worlds are built by people of power, not by insignificant little girls like you! You never, *ever* stood a chance of beating me!" Morg tilted her skull mask as the roots of her fern heaved Fox closer. "I see you for what you are, child. A miserable wretch with a thorny heart who lived unloved and will *die* unloved."

Fox's tears fell fast now. "Stop it!" she shouted. "*Stop it!*"

Heckle screeched in fury and Deepglint roared, but the roots only tightened round the panther and the parrot as they were thrust, along with Fox and the sloth, into the folds of the fern itself.

"Don't listen to Morg!" Deepglint panted as the fern began wrapping its leathery fronds round its victims. "You are loved, Fox. You—"

His words were smothered by the fern, which had now closed so tightly round its prey that Fox could no longer see or hear Deepglint or Heckle. She clung to the sloth's paws with all the strength she had left. But through the tiny crack in the plant she saw only Morg, her wings outstretched in triumph.

"Feast on them!" the harpy shrieked to the fern. "Feast on them all!"

Chapter 23

Fox's pulse thrashed beneath her skin. She was terrified of the fern and of what it was about to do to her and her friends, but she was also terrified by what Morg had said. That Fox had spent a lifetime being unloved and would now die that way too. That she had never stood a chance of finding the Forever Fern and saving the world. That she was foolish to even think she could.

Fox felt her limbs slacken and her breathing slow as a soul-shuddering despair overcame her. And though she could feel the sloth clutching her hands, she no longer had the strength to twist and turn to try and break free. This was the end. She could feel the fern sucking at the life inside her. Tears rolled down Fox's cheeks as the air turned cold and fizzed with curses.

But sometimes, as an adventure draws to a close, we find

unexpected things. Tiny jewels almost completely buried in the shadows. And somehow, somewhere—though she was bound in the clutches of the very worst magic—Fox found a flicker of hope still burning in the dark.

Her whole life she had buried her heart beneath thorns and hidden it behind walls, but something had changed out here in Jungledrop the moment she'd seen the quest for what it was: not some selfish opportunity to make a fortune, but an important mission to save two worlds. And she had seen her relationship with her brother more clearly too. They weren't rivals or business competitors. They were siblings, and they had a lot more in common than either of them had realized. Fox couldn't predict how the quest would end, or even if she'd manage to persuade Fibber to come home from Jungledrop with her, but she did know this: She had a brother who cared for her, and she, in turn, cared deeply about him.

And in Fox's learning to care—for Fibber, Heckle, Deepglint, Iggy, Goldpaw, and *all* the others she had met on her journey—the wall around her heart had come crashing down. So this quest hadn't been doomed from the start, whatever Morg might say. Not when so many here in Jungledrop believed in

Fox and had shown her kindness along the way that had kept the search for the Forever Fern alive.

Fox felt a tingling sensation tiptoe over her skin. And that's when the faintest sound began, only just audible beneath Morg cackling and the throb of the fern's dark magic. It was a tinkling sort of sound—the kind of noise starlight might make if you bottled a constellation—and with it came a familiar glow. One that Fox had last seen in Casper Tock's antiques shop, but which had been quietly growing in the shadows of her satchel from the moment she had turned Fibber into a sloth and vowed to work with her brother to find the Forever Fern for the sake of the world and everyone in it.

Fox was bound too tightly by the fern to lift the satchel from her shoulder and peer inside, but she could tell with every fiber of her being that the ancient magic of the phoenix tear was stirring. And it seemed Fibber could tell this too, because he was now twitching with excitement around her neck. The glow brightened until Fox was no longer shrouded in gloom, but bathed in a magnificent blue light. Seeing that light, so bold against the dark, filled Fox with renewed strength.

"There is a magic stronger than yours!" she shouted to Morg. Fox didn't know if her voice would travel beyond the fern's fronds, but she flung her words out anyway, because they were all she had left to fight with. "You say that this quest was doomed from the start and that worlds are built by people of power, not by insignificant little girls like me? Well, you're wrong, Morg!"

The glow was now so bright inside the fern that Fox was blinking into its light, and the sloth around her neck was squeezing her hands tight, as if willing her on.

"I used to think like you!" Fox shouted. "I used to believe that to be kind was to be weak and that stamping all over other people meant you got what you wanted. I was wrong. To be kind is to be strong. And if you're strong enough to pull down a wall around your heart, you can fight with the strength of a warrior, because then you will have learned to love!"

The sloth rubbed his head against Fox's neck.

"My brother and my friends in Jungledrop taught me that worlds are *not* built by people of power!" she cried. "Worlds are built by people who care! Kingdoms go on because kindness goes on." She took a deep breath. "You don't know my heart, Morg—whatever you might say—because *I* care. About our world and about all the people in it. I carried on with this quest even when I lost my brother and I wanted to give up. I set the glasswing butterflies free even though it could have cost me my life. I believed in Deepglint even though I risked everything doing it. And I went back for him even though the hunchbacks were closing in because that's what friends do."

And though she was still held in the grip of dark magic, Fox's heart stumbled across something else half buried in the gloom then. Something sitting alongside the flicker of hope and burning with just as much strength: grace.

She threw her last words out as loudly as she could with the power of the phoenix magic on her side. "I will not let you undo what others have taught me, Morg! I will not let you force a wall back up round my heart! So . . ." She bit her lip—she could hardly believe what she was about to say. "I forgive you for what you did to Iggy Blether and Doogie Herbalsneeze and all the other Unmappers and animals you locked away. I forgive you for what you are doing to me and my brother and Heckle and Deepglint right now. I forgive you for everything because kindness is stronger than hate, and I *will* win this quest even if every single odd is stacked against me!"

Fox could feel her satchel shaking now. And bulging. As if something inside it was struggling to get out. Then suddenly the satchel flung itself open, flooding the fern with light and burning through the fronds as if they were paper-thin. Fox and the sloth tumbled to the ground, and Deepglint and Heckle did the same on either side of them as the fern shriveled before their eyes until it was nothing more than a heap of black grit.

The satchel lay beside it, at the foot of the throne where Morg sat.

The harpy looked on in horror. "No," she murmured, leaping up so that she was standing on the throne. "What is this?!"

Fox gasped in disbelief. Creeping out of the satchel that she had carried for the whole quest was a silver fern that glittered and shone as if it had been dusted in frost. And suddenly Fox realized why the satchel had grown heavier and heavier during the course of their journey, and why there had been soil and leaves inside it when she'd opened it up back in Cragheart. All along there had been a fern growing inside it!

Fox watched, awestruck. The fern was growing fast now that it was out in the open. It set down roots that sprawled the length of the garden, and then it grew taller than the throne Morg stood on, taller than the biggest plant in the Night Garden, taller even than the walls that surrounded the antechamber. It stood before them, a tower of shimmering silver. And Fox knew, without a shred of doubt, that this was the Forever

Fern. She looked at the plant, hardly daring to believe it. How had it come to be in her satchel? How had it grown in there?

But Morg was on the move now, so any answers would have to wait. The harpy leapt up into the Forever Fern's fronds, which were as sturdy as if they belonged to a tree, and began searching frantically.

"The pearl!" Deepglint cried to Fox. "She's after the pearl!"

He swiped at Morg's talons, trying to stop her pursuit, but the harpy twisted away just in time and carried on tearing through the fern, plucking at its fronds and muttering wildly.

"It must be here!" Morg cried. "I'm so close to claiming all the Umapped magic!"

The harpy's words suddenly brought something back to Fox, something that Doogie Herbalsneeze had said in the Constant Whinge: "*The things you search for are often much closer than you think.*"

Fox dug her hand into the satchel. There was nothing left of the fern inside it now. Its roots were lodged in Shadowfall's soil. But the phoenix tear was still there, flickering quietly, along with Fibber's paintings. Fox had no idea how long the Forever Fern had been in her satchel, but she wondered whether somehow its growing had sparked the phoenix tear's magic into life. So could it be, then, that the phoenix tear *was* the pearl? That she had been carrying it all along . . . ?

Heckle was now hissing at Morg's heels, and Deepglint was charging up the fronds after her. Quickly, Fox raked away at the plants in front of her until she'd uncovered a small patch of soil. Morg glanced down just at that moment as she realized what was happening.

But unbeknown to the harpy and to Fox and her friends, the little sloth had been making his way up the Forever Fern as soon as it had sprung up because he sensed that Morg would want to search it for the pearl. So despite his fear of heights, Fibber had climbed into the fronds before the harpy had leapt into them and before even Deepglint had raced up after Morg. And as the harpy made to leap from the fern now and hurtle down toward Fox to ruin her chances of saving Jungledrop, the sloth had the chance to do something magnificent.

Clinging to the frond directly below Morg, he swung out his paw at the same time as the harpy launched herself from the fern. He was a little sloth, but his claws were sharp and they ripped a hole in one of Morg's precious wings, which sent her crashing off course into the plants beyond Fox. And because of her brother's quick thinking, Fox was able to plunge the phoenix tear into the ground and heap the soil back on top of it.

There was a tangle of claws and wings as Deepglint finally caught Morg and pulled her back. Then the magic of the phoenix began to blaze in all its glory, the Night Garden transforming before their eyes as every single black plant withered and thousands of glow-in-the-dark flowers and shrubs sprouted up in their place.

"No!" Morg shrieked. "No!"

The harpy wrestled free from Deepglint and rose, stumblingly, up into the air on wings that were now torn and ragged from her tangle with the sloth and the panther. But it was too late. She couldn't undo what Fox and Fibber had started. She could only watch as the garden flooded with color and a ring of blue bushes laden with berries surrounded the Forever Fern.

"Thunderberry bushes!" Heckle squawked.

Morg screeched with fury as her plan fell about her in ruins and she realized that her only option now was to flee. Her wings carried her up to the wall, but the harpy knew they would not take her any further. She looked out, desperately, over the rest of the Bonelands.

There came a rumble as the walls surrounding the hall

began to crumble, then the bone walls around Shadowfall collapsed as if everything was bowing to the ancient magic of the phoenix. Morg clattered to the ground, then gathered herself up to flee through the rubble on foot. But she hadn't anticipated what would be standing in her way.

The animals and Unmappers that had been Morg's prisoners in the crypt hadn't hidden inside the avenue of trees as they'd been told to do by Deepglint. They had surrounded the bone walls so that, when they crumbled, the prisoners formed a ring round Shadowfall. They were bruised and weak from being locked up, but they were no longer wispy and faint, as they had been in the crypt. The Forever Fern had restored their magic! And flying above them, albeit rather haphazardly, was Total Shambles, who had come back to fight on behalf of Fox and Fibber after all.

Morg darted toward her former prisoners, hoping that she could barge a way through them. Orangutans shrieked, gibbons beat their fists on their chests, and Unmappers roared. But Morg knew, despite the noise, that they were weak and drained from their time in her cages, while she still had the power left to destroy enough of them to forge a path through their midst. She rushed toward them in one last bid to escape.

And that's when Total Shambles, who hadn't been locked in a crypt and no longer had an injured leg, dived down.

He slammed into the harpy, battering her with his hooves and pecking at her wings with his beak. Fox had never really understood why the flickertug map had led her to the Constant Whinge if the pucklesmidge syrup had then been used by Fibber on the swiftwing so shortly afterward. But as Total Shambles fought Morg now, Fox wondered whether the map had known, all along, the path that needed to be taken to lead them all here.

Doogie had said the flickertug map showed a journey of the heart, not the feet, so maybe the twins needed to lose Total Shambles for the wall around Fox's heart to come down. And perhaps the map had also known that the swiftwing would come back, in the end, to protect the Unmappers who tried to stop Morg fleeing.

Deepglint was bounding over to the fight now, and so, with one final burst of strength, Morg wrenched herself free from Total Shambles. She staggered back through the glow-in-the-dark plants, into the far corner of the garden, and though Deepglint was hot on her heels, he wasn't fast enough to stop the harpy throwing herself down the well that stood there.

There was a flap of feathers and a terrible screeching. "This is not the end!" Morg screamed. "I will find another way to steal the Unmapped magic! My reign is coming, and when it does, it will swallow you all in its darkness!"

Fox raced over to the well, but when she peered down into it, she saw only black. A pit that seemed to go on and on forever more. There was no trace of the harpy at all.

Heckle fluttered onto Fox's shoulder. "Has—has Morg gone?"

Deepglint placed two heavy paws on the well, and as he breathed over the top, a stone lid formed, crunching into place over the pit.

The Lofty Husk turned to Fox. "The phoenix magic you brought here granted me the power to set an unbreakable spell over this well. Never again will Morg be able to find a way back into Jungledrop." He raised his chin and looked at Fox, not as if she was an insignificant little girl, as Morg had done, but as if she was his equal. "Because of the strength of your heart, Fox Petty-Squabble, and the strength of your brother's, the Unmapped Kingdoms and the Faraway are still standing."

There were cheers from the animals and the Unmappers ringing Shadowfall, and Total Shambles pulled off a highly risky but very impressive loop-the-loop before crash-landing in a thunderberry bush.

Fox felt herself sway. No one had ever congratulated her for anything back home. She'd never won an award or been praised for doing well. *This*, Fox thought, *this is happiness: knowing that, because you were brave enough to love, other people stuck around to love you back.*

"But—but how did the Forever Fern start growing in my satchel?" she murmured. "And why did the phoenix tear only save Jungledrop when the fern had grown? Why not before? I had it from the moment I set foot in this kingdom!"

Deepglint smiled. "I am only now grasping the truth of what must have happened." He paused. "A plant needs four things to grow: water, air, soil, and light. And a magical plant is much the same, with perhaps just a few little tweaks. So, can you think of an instance when water, or something like it, might have fallen onto the satchel?"

Fox shook her head, but from her shoulder, Heckle squawked. "Your tears in the bramble tunnel, Fox . . . Heckle distinctly remembers seeing them fall onto the satchel when you wept for your brother and for all those suffering at the hands of Morg!"

Deepglint nodded. "Water, then—with a magical twist . . ."

Fox blinked as she thought back to her quest, and for some reason she found herself remembering the ripple of air that had brushed against her skin as the butterflies she'd freed flapped round her. It had felt different from an ordinary breeze or a gust of wind—more magical somehow.

"I think the air that came from the wingbeats of the butterflies I rescued might have been filled with magic." Fox glanced at Deepglint. "And some of Cragheart's soil could have got nudged inside the satchel when I used it as a pillow that night we slept in the cave when we refused to give up on you being a Lofty Husk."

"Cragheart's soil is most definitely magical," Deepglint said. "For from it springs every Unmapper's fingerfern."

Heckle was now hopping from foot to foot. "And surely the magical light was the golden mist that rose up from the letters of your name, Deepglint! That light dried Fox's tunic, and the satchel was right beside her at the time!"

Deepglint smiled again as he looked from the parrot to Fox. "It would seem the Forever Fern started growing in your satchel when you and your brother started working together to find the fern for others rather than for yourselves. It grew, little by little, as your kindness grew. And it was the strength of heart you showed inside Morg's plant at Shadowfall that was the key to it bursting out of the satchel and activating the phoenix tear as the pearl to save Jungledrop."

Again, Fox thought of Doogie Herbalsneeze's words; the flickertug map really had sensed the journey of her heart. And of her brother's, too, it seemed. Fox glanced around for Fibber. In all the commotion, she realized she hadn't seen him since he'd torn a hole in Morg's wings. Where was he?

Heckle launched herself off Fox's shoulder to find Iggy while Fox raced toward the Forever Fern. Was Fibber still up in its branches, or had he fallen and hurt himself? Her pulse thrummed at the thought of what might have happened to him.

"Up there!" Heckle squawked from Iggy's side, and she pointed to the top of the Forever Fern with one wing. "Heckle can detect some very panicky thoughts about heights!"

Fox watched the uppermost fronds as they rustled to and fro. There was definitely something up there. She snatched a charcoal sketch from the satchel, then scrambled up the fern, higher and higher, hoping and wishing . . .

Until there was Fibber. Not a sloth anymore—perhaps the phoenix magic had broken that spell, too—but a boy again at last!

Fox threw herself at her brother, wrapping her arms round his neck. And he hugged her back with just the same strength as if, in this hug, the twins knew that they were making up for all the ones they'd missed out on before.

For a while, they sat together, looking out over the Bonelands: at the glow-in-the-dark garden glimmering before them, at the waterfall behind the temple, which was now churning out silver water, at the avenue of trees now bursting with colorful vines, and at the swamp in the distance, which was now shining turquoise beneath the moonlight.

Then Fox whispered, "I'm sorry, Fibber. For everything back home and for everything out here before the bramble tunnel as well. I've been a terrible sister."

Fibber looked down at his hands. "And I've been a pretty lousy brother." He held Fox's gaze. "I will never lie to you again, Fox. I promise."

Fox smiled through her tears, then she held out the sketch Fibber had drawn of the two of them laughing on the bridge back home. "You're so talented."

Fibber sighed. "Mum and Dad wouldn't think so." He plucked at his feather waistcoat, then said quietly: "But if I stay out here in Jungledrop, away from Mum and Dad, I can be myself." He looked at Fox. "I could be a Doodler here. I could paint every day! I could do what I love at last!"

Fox listened without saying anything. There had been times when she, too, had wondered whether she could stay in Jungledrop if the quest ended well. She was angry with her parents for lying to her and Fibber, and she dreaded going back to a home where conversations were limited to business, smiling was optional, and hugging was completely out of the question. But the only reason she had beaten Morg was because she had stood up to her. She had faced the harpy and she had discovered that she was worth something.

"We never once stood up for ourselves back home," Fox said after a while. "We just kept trying to be who Mum and Dad wanted us to be. But what if we did stand up for ourselves, Fibber?" She paused. "I've learned that a lot can happen when you speak out. So maybe, if we get home, you should show Mum and Dad your art and let them see how brilliant you are at painting. Tell them you're going to keep at it because it's what you love. You might not make billions, but you'll be happy. And I, for one, will back you all the way."

"You'd be with me if I told Mum and Dad?" Fibber asked.

Fox smiled. "Course I would. Because that's what siblings do: They stand by each other through thick and thin."

And Fibber grinned. Now that he had a sister, not a rival, by his side, suddenly the thought of going home felt a little less frightening.

Fox imagined being in the room with Fibber as he revealed his artwork to their parents, and she felt proud of him for finding something he loved and was good at. But a small part of her was sad that she'd have nothing to show for her time in Jungledrop. Just her word that she'd found a fern that had brought the rains back. And why on earth would her parents believe her when she herself had sneered at Casper Tock when he'd claimed something similar?

As if he could read his sister's thoughts, Fibber said: "You might not be going home with a satchel full of drawings, Fox, but I think you're leaving with something much more powerful." He looked out over Jungledrop. "You own a story. And not just any old story. The story of how you battled through the Bonelands and planted the pearl to save Jungledrop and the Faraway. Not because you were some fancy politician flinging words around or an important general in charge of an army or a businesswoman who got to the top by stamping on other people. You saved the world because you're kind and brave."

Fox felt a glow spread inside her.

Fibber went on. "Being a sloth gave me a lot of time to think. At school, the people who usually get noticed are the ones with the best marks in class, the most goals in sports, or the biggest parts in the end-of-term play. There's a lot of noise and hype around these kind of people. But away from all of that there are ordinary people, doing extraordinary things, purely because they're kind. *They* are the real world-shakers, the ones who start revolutions and overturn wrongs. And you're one of *them*, Fox. Your talent is that you're kind and that is enough. More than enough. Because the world is nothing without kindness."

Fox thought about this. During their quest, she had begun to understand the importance of being kind to others, but it turned out that almost harder than this was realizing that you needed to be kind to yourself, too. She had been convinced that she was unlovable, but now here was her brother saying that she was worth something. That she, Fox Petty-Squabble, who didn't think she had a scrap of talent to her name, was a world-shaker.

And just like that, something deep inside Fox healed. It had taken an adventure across a secret kingdom and almost losing her brother altogether, but Fox had learned what some grown-ups take a lifetime to understand: that being kind is the greatest talent of all.

Chapter 24

The twins climbed down the Forever Fern together, and it was obvious from the way Iggy and Heckle were twitching about in front of Deepglint that they, and very probably the Lofty Husk, knew something Fox and Fibber didn't.

"Look at the fern," Iggy cried as the twins' feet touched the ground.

Deepglint nodded. "Look closely."

Fox peered at the silver frond in front of her, and it was only then that she noticed the patterns that scored the leaves: tiny lines that looped and swirled, just like the loops and swirls she'd seen on the ferns inside Cragheart.

She looked at Deepglint with questioning eyes. "Fingerprints. I don't understand. . . ."

"As Heckle told *you*," the Lofty Husk said, "when an Unmapper is born, a fingerfern sprouts in his or her honor."

He looked from Fox to Fibber, and Fox felt her heart skitter as she looked at the patterns on the frond in front of her.

Heckle fluttered up onto the leaf. "We think the Forever Fern is a fingerfern—a very special one. We think it's *your* fingerfern, that it grew in honor of you both."

Fox held her palm up to the frond in front of her, and her eyes widened. The silver loops and swirls did indeed match her own fingerprints! And from the look on her brother's face beside her, she could tell that he had seen his prints on the frond before him.

"Wherever you are in the world," Deepglint said, "a part of you both will always be here in Jungledrop."

The twins smiled at the thought.

"Morg cannot find a way back into Jungledrop directly," Deepglint went on. "Planting the phoenix tear has meant that she is banished from this kingdom forever. For now, she is trapped underground, but she is not gone for good, so there is a chance that she will find her way into another Unmapped Kingdom. After all, there are more phoenix tears in the Far-away that will be waiting to bring others like both of you to our kingdoms to help us defeat Morg again, should the time come. Then, perhaps, a new phoenix will rise from Everdark and the world will be rid of the harpy forever."

Deepglint drew himself up tall. "Now, though, the Faraway and the Unmapped Kingdoms are safe, and if the thunderberry bushes have bloomed again across Jungledrop, as they have here, then we will have rain scrolls before long. So let us hasten back to Doodler's Haven to check that the scrolls are ready to be sent on to your world."

The Lofty Husk looked at Total Shambles, and the swiftwing picked his way over the rubble toward them.

"The Bonelands are rid of Morg's curses now," Deepglint said to the swiftwing, "and I thank you for your part in helping Fox and Fibber on their quest. But the animals and Unmappers are weak still, and I must lead them home. Can I trust that you will carry our heroes safely back to Timbernook?"

Total Shambles cocked his head at the twins, then he spread his wings before them as if that evening in the bramble tunnel had never happened. Fox and Fibber rushed over to him, and as Fox told the swiftwing how sorry she was for the lies she'd told him, he pressed his head into her chest.

Deepglint glanced at Iggy and Heckle. "If there is room on

your back for a very small Unmapper and a very talkative parrot, too, then that would, I have no doubt, be greatly appreciated, Total Shambles."

The swiftwing ruffled his feathers, then swished his tail, and as the twins, Iggy, and Heckle climbed up onto the swiftwing's back, Deepglint dipped his head at them.

"I will see you at Timbernook," he said. "It has been an honor to fight by your side."

Total Shambles wobbled up into the night sky until Deepglint and the other Unmappers were just specks down below. And though it was night now, the twins could see that Jungledrop was a glow-in-the-dark rainforest brimming with life and color once again. Trees had regrown, plants had flourished, and the kingdom rang with the sound of animals and magical creatures rejoicing in their newfound freedom.

For a while, Fox looked down at the canopy and marveled at where her adventure had taken her: over rivers and lakes, forests and ravines. But soon she and the others fell asleep, their arms locked round each other's waists and their bodies nestled in between Total Shambles's wings, as he flew on beneath the stars.

They knew they had arrived, several hours later, because the swiftwing's landing was as clumsy as ever, and it sent them toppling over Total Shambles's head into a heap at Goldpaw's feet. The group stood up by the edge of the lagoon in Doodler's Haven. Its water glistened in the dawn light, and Fox noticed there was a gravestone covered in flowers beneath a candletree. It marked the fall of the Lofty Husk called Spark.

"You were very much *not* what I was expecting when you arrived in Jungledrop," Goldpaw said to Fox and Fibber with a smile. "And yet a message from Deepglint tells me that it is, ultimately, because of you two that the thunderberry bushes have sparked back into life again and Morg has been banished from the kingdom. You achieved what none of us here could, and Jungledrop owes you the very greatest debt."

Fibber nudged his sister with pride. "It was mostly Fox. She's the one who tricked Morg's Midnights and worked out that the phoenix tear was the pearl all along. She's the real hero."

Fox blushed and Goldpaw laughed at the change in the Faraway children. Then she glanced over at the temple in the middle of the lagoon. "There is just one more thing," the Lofty Husk said, "concerning the rain scrolls. And I wondered whether I could call upon Fibber's help?"

Doodler's Haven was a bustle of activity compared to when the twins had last seen it. Dashers with bulging satchels were hurrying through the tunnel that led from Timbernook to Doodler's Haven and rushing inside the Bustling Giant. And within that huge tree, the twins could hear cauldrons hissing and spitting. Perhaps these were the marvels from Rumblestar that the Dunkers were mixing with the dye from the thunderberries, Fox thought. She listened as a gurgling sound bubbled inside the pipes leading into the waterfall, then torrents of ink, every shade of blue, surged out and cascaded down into the lagoon.

Fibber watched the Doodlers on the temple steps as they dipped little jars into the ink before rushing back to their easels to paint the canvases waiting there.

"They will be on the back foot," Goldpaw explained. "The best Doodler in the kingdom—Flavia Flickerpaint—was kidnapped by the Midnights, and though she is on her way back here with Deepglint, we cannot delay getting these scrolls painted. The dragons will be here soon, and the Faraway needs as many rain scrolls as possible to restore the damage of the drought." She turned to Fibber. "Deepglint said that you would be a match for Flavia Flickerpaint."

Fibber shifted. "But I—I've never seen a rain scroll before. How will I know if I'm doing it right?"

"There is no right or wrong with painting," Goldpaw

replied. "You just need passion and faith. So paint with everything in you, boy. Paint because your world depends on it."

Fibber took a deep breath, then he hurried over the bridge of vines that led to the temple. And it was clear, when he arrived, that the Doodlers were expecting him. One handed him a jar of ink while another led him toward a blank canvas.

Fox watched from the bank of the lagoon and felt nothing but pride as Fibber painted his scroll. Gone was the jealousy that had mounted over the years. Gone was the panic that usually rode up inside her whenever she saw Fibber excelling at something. Instead, she simply looked on, with Iggy, Heckle, and Total Shambles by her side, knowing that Fibber's rain scroll would be incredible.

Eventually, the scrolls were finished—a dazzling array of paintings showered in so many shades of blue, it was possible to see every kind of rain on the canvas: from the glitter of fine rain to the deluge of a downpour and the mist of a drizzly day. The Doodlers rolled the scrolls up and stamped them shut with wax seals, then they placed them in a large pulley basket that was hoisted across the lagoon and up into the canopy of the Bustling Giant.

There was a moment of quiet, as if everyone might be

waiting for something, then the *whoomph* of heavy wings, a glimpse of large, curled claws between the branches of the tree, a rustling in the leaves, and then, just like that, the rain scrolls were gone—carried off by the dragons to the Faraway.

Doodler's Haven erupted into cheers then as Dunkers and Dashers spilled out of the Bustling Giant, Doodlers clapped Fibber on the back, and the imprisoned Unmappers and animals came pouring out of the tunnel with Deepglint. And so it was that the kingdom of Jungledrop was brought together again, a jostle of extraordinary animals, magical creatures, and Unmappers all wanting to congratulate Fox and Fibber for being the heroes who saved the kingdom.

Great platters of food arrived with another batch of Unmappers, everything from pyramids of exotic fruit to goblets of juice and chocolate pastry towers, and everyone sat down on the banks of the lagoon and ate. Even a handful of trunklets appeared to join the celebrations, and Fox noticed they ate the platters and the goblets as well as the food and drink on offer.

Doogie Herbalsneeze sat beneath a candletree with the Lofty Husks who, it appeared, were telling jokes to one another, while the twins sat with Iggy (and Heckle, who was so overwhelmed by the amount of thoughts she could read in one place that she rather sensibly went to sleep in Iggy's hair) and his friends, who wanted to know everything about life in the Faraway. Apparently, there was only so much they could learn from the plant that grew newspapers. . . .

"Is it true that everyone in England eats hot cross buns for tea?"

"How do cars work without junglespit to power them?"

"Are Germans really on time for absolutely everything?"

"Should you smuggle a pretty-please plant home with you so that you can get pocket money on demand whenever you hold a hand under its leaves?"

Fox and Fibber answered the questions as best they could, though there was one that left them both stumped: "How on earth will you get home?"

And though magic is rarely on time—in fact, more often than not it is disgracefully late—that day it was rather prompt to show its face. Because as the last of the celebratory dingle-juices were drunk (a fabulous concoction that tasted of bananas and raspberries with a smattering of chocolate thrown in), there was a chugging sound, followed by a whistle blaring, and then, to everyone's surprise, the nose of a train poked through the undergrowth behind the candletree the twins sat beneath.

Fox watched as green smoke fizzed up through the branches of the tree, then a junglespook, wearing nothing but a loincloth, sauntered out of the undergrowth.

"Do I have a Fox and Fibber Petty-Squabble here?" Tedious Niggle asked. "Or did they get savaged by sticklebugs over in the Bonelands?"

The twins stood up before the junglespook.

Tedious Niggle rubbed his eyes. "You look different," he said. "Less clean. Less cross."

The twins laughed. Fox had imagined leaving Jungledrop many times, the Forever Fern's immortalizing pearl clutched in her hand, and so it felt strange seeing the way home right there in front of them and to be leaving empty-handed. But then she thought back to her and Fibber's journey, of all they had seen and done to set things right. And she realized that she wasn't really going home empty-handed at all; she was returning with a brother who was a friend, not a rival, and she was returning with a surprising amount of self-belief *and* a world-shaking story. Fox blinked. She was, in fact, leaving with so many brilliant things she felt a little bit greedy.

"I won't ever forget you," Iggy said to the twins. "You've been the most wonderful heroes."

On the Unmapper's shoulder, Heckle cocked her head. "And the most brilliant friends. Heckle will miss repeating your thoughts all day long."

Fibber ran a hand over the parrot's head and Fox stroked her wing, then they hugged Iggy tight.

"We'll miss you both so much," Fox said.

Deepglint padded over to the twins. "Your names will go down in Unmapped legend, as Casper Tock's did in Rumblestar, and Smudge and Bartholomew's did in Crackledawn."

Fox gazed at the Lofty Husk. He was so big and strong and wise and kind, and the thought of not having him around made her heart tremble. She tried to say something, but her voice was all choked up inside her.

Deepglint burrowed his head against hers. "You brought my magic back to me, Fox. You forged a bond between us that even being in different worlds cannot break. And so, whenever you fall asleep back home, whisper for me in your dreams and you will find me there."

Fox wrapped her arms round Deepglint's neck. How she wished he could be by her side when she faced her parents and told them she wouldn't be coming up with a fortune-saving business plan but was hoping to turn all her efforts into helping others. There was a Save the Planet club at school that previously she'd dismissed as a waste of time, but which now she wanted to get involved in. And apparently there was a fundraiser next term for the old people's home beside the school, which she had a few ideas for. And then there were her classmates in general; she knew it was time, at last, to start making friends, even though the thought made her palms sweat.

As if the Lofty Husk could sense Fox's fears, he whispered: "Be yourself back in the Faraway and those around you will come to see you for who you really are." He lifted a paw to hold Fox close to him. "It is impossible not to love someone as wonderful as you, Fox Petty-Squabble."

Fox hugged Deepglint once more, and when she drew back, she saw a tear slip from the panther's eye. She thought of how the Lofty Husk had hidden his tears when he learned of Spark's death but was making no attempt to do so now. *Perhaps even grown-ups learn things about love on adventures*, Fox thought.

She smiled at Deepglint one last time, then she stepped onto the train after Fibber.

Tedious Niggle was on board already, plumping up cushions in the carriage before them. "I have to say I am glad to see you changed out of those ghastly business suits. And congratulations for beating Morg, by the way; I *was* rather worried you'd just get sunburned instead."

He swished through the carriage to the far door, then turned. "Could I please ask that you sit down in the snugglers and hold on, tight, for the departure of this service? The Here and There Express tends to lurch off at speed, which is important if we're to be back in the Faraway with only a few hours having elapsed since we left."

Fibber placed the satchel containing his paintings by his feet and sat down in the armchair before him, which changed immediately into a park bench laden with cushions. And Fox found her armchair morphing into a snug beanbag again. There was no sign of an office chair or a spiked throne this time.

The twins glanced out of the window to see the huge crowd, fronted by Deepglint, Iggy, and Heckle, waving them off, then the train jerked forward, and before the twins could even catch their breath, it was whisking them through the rainforest at breakneck speed.

The Here and There Express raced along until they were soon back at Snaggletooth Cave, charging headlong into its mouth. The train rattled on and Fox thought back to how frightened she'd been when they'd plunged into this tunnel a week ago. But this time, in the drawn-out darkness, Fox felt her brother's hand squeeze hers. Their adventure in Jungledrop was coming to an end, but their adventure back home was just beginning. Fox felt a flutter of excitement at the thought.

The train burst out of the tunnel, and Fox and Fibber blinked in surprise to see that they were wearing ordinary clothes once again. Not business suits, as they had been when they set out on their adventure, but clothes that regular eleven-year-olds might wear during the summer holidays. Shorts and T-shirts, socks and sneakers. There wasn't a tie or a briefcase in sight.

The twins looked out of the window. They were moving so fast the countryside was a haze around them. But then the train slowed a little and their surroundings came into focus. Meadows strewn with flowers, wooden chalets clustered round lakes, mountains rising up into the distance.

"Germany!" Fibber cried.

Fox shook her head in disbelief. "We made it back!"

It was raining—great torrents of water pouring down onto the countryside—and this was drawing people, hundreds of them, out of their houses and into the meadows and fields. They were dancing, whooping, and kicking through the puddles while holding up open hands as the rains fell and fell.

"We did that," Fox said, smiling. "All this rain—because of what we did in Jungledrop!"

The twins sat back and tried to take it all in as the train sped on toward Mizzlegurg.

Far, far away, in the depths of a well, the harpy screeched with fury. She had lost her hold on Jungledrop and her rage swirled inside her. But when she had created the Night Garden, she had placed this bottomless well in the corner, and she knew that even bottomless wells did, eventually, lead somewhere. Even if that somewhere was so deep underground the only thing living there was the darkness itself.

But Morg was a creature who clung to the dark, who knew how to use it to weave terrible spells. As she fell down, down, down into the well, she vowed to herself that she would stop at nothing until she had conjured a doorway into Crackledawn—an Unmapped Kingdom that still housed a few of her followers from her fleeting visit there many years ago. And if she could find a way into this land again, as she had done on the night she rose up from Everdark, and rally her followers, then one final opportunity would arise for her to steal the magic of both Crackledawn and Silvercrag—the last two Unmapped

Kingdoms she hadn't yet been banished from. Then she could begin her reign in earnest. . . .

Morg fell still further into the dark while the Here and There Express carrying Fox and Fibber rushed still farther into the Faraway.

Chapter 25

The twins saw Mizzlegurg's clock tower first, rising up above the village, and Fox noticed that it said 7 p.m. Not only was this the same day they had left but, as Tedious Niggle had said, only a couple of hours had passed while they'd been away!

The train pulled to a stop at the station, which was as empty as it had been when the twins left. The carriage doors swung open, Tedious Niggle shooed them off, and then Fox and Fibber were standing on the platform—their sneakers planted in a large puddle—as the Here and There Express pulled away.

Beyond the platform, where the station led out onto the street, Fox could see a large crowd had gathered to celebrate the rains. And thundering through the middle of this crowd, barging with their elbows and ramming with their briefcases, were Mr. and Mrs. Petty-Squabble. Fox tensed at the sight of her parents, and as Bernard and Gertrude caught sight of their children and stormed across the platform, Fox felt a familiar fear scuttle through her.

"We can do this, Fox," Fibber whispered beside her. "You and me—we're a team."

Bernard thumped his briefcase down in a puddle and raised himself up before his children. "We expressly told you to stay in the penthouse suite of the Neverwrinkle Hotel."

Fox stared at her father. There was no mention of the rains returning, of the world having been saved from certain doom.

Gertrude straightened her tie. "Your father and I have always prided ourselves on raising predictable children. We tell you to stamp on other people—and you do it. We tell you to work on a business plan—and you do it. We tell you to stay in one place—and you do." She raised an eyebrow. "Why, then, do we suddenly find you on the platform of an ancient train station dressed in shorts and T-shirts?"

Fox looked her parents up and down. She had always thought of them as people to be feared. But standing in front of them now, with her brother by her side and all that she'd learned about love, self-belief, and courage bubbling inside her, she thought they seemed smaller than they had done before. And she felt almost sorry for them, because they would never see the world in the bright and wonderful way that she did now.

"You lied to us," Fox found herself saying. "You pitted Fibber and me against each other in the hope of making money. And though we may only be half your size and a quarter of your age, we matter. Just as everyone around us matters too, whatever you may have led us to believe." She took a deep breath and channeled her firmest voice yet. "Bullies and liars often go from strength to strength until someone is brave enough to take them down. And, well, Fibber and I aren't going to be bullied anymore."

Fox couldn't believe the words had come from her. Indeed Gertrude was rubbing her ears so hard, and Bernard blinking so madly, that Fox realized her parents couldn't believe the words had come from their daughter either.

"And we won't be stamping on other people's feelings either," added Fibber.

Bernard stepped forward as if to say something, but Fibber merely held up his hand and carried on talking, which Fox thought was the slickest and most businesslike thing she'd ever seen him do.

"We won't be spending all of our time coming up with ways

to save the family fortune. Or ignoring the fact that we could do more, every day, to save our planet and to care for the people in it. And we definitely won't be allowing you to mail either of us to Antarctica. Because"—Fibber swallowed—"that's just not what families do. They look out for each other. And we're a family, even though up until now we've not done a very good job of being one. Fox is my sister, not my rival, and I think she's brilliant. So from now on we'll be treating each other with respect, whether you like it or not."

Bernard and Gertrude seemed to grow smaller and smaller with every word Fibber said. Indeed they were so stunned by this change of character in their children that they were, for once, completely lost for words. And that was probably just as well. Because when terrible parents run out of things to say, it creates a little room for sense.

"Please go back to the penthouse suite and wait for us there," Fox instructed. She had seen someone in the crowd behind her parents, someone she knew she and her brother would very much like to talk to.

Fibber, too, had caught sight of the old man with dark, wrinkled skin who was peeling away from the crowd and hobbling toward them.

Fox eyed her parents, who seemed to be locked in a state of shock at this turn of events. She knew that she and Fibber still had so much more to tell them, but she imagined the hardest things about tricky conversations were the beginnings, and now that she and Fibber had begun, perhaps the rest would be a little easier.

"There's rather a lot we need to say back at the hotel," Fox added, "so I suggest you put the kettle on. I think the truth might be less distressing if you're both armed with a cup of tea."

Bernard and Gertrude looked at their children with an expression that was an extraordinary mix of outrage, surprise, and—for the briefest of moments—tenderness. As if the twins' honesty and courage had awakened something inside the Petty-Squabble parents that they had assumed was long dead.

Then Fox and Fibber watched as their father picked up his briefcase and followed his speechless wife back through the crowds with a fraction less barging and ramming than they had displayed earlier.

The children turned their attention to the old man making his way toward them. Casper Tock had sensed the presence of magic before, and so he knew when it was hovering close by again. He stopped in front of the ticket office and looked at the twins standing on the platform. To him, it felt just like yesterday that he had stumbled into Rumblestar and saved the world, and yet before him now were two more children, the unlikeliest of heroes, who had journeyed to an Unmapped Kingdom and restored hope to the Faraway.

The crowds in the street had no idea that Fox and Fibber Petty-Squabble had been the ones to bring rain back to their world, but the antiques collector knew.

"So you found your way into an Unmapped Kingdom," he said quietly.

The twins nodded as the rain fell about them, full of promise.

Casper raised a wrinkled fist in triumph, then he chuckled. "However did you beat Morg?"

Fox thought of all that had stood in their way during their quest to find the Forever Fern: cursed monkeys, nightcreaks, hog-nosed vipers, witchcrocs, hunchbacks, giant apes, hexed ferns, *and* the harpy herself.

"By being kind," Fox replied. "And by believing, full tilt, in magic."

The antiques collector shuffled closer to the twins until he was standing before them. "I saw many astonishing things during my time in Rumblestar, but you two have reminded me that the most astonishing creatures of all are, in fact, children. Because what they lack in size, they make up for in spirit."

There was no podium or victory speech, no orchestral music or bubbling wine, as Fox had once imagined. Just the antiques collector's words. But they made Fox's heart swell with pride. And together with Casper Tock and her brother, she watched as the Here and There Express melted into the rain and the last of the junglespit drifted away with the clouds.

Acknowledgments

Fox Petty-Squabble's list of people to write thank-you letters to following her quest in Jungledrop:

1. *The brilliantly talented and endlessly dynamic team at Simon & Schuster for championing me and my story long before I started championing boglets and brothers, parrots and panthers: Eve Wersocki-Morris, Sarah Macmillan, Dan Fricker, Laura Hough, Rachel Denwood, Stephanie Purcell, Jane Tait, Mara Anastas, and, finally, Jane Griffiths and Sarah McCabe—whose editorial prowess helped Abi bring my quest to life.*
2. *Illustrator-extraordinaire Petur Antonsson for not making me look too bratty or spoiled or stampy on the front cover.*
3. *Literary agent superstar Hannah Sheppard for her unfaltering support of the Unmapped world and her excitement and expertise regarding adventures ahead.*
4. *The wonderful teachers, librarians, booksellers, and parents for placing my and Fibber's quest into the hands of kids all over the globe.*

5. Abi's author friends (particularly Piers Torday, Lauren St John, Katherine Rundell, Katie Webber, Mel Taylor, Abie Longstaff, and Perdita Cargill) for their humor and wisdom—wisdom to rival that of the Lofty Husks, I might add. . . .

6. Abi's family for their love and patience, and her husband, Edo, who taught her more about kindness than anyone in the Faraway—which she then handily passed on to me for the quest.

7. Abi's Coram Beanstalk past and present book clubs at Oxford Gardens Primary School—Adil, Tristan, Islam, Munirah, O'shiannah, Tolmon, Tasneem, Lacey, Khawla, Raphi, Jack, Shyan, Fatima, and Mimi—and the Reading Gladiators at Fox Primary School in Notting Hill, for reminding Abi why kids are infinitely more fun than grown-ups and channeling that playfulness into my story.

8. Laura and Faith Jackson for naming Jungledrop's secret cave, Cragheart, so well.

9. Toby and Mark Nieman for letting Abi stay a night in the exquisite Elham Treehouse in Kent so that she could imagine what it might be like for me and Fibber sleeping up among the trees in Jungledrop. (To book a night in their tree house, visit: www.elhamtreehouse.com.)

10. The fabulous Joy Court for giving Iggy Blether such a perfect surname.

Turn the page for a peek at
an exciting new adventure in
the Unmapped Kingdoms!

Zebedee Bolt was good at running away from home. He'd done it enough times, after all. And not the half-hearted wandering off that involves shouting at your parents, storming to the bottom of the garden, then slinking back in time for tea. When Zeb ran, he crossed bridges and raced through unfamiliar parks, safe in the knowledge that he had memorized all the latest tricks from the Tank (a survival expert who did deeply uncomfortable things, like drink his own sweat and make rescue ropes out of his beard hair, on his television show).

But Zeb was always discovered in the end. And this was because he found it almost impossible to rein in the Outbursts. These episodes came upon him without warning and consisted of an embarrassing amount of sobbing on street corners.

By the time he'd got a grip of himself, various grown-ups were usually stepping in to bring his getaway to a close.

You see, Zeb wanted to be tough. He longed to be like the Tank, who could escape any situation, like surviving weeks in the wild on a diet of grasshoppers, or emerging from a tussle with a bear with nothing but a bit of light bruising. But when you've got no money, a limited supply of food, and no friends to fall back on if things go wrong, it is a bit harder to remain upbeat.

So, while Zeb's getaways always started well, it wasn't long before the fear and panic kicked in. Where, really, was he running to? What hope was there for an eleven-year-old boy alone in New York? Who actually cared about what happened to him? Not that he ever talked about his feelings to the grown-ups who found him, the social worker in charge of him, or the foster families he'd lived with. Because talking meant trusting. And trusting other people had gone out the window years ago for Zeb.

Tonight would be different, though. Tonight he had remembered cookies. And he had made a solemn vow in front of the mirror that he wouldn't burst into tears and get found, not even when it got dark, or a little bit scary. Because Zeb had had enough of being passed around people's homes like an unwanted package, enough of hearing the same things whispered about him by the foster families he'd known: *He's so quiet. Why does he never smile? Is he always this moody?* And, overheard this morning, from foster parents Joyce and Gerald Orderly-Queue of 56 Rightangle Row, Manhattan, while on the phone to his social worker: *We've had him for six months now, and it's simply not working. He doesn't smile; he doesn't laugh; he barely even talks! And he spends so much time shut away in his bedroom, he is almost certainly plotting something dreadful. So before he poisons us in our sleep, or worse, sprays graffiti all over the sitting room, we'd very much like to hand him back.*

Their words jostled in Zeb's ears as he ran over the Brooklyn Bridge. It was always the same thing; he was never what foster families wanted. And while the welfare agency in charge of him had placed dozens of other children in loving homes, those—like Zeb—under the care of social worker Derek Dunce hadn't had the same luck. Derek Dunce was a buffoon of a grown-up who was capable of messing up even the simplest of things, like walking down a corridor. Finding loving families to nurture and understand vulnerable children was completely beyond him. So, like a disappointing meal in a restaurant or a faulty coat from a department store, Zeb was always sent back to the welfare agency in the end.

Zeb had crept out of Number 56 Rightangle Row for good

over an hour ago, as soon as he'd gobbled down his dinner and finished talking to himself in the mirror. Now he was on the run, and though he wasn't sure where he was running to, he kept going, even as the dark settled in and the city lights began to glitter. He pulled the hood of his jacket up, partly because he'd once seen the Tank do the same, moments before facing down a lion, and partly as a precaution. If the Orderly-Queues had sounded the alarm and the police were out looking for an eleven-year-old boy with blond hair, green eyes, and a fondness for hysterical crying, Zeb wanted to be disguised.

He turned off the bridge and hurried into the heart of Brooklyn. The place was buzzing. People poured in and out of restaurants, music sailed through open windows, and taxis honked. For a second, Zeb allowed himself to wonder what belonging to a neighborhood like this, with family and friends around him, would be like. Bike rides with a mom and a dad in the park? Weekend cinema trips with kids from school? Sleepovers at the neighbor's house?

A longing grew inside Zeb and with it, a lump in his throat—the first sign of an Outburst. He swallowed it down, then did what the Tank did when the going got tough: some jaw clenching, followed by a grunt. Instantly, he felt better, and as he made his way on through the crowds, he reminded himself that dreaming up family and friends was pointless, because you could never count on other people. Not when they'd let you down time and time again. Humans, Zeb had come to learn, were a bit like vegetables. They claimed to be full of all sorts of good things but ultimately, they were pretty disappointing.

According to Derek Dunce, Zeb had been born in the Bronx, his mother had died when he was only a few months old, and his father had wanted nothing to do with either of them. At first, those responsible for Zeb had hoped that the foster homes would be temporary, that he might soon be adopted into a loving family. But because Derek Dunce was entirely unqualified for his job, the foster parents Zeb had encountered were the sort of grown-ups who only really wanted uncomplicated children, the types who may throw the odd tantrum around mealtimes and get in a flap about having their toenails cut, but who generally just got on with growing up.

Zeb was not one of these children because it is hard to get on with growing up when being loved hasn't happened first. His Outbursts led to him being labeled a "difficult child," and at the string of schools Zeb had been to, he'd never made friends. He kept to himself to himself, too wary to let his guard down even for a moment. It was a lonely business, but it was better than trying to make friends only to move again.

Zeb slowed to a walk as he made his way on into the city alone. He left the bustle of restaurants and bars behind him and turned onto sleepy side roads lining closed parks, until the neighborhood began to fray and become a less-visited sort of place. Zeb gripped the straps of his rucksack. This was the farthest he'd ever come by himself. He contemplated a brief sob before thinking better of it and walking on through the trail of autumn leaves.

It was quieter here—and darker. Many of the street lamps had fizzled out, and the moon was tucked behind the clouds. Zeb went on into the shadows, unknowingly drawn by the pull of magic. The streets had emptied, and now the night belonged to strays: a prowling cat, a dog hunting for scraps, and a rat scampering into the gutter.

Zeb stopped again, and the panic swelled inside him. He had pinched a sheet of tarp from the Orderly-Queue's garage because the Tank was always talking about thinking ahead when building a shelter. But how did you know where to set up camp? Should you just curl up beneath the tarp with your cookies and hope for the best?

As if the city could sense Zeb's unease, a breeze came out

of nowhere, stirring a handful of leaves at his feet before nudging them on down the road. Zeb found himself following the leaves as they tumbled one after the other down the street and across another road.

He passed a discarded newspaper and only half-registered the headlines:

GLOBAL TEMPERATURES SOAR
POLAR REGIONS MELT AT RECORD SPEED
ARCTIC ANIMALS FACE EXTINCTION
SEA SWALLOWS COASTAL TOWNS

In the last hundred years, there had been two major climate disasters. A series of hurricanes which had nearly torn the world apart, then a drought that had starved the planet of rain for months on end. And now huge chunks of polar ice were melting each day; the polar bears and beluga whales were almost extinct; the rising sea was flooding entire cities; and the hottest summer on record had seen raging wildfires across the world. Millions had lost their homes, thousands had lost their lives, and the Arctic and the Antarctic were disappearing at terrifying speeds. Everyone living in a city by the sea was nervous—everybody except Zeb. Because stopping global warming wasn't top of his agenda tonight, or any night really. Preventing an Outburst and finding a place to hide was.

Zeb followed the leaves until they settled at the foot of a signpost that marked the start of a street so dark, it looked like the mouth of a cave. Zeb felt his knees wobble and a familiar lump slide into his throat. To prevent an episode of uncontrollable howling, he puffed out his chest, raised his chin, and focused on the fact that there was nothing and nobody waiting for him if he let an Outburst loose now. Joyce and Gerald Orderly-Queue had shown more affection for the Saturday crossword than for him. He *had* to go on. He had to start a new life on his own.

He looked up at the street sign. It was rusted at the hinges and the lettering was chipped, but he could just make out the words.

"Crook's End," he murmured.

He took a small step closer. There were more signs nailed to the buildings: PABLO'S PIZZAS, PASTA HEAVEN, BROOKLYN BURGERS. But these restaurants looked like they'd been boarded up for a while now, and at the end of the street, closing the road off into a dead end, was another building. It was taller and wider than the others, and the stonework above the old wooden door was a little fancier.

Zeb glanced at the faded sign hanging above the door: THE CHANDELIER, it read, and beneath it was a list of what appeared to be outdated showtimes.

"A theater," Zeb whispered. "All the way out here." He eyed the door which had been padlocked shut. "Grown-ups, they always focus on the doors. . . ."

But Zeb knew, from personal experience, that if you could escape a building in a number of ways: out of a window, via a skylight, down a fire escape—then there were multiple points of entry, too.

He settled for a ground floor window now, one covered with planks that had rotted through. He pulled them away to find a grubby pane of glass, and he hadn't expected to see much when he pressed his face up against it. But at that precise moment, the moon edged out from behind a cloud. And because the roof of the theater was in need of repair, the moonlight slipped in through the cracks and shimmered on the most enormous chandelier Zeb had ever seen. Hundreds of glass droplets hung from the domed ceiling, glinting silver like a giant's crown.

The moonlight was so bright that Zeb could see quite clearly inside now. Beyond a tiny foyer, the theater opened to reveal a balcony of seats up high, and down on the floor, more seats arranged in rows and draped in cobwebs. These led up to a stage fringed by tattered curtains and covered in dust. The stage was empty but for one thing. And when Zeb saw what it was, a small smile escaped his lips.

"A piano," he breathed.

You see, Zeb had not been brewing poison or shaking up cans of graffiti paint inside his bedroom on Rightangle Row. He had been teaching himself to play the keyboard he'd found under the bed there. Music, it turned out, was the one thing that could blot out everything else for Zeb. As soon as the first few notes of a song sounded, the rest of the world fell away. And while music didn't seem to be a priority for the Tank, Zeb *had* watched an episode where the survival expert fashioned a rescue horn out of an ox's thighbone, so he decided it must be all right to play a few sonatas from time to time.

Zeb gazed at the grand piano, sleek and black, as if it had been cut from midnight. And suddenly he forgot all about Outbursts and disappointing foster homes. He heaved the window up until there was space enough to climb through. Then, throwing one last look down Crook's End to check that he hadn't been followed, he squeezed himself into the theater and closed the window behind him.

About the Author

ABI ELPHINSTONE grew up in Scotland, where she spent most of her childhood running wild across the moors, hiding in tree houses, and building dens in the woods. After being coaxed out of her tree houses, she studied English at Bristol University and then worked as an English teacher in Tanzania before returning to the United Kingdom to teach there. When she's not writing, Abi volunteers for the Coram Beanstalk charity, speaks in schools, and travels the world looking for her next story. Her latest adventures include living with the Kazakh eagle hunters in Mongolia and dogsledding across the Arctic.